THE PRIVATE
BLOG OF
JOE
COWLEY
RETURN OF THE GEEK

For Mom, Dad, Vikki, and my best man, BECKY.

OXFORD
UNIVERSITY PRESS

Great Clarendon Street, Oxford OX2 6DP
Oxford University Press is a department of the University of Oxford.
It furthers the University's objective of excellence in research, scholarship,
and education by publishing worldwide in

Oxford New York

Oxford is a registered trade mark of Oxford University Press
in the UK and in certain other countries

Text Copyright © Ben Davis 2015
Illustrations Copyright © Mike Lowery 2015

The moral rights of the author and illustrator have been asserted

Database right Oxford University Press (maker)

First published 2015

British Library Cataloguing in Publication Data

Data available

ISBN: 978-0-19-273696-3
3 5 7 9 10 8 6 4 2

Printed in Great Britain
Paper used in the production of this book is a natural,
recyclable product made from wood grown in sustainable forests.
The manufacturing process conforms to the environmental
regulations of the country of origin.

Inside photography:
Football boots - Lee Torrens/Shutterstock.com
Chihuahua and Macaw – Eric Isselee/Shutterstock.com
Pigeon: lineartestpilot/Shutterstock.com
Sick bag: Zern Lieu/Shutterstock.com
Monster Munch: Aaron Amat/Shutterstock.com
Dog bin: Steve McWilliam/Shutterstock.com
All other images OUP

THE PRIVATE BLOG OF JOE COWLEY

RETURN OF THE GEEK

WRITTEN BY
BEN DAVIS

OXFORD
UNIVERSITY PRESS

Monday 3rd September

Hello, blog.

Haven't seen you in a while.

I know, I've been neglecting you, and I'm sorry, but that's because the whole reason I started you was to try and sort my life out, and to be honest, it has been sorted. This past summer has been the best ever. Here's why:

- I spent it with my girlfriend Natalie who is brilliant, and still makes me go all warm and tingly when she looks at me and—blah, blah, blah—all that girly crap.
- Not only did my best mates Harry and Ad not mind Natalie hanging around with us, they actually encouraged it. Ad said to her, 'It's almost as if you're a lad . . . No offence.'
- We all went to Coasterville and I rode the Beast without throwing up even a little bit. Admittedly, I did have to sit with my head between my knees for about twenty minutes afterwards, but still.
- If I do say so myself, I have got proper good at snogging. Natalie has noted an improvement in my technique. It's all down to lots of practice, and an article on Men's Domain called 'Becoming the Master of the Mouth'.
- Me, Harry, and Ad went for a bike ride into the country-side. We found this donkey tied up next to a load of old sacks, and Ad had the idea of playing 'Real-Life Bucka-roo'. I don't think I need to say how that ended.

- Natalie got her lip pierced, which meant having a kissing break, but once it healed, it made it a bit more exciting. It made her talk funny for a while as well, and I teased her, saying she was 'thuper thexthy', because that's the kind of HILARIOUS guy I am.

- When Harry and Ad retired to Ad's garage to start creating their own tracks as the SOUND EXPERIENCE (their embarrassingly hopeless DJ business), me and Natalie got to have loads of time alone. And there was this moment in the park, when she had just bought three 99s—one for me, and two for her to soothe her lip—and the sun made her hair glow bright purple, that I realized I was happier than I had ever been. Then a Canada Goose chased me for my cone and pecked holes in my calves, but when I look back on it in years to come, I'm sure my brain will edit that part out.

« Older posts

Anyway, all things must come to an end, and that includes the holidays, so it was back to stinking school today to begin Year Eleven. The last year before I can leave and never go back. I considered crossing out the days on my **STAR TREK** calendar, but writing on it would decrease its value.

'I agree that it has been a terrific summer,' said Harry as we trudged to school. 'Exemplary, in fact. But in a way, it was also a failure.'

'Why?' I said. I couldn't believe he'd ever say something so ridiculous, and as someone who is obsessed with both the Second World War and electro music, he is pretty damn ridiculous.

'Yeah, what you on about?' said Ad.

Harry got his empty pipe out and took a few thoughtful puffs. 'It was a failure for one reason: it was yet another summer when we didn't go to Buzzfest.'

Ah, *BUZZFEST*—the best music festival in the universe. We've been wanting to go there since forever. Despite Harry and Ad's get-rich-quick schemes, we've failed to get enough money for tickets every single year.

They keep going on about sneaking into the archaeological dig at the park next to the old war bunker. Harry reckons there must be loads of old coins buried under there that would pay for a trip to *BUZZFEST* many times over. Yeah right. I'm more worried about the idea of an open pit in the park. Ad is bound to fall into that, statistically speaking.

'This again,' I said. 'Look, we might as well just face facts: I will never be Captain of the *ENTERPRISE*, Ad will never figure out how to tie his shoelaces properly, and we will never go to Buzzfest.'

'How do you know?' said Harry.

I didn't have to answer because Ad then tripped over his shoelaces and smacked into the side of a parked van.

'See?'

'That doesn't mean a thing,' said Harry. 'Next year, we'll be going. You, me, Ad, even Natalie if she fancies it.'

'Yeah,' said Ad, rubbing the side of his face that made impact. 'Anyway, ain't Nat's family minted? Couldn't you just sweet talk her for some money?'

'No,' I said. 'Besides, I don't know if her family are all that rich.'

'Why?' said Harry. 'Is her dad secretly Mad Morris who lives down the park?'

I hoofed a pebble at him. 'No. At least, I hope not. I've never actually met her parents.'

Harry narrowed his eyes at me and took a long drag on his pipe. 'Interesting . . . '

'What's that supposed to mean?'

'Nothing,' said Harry. 'It's just perhaps Natalie has talked you up too much and now she's realized you won't live up to it. Maybe she's told her folks you're an heir to a fortune, and six foot three, with a healthy investment portfolio . . . '

'Yeah, and a massive kno—' Ad cut in.

Harry held up his hand to silence Ad. 'This is irrelevant, anyhow,' he said. 'Our main focus this year must be getting to Buzzfest.'

'Um, shouldn't our main focus be our GCSEs?' I said.

'That as well.'

What he said about Natalie's parents did bug me a bit. Why have I never met them? I mean, it's not something I was particularly looking forward to anyway, because knowing my track record, I'd probably end up asking her dad if he liked wearing bras or something, but still, it's odd that we haven't been introduced.

Whenever I mentioned going to hers over the summer, she'd always change the subject. But then, I suppose I was concentrating so hard on not messing up that I didn't let it get to me. I was determined not to let our disastrous first date happen again.

We went to Water World (NOT MY IDEA) and all these buff guys kept doing super-technical dives off the high board. I went up there and tried to do one, but I ended up falling off and bellyflopping. My chest was bright red for three weeks and I lost my goggles. Then, on the way home, I tried to do that tucking her hair behind her ear thing that you see in films but somehow ended up poking her right in the eye.

And this leads to another problem: now summer is over, we have an earlier curfew, which means me and Natalie are going to have to start hanging out at mine again. This is not good. Because to call my house a mad house would be an insult to mad houses everywhere.

Take Mum for instance. Because she's preggers with twins, she's dropped her hours at work and is around the house all the time. Last night a toilet roll advert with a load of puppies came on and she started crying. Not just a tear either, I mean runny mascara, snot—the whole shebang. I didn't realize having people growing in your belly sent you insane.

If that wasn't bad enough, I'm still having to share my bedroom with Gav, who is like Shrek's stinkier twin. He used to be my school bully and moved in when his dad, Jim, got engaged to my mum. And in what I see as an admission that we're going to be sharing a room until the apocalypse, Mum and Jim got rid of my portable mattress and bought us a bunk bed. It's as if I'm nine years old.

What's worse is Gav bagsied the top bunk, even though he weighs the same as two of me. It's horrendous, lying

awake at night and hearing every fart exploding above me, like some kind of disgusting firework display.

The wait for his nan, Doris, to move back into her flat is never-ending as well, and I can't see it ever happening. She still thinks a plastic doll is a real baby, and last week I caught her trying to wrap next door's cat in tinfoil. When I challenged her about it, she said, 'Well you don't want it to go stale, do you?'

I've got to think of another place where we can go, because Natalie will surely get fed up sooner or later. If we hang out in my room, Gav would come barging in, blasting crappy music. If we hang out in the lounge, Mum will sit between us and alternate between laughing and crying at two-minute intervals, or Jim will come in and start doing DIY, or Doris will shuffle in, chuntering on about getting the doll some gripe water. And to top it all off, in just a few months, there's going to be two REAL ACTUAL babies. WHERE THE COCKING HELL ARE THEY GOING TO GO? IN THE SHED?

Tuesday 4th September

Turns out we've got PE with old Boocock again this year. Great. When he saw me he actually rubbed his hands together with glee. We did football and he made me be a goalpost. My face is still stinging. If I didn't know any better, I'd say people were aiming for me. Especially Gav.

He'd normally be skiving, but Mr Pratt has forced him onto this good behaviour bond, meaning he has to attend every day in perfect uniform or he gets suspended. Jim has to personally escort him to the door every morning.

Anyway, when I complained that being a goalpost was a breach of my human rights, Boocock made me do ten laps, and replaced me with a cone. He said the cone was better because it didn't bitch and moan as much.

I've got a feeling this school year is going to be even worse than the last one. But at least everything is hunky cocking dory in my private life, correct?

9 p.m.
COR-WRONG!

Natalie came over to mine to do some 'homework'. We started off nicely in the bedroom, but then Gav came in, stuck his hand down his pants and unleashed a sonic boom burp that shook the windows. I asked him if he could leave us alone and he replied, 'Yeah. If you make me.'

Hmm. Maybe I should invest in a harpoon, or something.

Then we went in the lounge, but Mum was in there crying. FOR A CHANGE.

'What's the matter?' I said, which is becoming my most-used three-word phrase in this house, knocking, 'That stinks, Gav,' off the number one spot.

'Jim said I'm fat,' she sobbed.

« Older posts

Jim looked like he'd just survived being mauled by a panther.

'I didn't say that, Joe,' he said. 'Your mother asked if I thought she was fat, and I told her I love her just the way she is.'

I facepalmed.

'Ouch,' said Natalie.

Jim's sigh sounded like a bouncy castle going down. 'I should have just said no, shouldn't I?'

It was still warm-ish outside, so we went into the back garden, but Doris was out there, walking Ivy the doll in a pushchair.

'Don't mind me, I'm just getting the baby to sleep,' she said. And then started singing lullabies really loud and out of tune.

Lastly, we tried the kitchen—the one peaceful room in the house since Syd the parrot moved out. Pregnancy made Mum allergic to his feathers so he's staying with my weird Uncle Johnny. God knows what he'll be saying by the time he comes back. Anyway, it was going OK in there until Jim came in and started fitting baby-proof locks to everything.

Maybe I could cover the pit in the park with some canvas and turn that into our place? No, Natalie's used to a high standard of living, there's no way she'll go for that.

Still, at least she's seeing the funny side. For now.

'Your family is amazing,' she said. 'Like totally surreal.'

And she hasn't even met my dad yet.

God help me.

Wednesday 5th September

'Have you seen this, old boy?' Harry shoved a sheet of paper in my face as soon as I opened the door. 'It's bloody incredible!'

'Wow, paper,' I said. 'Those Ancient Chinese were an inventive people.'

'Just read it, smart-arse.'

Ad nodded at me like an excitable puppy that had just scarfed a bag of sugar.

I skimmed it as we walked down my garden path:

COULD YOU BE THE NEXT SUPERSTAR DJ?

Oh sweet Jesus.

Bangaz Radio are searching for the next big thing in clubland. We'll be holding heats at venues across the country, culminating in a wicked grand final in London, judged by the legendary DJ Swizz.

The winner gets to play the dance stage at BUZZFEST, the hottest party of the summer, and runners-up will receive VIP weekend tickets.

Send a demo MP3 to our website by Saturday 8th September to be in with a chance to audition.

« Older posts

'What do you think of that, soldier?' said Harry. 'This could be the answer to our prayers!'

There's no way the *SOUND EXPERIENCE* stand a chance. They did such a horrific job at the prom, the school would only pay a hundred pounds of the agreed two-fifty. Apparently, Mr Pratt had to have counselling for post-traumatic stress.

I tried my best to get them to drop the idea, but I couldn't. Their adventures only lead to pain and humiliation. Like the time Harry bought us fake moustaches so we'd get served in a pub. To my amazement, it worked, but then Ad sneezed his off right in front of the landlord.

'This has to be a sign,' said Harry. 'Just as I was saying we had to go to *BUZZFEST*, this comes along. Tonight, we are recording our very first demo.'

I'm not too worried. There's no way that pair of amateurs will have a demo ready by Saturday, let alone get an audition.

As well as all this crap, I have a dentist appointment later. I was hoping to weasel out of it, like I did the last five times, but now Mum is making me go. Actually taking me there. I thought about debating it with her, but that'd be like poking a grizzly bear with a pointy stick.

7 p.m.

I HATE DENTISTS.

Old Dr Priss seemed a bit racked off that I hadn't been in three years, and I swear he was being unnecessarily violent with his scraper. What's worse is that secret language he talks to the nurse in:

'A1, A2, A3, C1, D4, E1, E2, F4, F6, G1, G3.'

Now I can see why people get annoyed when me and Natalie speak Klingon to each other. I bet the secret language is something like:

A1: I

A2: Am

A3: Going

C1: To

D4: Be

E1: Extra

E2: Rough

F4: With

F6: This

G1: Little

G3: Geek

And then he kept asking me questions while he had his fingers in my mouth.

Anyway, when I was done, he sat me up in that weird chair thing and took his face mask off.

'Well, Joe,' he said. 'Do you want the bad news or the bad news?'

FIVE FILLINGS!

First of all, he injected my gums with the sharpest needle in the world, then I had to sit in the waiting room and read magazines that were printed before I was even born. Then, when my face went numb and I started to dribble, he called me back in, drilled the insides of five of my teeth out and replaced them with this weird silver stuff, before making me rinse and spit with that horrible purple liquid.

But that's not all. Next week I have to go back.

FOR BRACES.

Well, you know, I already have bad skin, bad hair, and bad fashion sense, so why not complete the look with some wire sticking out of my face? My life is over. Natalie will refuse to be seen with such a monstrosity and I will have to go and live in the sewers, singing and playing the organ. Mum reckons I'm overreacting BUT WHAT THE COCKING HELL DOES SHE KNOW? SHE ISN'T ABOUT TO HAVE A HIGH SPEED RAIL LINE INSTALLED IN HER GOB.

I met Natalie at Griddler's afterwards but didn't have the guts to tell her about next week. I looked at her across the table and realized I'm really going to miss her when she dumps me. Then she leaned over and wiped my chin with a serviette. It turned out I'd been dribbling my milkshake. Stupid numb face.

Thursday 6th September

Fuming is what I am. Steaming, in fact.

Everything was perfect tonight. Mum and Jim had fallen asleep on the sofa, Doris was tucked away in her room with Ivy, and Gav was out somewhere with those idiot Blenkinsop twins, probably harassing community support officers or something. We had no chance of being disturbed.

Natalie brought her iPod over and played something called *Godspeed! The Tears of a Thousand Orphans*. Not exactly what I'd call 'mood' music, but never mind.

Anyway, we were sprawled out on my bunk and we had

a nice kissing rhythm going. I had 'Master of the Mouth' printed out and ready to consult at a moment's notice.

Even though I'd been trying to phase them out, the men in the control room in my head leapt into action.

Now, I probably should explain here that I don't literally think there are actually men in my brain—the idea just helps me make sense of the crazy crap that goes on in there. The amount of control room workers vary, but there are always two running things—Norman and Hank.

You know what she'd love, man? said Hank, the crazy American one. *If you squeezed her ass.*

Oh don't be so vulgar, said Norman, the sensible one. *Keep it above the waist, Joe.*

Well, how about—

And not THERE, said Norman. *Let's try and stay family friendly.*

Anyway, because of this, or maybe because of the screamy music, I didn't hear Mum or Jim wake up and answer the front door. And I definitely didn't hear footsteps coming up the stairs.

'Easy, old boy!'

I shot up, smacking my head on the top bunk and sending Natalie rolling off the bed.

'What the hell are you two doing here?' I held my forehead to try and stop the throbbing.

'We've brought you our demo,' said Harry. 'As our manager slash roadie, it's important you have a say.'

'All right, Nat?' said Ad. 'Hey, Joe, why are you holding a pillow over your lap?'

'Shut up, Ad,' I said. 'Haven't you heard of knocking?'

'Pay no attention, old son,' said Harry. 'He's just annoyed because he's knocking on the inside of his zip.'

They switched *Godspeed!* off and put their demo on. I sat and half-listened, wishing them to go away.

'So what do you think?' said Harry after it finished. He fiddled with his pipe.

'Um . . . I don't know,' I said, trying to remember anything resembling a tune in amongst all the drums and twirly noises and explosions. 'It sounded . . . modern.'

'It was so *real*,' said Natalie.

I spun around and stared at her. She seemed actually moved by it.

'I loved it. It really spoke to me.'

Harry and Ad grinned like a pair of loons. I tried to make

« Older posts

eye contact with Natalie to see if she was just taking the piss, but she had this faraway look in her eyes, as if she'd undergone a deep spiritual experience.

Anyway, I practically shoved the *SOUND EXPERIENCE* out of the door after that, but all Natalie would talk about was how brilliant the demo was.

'I think they could win,' she said. 'And we should support them because if they do, we could go with them. Imagine—VIPs at Buzzfest. That would be amazing.'

Well, if it makes her happy.

11.50 p.m.

Gav is asleep now, but has just emitted a fart so heinous that it has seeped through his mattress and offended all five of my senses. Yes, it was so bad, I could almost touch it. Maybe a weekend away from this hellhole wouldn't be such a bad idea.

Friday 7th September

'Hey, Joe,' said Jim as he sat down to breakfast. 'What did Obi-Wan Kenobi say to Luke Skywalker when he was having trouble with his chopsticks?'

I sighed. 'Use the fork?'

'Use the fork,' he boomed in a terrible Obi-Wan voice. 'Thought you'd like that one, being a *Star Trek* fan.'

'That's *Star Wars*, not *Star Trek*,' I said.

Mum threw her Marmite and bananas on toast back down on the plate. 'Why can't you be nice for once, Joe? Why must you be so HATEFUL?'

Me and Jim shared an 'oh crap' look. Then Mum burst into tears. Again.

'I'm sorry, son,' she said. She leaned over and hugged me and the smell of her disgusting breakfast almost made me gag. 'It's just these hormones.'

Jim looks like he's aged about ten years.

It's times like this I miss Syd the parrot. Then I remember what he used to say about me and I learn to cherish the silences.

I spent break on the bench with Natalie. It was nice to have some time alone. And by 'time', I mean about eight seconds.

'Hey, it's the emo and the freako,' said Pete Cotterill, swaggering over like he'd just cacked himself. 'Been worshipping Satan together?'

'We tried to,' said Natalie, 'but our coven isn't so hot on spelling, so it turns out we've been worshipping Stan.'

'Yeah,' I said. 'And Santa.'

We proper laughed at our HILARIOUS jokes, but Pete just looked confused and walked away. I remember a short period when idiots like him left me alone and even pretended to like me. That changed pretty soon after I dumped the mega-popular Lisa for Natalie, though.

We sat in silence for a moment. Natalie seemed a bit distracted. Surely she wasn't still stunned by Harry's and Ad's musical brilliance?

'Joe,' she said. 'We need to talk.'

The sound of air raid sirens screamed through my brain. *WE NEED TO TALK?* If TV and films had taught me anything, it's that that sentence can only mean bad things. The girl says 'we need to talk' before dumping her boyfriend. The Mafia bloke says 'we need to talk' then BLAM! Brains all over the dashboard.

Red lights flashed in the control room.

Calm down, Joe, said Norman. *Don't automatically think the worst.*

Are you kidding me? said Hank. *Brace yourself, my man. And try not to cry when she does it. You don't want to look like a sissy.*

'Talk,' I said. 'T-talk. Yes, absolutely. Let's talk. You can't beat a good talk, can you? In fact, I believe our home internet package is with TalkTalk. It's so good, they named it twice. Please don't dump me.'

She laughed and smacked my shoulder. 'I'm not dumping you, idiot.'

'Oh.' I allowed myself to breathe again. 'Good.'

Her smile faded. 'It's just, something bad's happened.'

I'd been dreading this day for ages. I thought maybe her parents had found her another fancy-pants private school. Or even worse, they were moving abroad.

'What is it?' I said. 'This can still work long distance you know, with Skype and everything.'

'What are you talking about?' said Natalie, brushing her fringe out of her eyes.

'I don't know.'

'The thing is . . . ' She stopped and took a deep breath. 'It's my parents. They want to . . . meet you.'

'Oh,' I said, the relief washing over me in waves. 'OK. So what's the problem?'

Her eyes filled with terror. 'They're insane, Joe,' she said. 'Why do you think I haven't asked you back to mine yet?'

'I assumed it was because a lower-class serf like me would offend your butler.'

She whacked me again. 'We don't have a butler, we have a *gardener*.'

I put my arm around her and held her close. 'Don't worry about it,' I said. 'You've met my family, remember? They're crazier than a sack of tramps.'

'I know, but they're mad in a nice way,' she said. 'My family are mad in an it-makes-you-want-to-stab-yourself-in-the-eye-with-a-rusty-fork kind of way.'

'I'm sure they're not that bad.'

Natalie kicked a crushed can away from the bench.

'You'll see,' she said. 'Anyway, they've invited you up for Sunday lunch, so . . . '

I was about to remind her that Sunday is my court-appointed day with Dad, but then I remembered he's on holiday. In Ibiza. Clubbing. With his twenty-three-year-old girlfriend, Svetlana.

There is no way anyone's family is as mental as mine.

Saturday 8th September

Natalie popped around my house on her way into town this morning. She arrived just in time. And by that I mean she couldn't have picked a worse moment if she'd had a hundred goes. Yesterday, Mum and Jim took Doris to see Dr Chang, and she said that Doris needed more activity to keep her brain going, and recommended that she goes to some kind of old people's club at Morningside.

'Look, Helen, no one's saying you can't care for Mum,' said Jim. 'This is just to keep her mind active, like the doctor said.'

'I know,' said Mum. 'But who's going to take her? You usually work late and I'm the size of a house . . . '

'How about you, Gav?' said Jim. 'Fancy spending some time with your nan?'

Gav looked like he'd just been asked to slather himself in blood and go for a dip with some great whites.

'Nah, man,' he said. 'Old people freak me out.'

We all stared at him. 'Why do old people freak you out?' said Jim.

'It's their skin, innit?' he said. 'It's like tracing paper.'

Jim rubbed his eyes. I would feel sorry for him but if he didn't want the stress, he shouldn't have got my mum up the duff.

'We'll take her,' said Natalie.

I spun around so fast, I nearly snapped my neck.

'What?' I whispered.

'It'll be fun,' she said. 'Besides, I'm doing my work experience at Morningside, so I'll be used to the place.'

Oh crap. Work experience. I still haven't sorted mine. I realize I had all summer to do this, but I had more important things on my mind. Like figuring out what kind of black magic is responsible for working bra straps.

'So you're happy to take Doris to this club?' said Mum.

I glanced at Natalie. 'Yes,' I said. 'We'll take her.'

As I walked Natalie to the door, I asked her why she'd volunteered us for that.

'Well, you know I want to be a therapist, so it'll be good experience,' she said. 'Plus, we'll get to spend some time together.'

'Yeah, surrounded by geriatrics,' I said.

She kissed me. 'You're welcome.'

« Older posts

After Natalie left, everything went back to normal. And by normal, I mean cabbage-kickingly insane. Mum went up to our room, screamed and came stomping back down.

'What is that?' she yelled. 'The leaning tower of bloody Pisa?'

I knew what she was talking about. It was mine and Gav's washing hamper. The idea was, when it got full, we were supposed to take the dirty clothes downstairs, but it was always me that did it. Every time.

I decided that I'd had enough and refused to take it again. I thought eventually Gav would snap and just do it. Turns out I underestimated his tolerance for mess. I don't know why—this is a person who once left a pizza slice on top of our wardrobe for two whole months.

When Mum discovered the pile, it was nearly as tall as me. I'd been improvising to get around my lack of clothes. Like when Dad took me shopping before his holiday, I got him to buy me loads of underwear. Yes, it probably seems like a lot of effort to avoid moving some washing, but it's the principle of it.

Anyway, Mum said she was refusing to move it and that it was our job. Me and Gav eyed each other up. He didn't look like he was going to budge. Neither was I.

'So you're not going to do it?' said Mum.

We didn't speak. It was like a shoot-out from one of those old cowboy films.

'Fine,' said Mum. 'But if you think I'm going to move it, you can forget it. Then we'll see how long either of you last without clothes.'

My supply of pants and socks is still pretty healthy. I'm better equipped to deal with this situation than Gav.

Met Harry and Ad at Griddler's. They were still buzzing about this DJ competition.

'Think of the girls we'll get, Harry,' said Ad, with a mouth full of burger.

'So you've given up on Joe's mum then, old boy?' said Harry.

'Well, she's preggers now so she's off limits,' said Ad. 'Actually, I'm thinking of getting in touch with Jezza Kyle for one of them DNA tests. If them kids are mine I want visitationals.'

I balled up my sandwich wrapper and bounced it off his forehead.

Harry finished his drink and took his pipe out of his pocket. 'The Sound Experience must appeal to girls, old son. I mean, you saw Natalie's reaction.'

'I was surprised about that,' said Ad. ''Cause I thought she was into, like screamo, or whatever you call it. She must have weird tastes.'

Harry looked me up and down. 'Yes, she must.'

I shot him a quick middle finger.

« Older posts

'Anyway, enough of that, old boy,' said Harry. 'I'm sure you'll be pleased to hear that the Sound Experience's demo is with Bangaz now.'

'Right,' I said. 'Well, fingers crossed and that.'

'You don't need to cross anything,' said Harry. 'They'll love it.'

'Hope they do,' I said. 'I could do with a weekend away.'

'I don't know if managers can come, Joe,' said Ad. 'Maybe you'll have to be our dancer.'

Harry laughed. 'Are you pulling my plonker, old bean? Joe "I-have-the-coordination-of-a-jacket-spud" Cowley? We might as well have a brain damaged octopus flapping about on stage.'

'Hil. Ar. Ious,' I said. 'Anyway, shut up a minute because I've got a problem.'

Harry chuckled. 'What is it, old son? Are you worried Natalie will go for a rummage in your undercarriage and come away empty-handed?'

Ad spat Tango across the table, missing me by inches.

'No, you knobber,' I said. 'I'm meeting her parents for the first time tomorrow.'

'Ah, mate, it'll be like that film,' said Ad, wiping his chin.

'What, *Meet the Parents*?' I said.

'No. *Die Hard*.'

'Right,' said Harry, after a pause. 'Well anyway, you're in luck, soldier, because I can help you.'

'How can you help me?' I said. 'When have you ever met a girl's parents?'

'Last year,' he said, as if he were talking to an idiot. 'When I went out with Amelia Danson. When you were off for two weeks with chicken pox.'

'That's right,' I said. 'You "went out" with Amelia Danson, and yet she denies all knowledge.'

'Well, things ended badly,' he said, waving me off. 'Anyway, I shall give you the benefit of my experience because that's the kind of chap I am.'

'All right,' I said. 'But she reckons they're mental so . . . '

'Everyone says their family is mad, old boy, but they never are,' said Harry. 'Except Ad's, they really are.'

'Can't argue with that, mate,' said Ad.

'OK,' I leaned forward. 'Let's hear your tips, then.'

Sunday 9th September

So nervous. I'm terrible at meeting new people. I'm worried that I'll get so tense that my problem will flare up. The problem where I don't know what to say, and the control room takes over and I end up blurting out any old rubbish.

I've written down Harry's tips and I'm taking them with me just in case. They are:

1. Be charming to the mother. Be sure to say, 'You have a lovely home.'

« Older posts

2. Be respectful to the father. Make sure your handshake is firm, but not too firm. You have to let him feel like he is top dog. Even though you are shtupping his daughter.
3. Present yourself as a reliable, honourable young man who has only the best intentions for their little girl. Even though you have been vigorously shtupping her.
4. At the end of your visit, thank them for their hospitality.
5. Giving Natalie a friendly kiss on the cheek before you leave is acceptable, but under no circumstances refer to the fact that you are shtupping her.

Thing is, we're not actually 'shtupping', but now he's got that word in my head, I'm probably going to end up saying it.

Right, it's time to leave. You can do this, Joe. You met Lisa's parents before, remember?

But they weren't insane.

Oh God.

10 p.m.

Well, that was interesting.

10.30 p.m.

OK. I'll start writing this up now. Maybe it'll help me make sense of it all.

I stood outside the front door, shaking. Gav giving me a 'good luck' wedgie right before I left didn't exactly help matters.

Natalie's house is huge. I knew her family had a few quid, but I didn't realize they were that loaded.

It's almost not fair, if you think about it. I mean, there's only four of them rattling around in that giant barn, whereas there's five—soon to be seven—in our little house. Eight if you count the doll.

Before I could think about suggesting a house swap, the door opened and a small boy stood there. Balls. I'm cack at talking to little kids.

'Hello!' I said, bending down and talking to him like he was tapped. 'You must be Charlie . . . You know, I used to have a guinea pig called Charlie. Lovely, he was. Froze to death one winter. Very sad. We all miss him terribly.'

It begins . . . said Hank.

Charlie frowned at me and pushed his glasses up on his nose.

'Anyway,' I said, giggling like some sort of idiot. 'Is your sister there?'

'You're the boyfriend then?' He looked me up and down. 'Good luck.'

He opened the door and beckoned for me to come in. He went straight upstairs, and I wasn't sure whether I was supposed to follow him so I just stood in the hall like a plank.

This hall really was a hall, too. It was bigger than my

« Older posts

bedroom. Somewhere in the outer reaches of the house, I could hear voices. My eye started twitching.

A door opened next to me. *Please be Natalie. Please be Natalie.*

It wasn't Natalie. It was an old bloke wearing a hat. I reasoned it must be her dad, but something didn't seem right.

'Good afternoon.' I spun around and stuck out my hand for a firm but not too firm handshake. 'I'm Joe. You must be Mr Tuft.'

His big smile started to fade. 'What did you say, son?'

My eye twitch started up again. 'I, um, I said, I'm Joe, and you must be Mr Tuft.'

He looked at me, puzzled for a second, then threw his head back and laughed. 'You think I'm Mr Tuft—Natalie's father?' he said. 'Seems unlikely, no?'

Ah. Yes, he was black. And had a Jamaican accent. Probably should have realized.

'Ah ha ha,' I spluttered. 'No, I'm, uh, colour blind, you see. Which is why I can never learn to drive. I'd never know when to stop and go. Carnage. That's what it'd be.'

You don't get any better, do you? said Hank, holding his head in his hands.

Luckily, the old guy laughed. 'You must be Joe,' he said. 'Heard so much about you. My name's Clifton. I'm the gardener.'

He shook my hand again, and this time I wasn't as firm.

Had to save some power for the big dog.

He led me through the house and, before he ushered me through some grand double doors, whispered, 'Good luck.'

That was the second time I'd heard that.

Don't worry, Joe, said Norman. *They're probably just being friendly.*

Right, said Hank. *And the shark from* Jaws *was just an innocent fish and those people fell right into his mouth. Jeez.*

The living room was huge, too. This bloke who must have been her dad sat in a chair squinting at a BlackBerry, while her mum, who I vaguely recognized from the toy shop she runs in town, sat reading a newspaper. They obviously didn't know I was there. I cleared my throat. Nothing. I was starting to wonder whether they were waxworks, when Natalie came running in from outside. With her purple hair, black lipstick, and Oh, Inverted World T-shirt on, she looked like she was from a different planet.

'Joe!' She grabbed me in a bear hug and kissed me all over my face. The waxworks finally got up from their seats.

'Please, Natalie,' I said. 'I don't want your parents to think we're shtupping.'

'To think you're what?' Natalie's dad stood there frowning at me.

'Sh, sh, shnogging,' I said. 'Shnogging.'

He stared at me for an uncomfortably long time, then said, 'Quite.'

'I'm Catherine,' said Natalie's mum. 'You must be Joe.'

'Um, yes,' I said. 'I think so . . . Yes, I definitely am. Joseph. Joseph Marvin Cowley.'

Natalie frowned at me and mouthed, 'Marvin?'

Damn. I'd kept that a secret for six cocking months.

'Desmond,' said her dad. I held out my hand for a shake, but he'd already started to walk away. I looked down at my hand for a second, then pretended I had an itchy nose. Natalie raised her eyebrows at me as if to say, 'See what I mean?'

'I'm going to show Joe around the garden,' said Natalie.

'OK, but dinner's in ten minutes!' said Catherine.

'And don't disturb Clifton,' said Desmond. 'If he goes any slower, the hedges will start growing again before he's finished.'

We walked out into the garden. It was like something off the telly: hedge animals, fountains, even an actual lake! The closest thing we've had to a lake in our garden was when Gav locked himself out of the house and had to wazz into a bucket.

I ran my hand along a sculpted hedge. 'Wow.'

'I know,' said Natalie. 'Clifton's brilliant. I don't see why Desmond has to have him in on a Sunday, though.'

Before I had chance to ask why she calls him Desmond, she pulled me behind a hedge shaped like a lion. Clifton gasped and hid a book behind his back.

'Oh, it's you, Natalie.' He held his hand over his chest.

'What you reading now, Clifton?' she said. She slipped her arm around my waist.

'*Crime and Punishment*,' he said.

'Clifton's working his way through the Russian classics,' said Natalie. 'Clifton, this is Joe.'

'We've met already,' said Clifton. 'I think young Charlie abandoned him in the hall.'

'Sounds about right,' said Natalie. 'Little git.'

'Now, Natalie, you mustn't talk that way about your brother,' said Clifton.

'Careful, you're starting to sound like Catherine,' said Natalie with a smile.

Clifton held his stomach like he'd just been shot and then creased up laughing.

We left him to it, promising we wouldn't grass about him reading on the job and walked to the lake at the bottom of the garden. We sat down on a posh stone bench.

« Older posts

'It's nice here,' I said. 'You can't beat a good lake.'

'It's not a lake, it's a pond,' said Natalie.

'See, this is why I failed Geography.'

Natalie held my hand tight. I leaned in for a kiss but we were interrupted.

'Natalie, it's time for lunch!'

Balls.

'Here we go,' said Natalie as we got up. 'Good luck.'

Why does everyone keep saying that?

'So, Joe,' said Desmond as we started on our dinners. 'What line of work do you want to go into when you've completed your education?'

'I, I don't know really,' I said.

This was not good. I was supposed to be impressing them, and so far it was not going well. *What do I want to be when I grow up?*

Just say something, man, said Hank. *ANYTHING!*

'I, um, quite enjoy . . . drawing,' I said.

'Drawing?' Desmond scowled at me as if I'd said 'strangling kittens'. 'No future in that. Unless you consider dying of gonorrhoea in some godforsaken garret a future.'

My mouth went dry. Natalie squeezed my leg under the table.

'That's why I'm so glad our Charlie is technically minded,' said Catherine. 'You know, the other day he explained to me the concept of electro-conductivity. It was fascinating. For a seven year old he is remarkably gifted.'

I heard Natalie mumble 'Jesus Christ' under her breath.

I tried to remember the list. Rule one.

'That's great,' I said to Catherine. 'And you have a lovely home, by the way.'

She didn't say anything. I wasn't sure if she'd heard me. I started to panic.

'So,' I said to Charlie. 'Electro-conductivity, eh? How long would it take for you to explain that to me?'

'Probably a verrrry long time,' he said, without looking up from his book.

'Great,' I said. 'That's great.'

How many times do you want to say 'great', man? said Hank. *You sound like Tony the freakin' tiger.*

More silence. I glanced out of the window and saw Clifton replanting a hanging basket. He made brief eye contact then looked away.

'Soooo,' I said. 'Desmaaaa . . . Mr Tuft. What, um, what do you do? You know, for a living?'

Desmond leaned forward with his elbows on the table.

'I am the owner of the region's biggest supplier of public conveniences. You name them, I've sold them toilets. You been in the town hall?'

'Um, I don't think so.'

'The civic centre?'

« Older posts

'Errr.'

'The theatre?'

'I think I watched the *Teletubbies* there once, but I, er, didn't stay for the whole show.'

'Doesn't matter,' he said. 'I started off thirty years ago as a fitter, and now I'm a captain of industry.'

I took a sip of squash and tried to stop my hand shaking.

'Self-made man,' said Desmond while I started to regret even asking. 'To get to where I have, you have to work hard, apply yourself, and be a good manager of men.'

Natalie tutted and speared a carrot with her fork.

'That's interesting,' I said, sensing an opportunity for some common ground. 'Because I'm kind of a manager.'

Desmond glared at me while sawing at his beef.

'Y-yes, my friends are DJs,' I said. 'A-and I manage them. In fact, they've just entered this competition and . . .'

Before I could stammer the rest of the sentence, the dining room door opened and this kid walked in. He was wearing skinny jeans and had one of those trendy hair-cuts. A bit like the terrible one I had last term, but I got the impression he probably asked for his. He looked vaguely familiar, too. I couldn't figure out where from.

'Hey, guys, sorry I'm late,' he said.

Desmond practically levitated out of his chair and floated over to him.

'Seb, my boy, so glad you could come,' he said, shaking his hand. 'Catherine, fix Seb a plate, will you?'

Natalie gripped her knife so tight I could see tendons popping out.

'Charlie boy!' said Seb. 'How's it going, my man?'

'It?' said Charlie. 'How amusing.'

Seb smiled and shook his head.

'Hey, Nats,' he said. 'Looking killer as always.'

'Whatever,' she said. 'This is Joe, my boyfriend.'

'S'up, Joe,' he said, squinting at me. 'Hey, don't I know you?'

'I don't know,' I said. 'Maybe . . . '

'Oh, I do know you,' he said. 'You're that kid that broke Mr Boocock's ribs.'

Desmond glared at me. As did Catherine, returning from the kitchen with a plate. I could tell what their looks were saying. 'No daughter of mine will be associated with a teacher-assaulting thug.'

'That's not exactly true, *Seb*,' I said. 'It was one of my classmates. I was there when it happened, albeit completely uninvolved.'

'Cool,' he said. He sat down opposite Natalie.

'Really appreciate this, Catherine,' he said, gesturing at the plate which looked way fuller than mine. 'It looks delicious.'

'Don't be silly,' said Catherine. 'This is a surprise though; I didn't realize you were coming.'

'Well, Desmond asked me and—'

'Anyway,' Desmond cut in. 'Let's leave the boy to eat, shall we?'

It was then I realized where I knew Seb from. He's that sixth former who drives the gold Jag.

'Seb here is my protégé,' said Desmond. 'I'm showing him how to succeed in business. The boy's got it all—intelligence, determination, a good attitude. Reminds me of me when I was his age.'

They both laughed it up like it was hilarious.

'Yes, he's got it sorted,' said Desmond, looking straight at Natalie. 'He'll never want for cash. Not now he's learned the most important thing in life.'

'You've got to win at all costs,' said Seb. 'There's no prize for second place.'

'All those Olympic silver medallists would probably beg to differ,' is what I would have said if I'd have thought of it at the time. Stupid slow brain.

Seb smirked at Natalie. I'd only just met him, but I was already having graphic fantasies about gutting him with my dessert spoon.

'How's your old man, anyway?' said Desmond. 'Still sticking it to them in Westminster?'

'Seb's father is the local MP,' said Catherine.

'Wow,' I said. 'Great.'

Can someone get this kid a thesaurus?

'That's why the poor bugger has had to go to that awful school,' said Desmond. 'It wouldn't do for a politician to send his kid to a decent private academy, would it?'

'That would be terrible,' I said, just trying to join in.

They all stared at me. I felt like a museum exhibit.

'So, do you have any other hobbies, Seb?' I said. 'I mean, you can't just be into, like, business, can you?'

'Not at all, dude,' he said. 'I have other passions.'

I'm sure I saw his eyes flick over to Natalie.

'I'm a DJ,' he said.

No cocking way.

'And a bloody good one, too,' said Desmond. 'With his business skills and musical brilliance, he could be the next Slimboy whateverhisnameis.'

WHY DON'T YOU JUST MARRY HIM, DESMOND????

'And how about this contest?' said Desmond. 'Got your entry in yet?'

'Oh yeah, I sent it in last week,' said Seb.

'Well, with chops like yours, there's no way you can lose,' said Desmond.

'Is that the Buzzfest one?' I said.

Seb nodded. Desmond just swigged his wine.

'My, um, friends have entered that.'

'Really?' said Seb. 'What are they called?'

'The Sound Experience.'

Seb clicked his fingers. 'Wait a minute. Isn't that those kids that deafened the headmaster?'

Desmond and Catherine both gave me the evils. So apparently I'm part of a gang that goes around our scummy little school physically harming the teachers. This couldn't have gone better.

'Um, yes,' I said. 'But it was an accident.'

'Doesn't sound like you've got anything to worry about, Seb,' said Desmond.

'That's where you're wrong.' Natalie threw her knife and fork down. 'They're brilliant. The best.'

Desmond chuckled. 'Well, with what you listen to, that's not saying much.'

Natalie folded her arms. 'They are good, aren't they, Joe?'

I looked at Desmond, then Seb, then Catherine, then back at Natalie.

Hey, don't look at me, said Hank. *You're screwed no matter what you say*.

'I, um, I don't know,' I said.

As long as they beat that awful tossbag I don't care.

Monday 10th September

'So, how's it going?' I said to Harry and Ad on the way to school. 'Are you rehearsing? Sounding good?'

'We're doing OK, thanks, old boy,' said Harry.

'Just OK?' I said. 'Not brilliant?'

'Why the sudden interest?' said Harry. 'I was under the impression you weren't that bothered.'

Before I could say anything, a gold Jag pulled up alongside us.

'Hey, Joe!'

I turned and saw that greasy moron Seb hanging out of his window.

'Hello, Seb.'

'Good to see you, man,' he said. 'Is this the Sound Experience?'

'At your service,' said Harry.

'Nice pipe,' said Seb. 'Hey, have you guys got your audition yet?'

Harry and Ad exchanged worried glances.

'No,' said Harry.

'That's weird, 'cause I have,' said Seb, with that smug grin.

'You a DJ, then?' said Ad.

Seb laughed. It sounded like a posh donkey. 'Well aren't you a sharp cookie? I'm DJ Filthybeatz. My audition's at Scutty's, Friday the eighteenth.'

'Well, I'm sure they'll be getting in touch any minute now,' said Harry.

'Course they will,' said Seb. 'Anyway, it'd be wicked if we got the same audition. You could bring Nat along, matey.'

'Hmm, maybe,' I said.

« Older posts

'You're a lucky boy,' he said. 'Very lucky. Anyway, catch you guys later.'

He gunned his stupid knobmobile out into the street, giving us a face full of fumes.

Harry chuckled. 'Now I see why you want us to win so much.'

'What do you mean?' I said.

'Come on, you want us to rub posh boy's nose in it, don't you?'

I kicked a stone into the drain and shrugged. 'Maybe a bit.'

Harry smiled. 'I think we could manage that, couldn't we, old bean?'

'S'pose so,' said Ad. 'Except we haven't even got an audition yet.'

'Just a matter of time, comrade. Just a matter of time.'

I couldn't stop thinking about that arse Seb all day. His smug face. His stupid hair. And what did he mean by me being a lucky boy?

I met Natalie for the post-mortem of yesterday's lunch. I tried to play it casual to begin with.

'So, did your parents say anything about me?'

She stared at the floor. 'Not really.'

'Oh.'

'I haven't spoken to them since, anyway,' she said. 'I am steaming at Desmond for inviting Seb over. It was supposed to be about you.'

I thought back to how pleased they were to see him compared to me.

'Do you think they'd prefer it if you were going out with him?' I said.

'I don't care what they'd prefer,' she said. 'Our families have been friends for years but I've never liked him. He's always been a tosser.'

'I'm used to people not liking me,' I said. 'But because it's your dad, I kind of want him to.'

She kissed me. 'Don't worry about it,' she said. 'Because if you become the type of person *he* likes, I'll probably chuck you.'

I laughed, but deep down I still feel this urge to make him like me more than Seb.

After school, I went straight up to my room, nearly knocking the washing stack over as I walked in. That was close.

I found Gav playing a football game on my Xbox. He was playing as Aston Villa and was beating Barcelona six-nil. I'm clueless about football, but even I know that's bull. He's really starting to stink, too. I think he's been wearing the same pants for three days. I've never encountered such a stubborn adversary.

'Gav?' I said.

'What is it, man? Can't you see I'm busy?'

His tracksuit bottoms were falling down and I could see his disgusting hairy bum crack.

'I need to ask you something.'

'Yeah, go on.' He didn't take his eyes off the screen, where he'd just scored another unlikely goal. 'GET IN!'

'I'm serious, Gav.'

He huffed and paused it. 'All right, but I ain't checking your balls for lumps, man.'

'What? No, it's not that.' I sat on my chair. 'You know when you were going out with Lisa?'

'Mmhh.'

'Well, her parents didn't like you, did they?'

He shrugged.

'How did you deal with that?'

'I didn't give a rat's batty, blud,' he said. 'If they can't deal with the way the G-man operates, they can suck it, you know what I mean?'

'The G-man?' I said. 'Who calls you that?'

'Everyone.'

'I've never heard anyone call you that,' I said.

'Listen, man.' He looked like he was about to say something deep. Then he screwed his eyes shut and let out an enormous quacking fart.

'Thanks, Gav,' I said. 'This has been very useful.'

'Seriously though, bruv,' he said, as I was halfway out of the door. 'Maybe find out what they're into or something and talk to them about that.'

'Hmm, actually that might not be such a bad idea,' I said. 'Cheers.'

'Oh, and another thing,' he said.

'Yeah?'

He screwed up his face and let another ripper go.

'Brilliant,' I said. 'By the way, have you given any thought to taking the clothes hamper down?'

'I thought about it,' he said.

'And?'

'That's it.'

Oh, he'll take it down. I'm going to make this my life's work.

« Older posts

Tuesday 11th September

The smell in our bedroom was unbearable this morning. I think it's a combination of Gav and the dirty washing. There's no way I can bring Natalie here now. Not that that matters, anyway. Once Dr Death installs the national grid on my teeth, she'll be a distant memory.

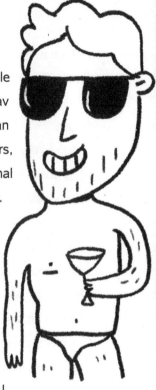

To make matters worse, I'm now down to my last pair of pants. This is getting desperate. I thought I had more, but it turns out me and Dad must have got ours mixed up and now they're all too big for me. This means he is in Ibiza right now, with loads of undersized undercrackers. The sick thing is, he'll still wear them. I swear to God, he was threatening to buy Daniel-Craig-style budgie smugglers for the beach.

Anyway, I had a brilliant idea at school. An idea that would bring an end to this madness once and for all.

8 p.m.

At least, that was the theory.

Before Gav got home, I put all the washing into two black bin bags, then carefully laid his pirate DVDs on top. I put enough in there to create the illusion that it wasn't mostly dirty clothes.

I sat in the shed, waiting for him to get home. When he finally did, I rang him.

'Gav,' I said. 'You need to get those DVDs out of the house.'

'Uh? Why?'

'Because the, um, piracy police have raided the house. They've taken me in for questioning. This is my one phone call. If you can get those bags out, they won't have a case against us.'

He swore and I could hear the bags rustling. I left the shed, to be ready in the kitchen to tell him I'd got him good. I looked up and saw my bedroom window open.

I dived back into the shed. 'Make sure you take them downstairs through the kitchen,' I said. 'We don't want the neighbours to see.'

I peeped out of the window and watched him drag the bag back in.

Are you sure this is worth it? said Norman. *Why don't you just take the washing down yourself?*

Because Joe has his principles, Norm, said Hank. *And what is a man without his principles?*

I don't know, but he's definitely not hiding in a shed, pretending to be in police custody, said Norman.

I ran across the garden and into the kitchen. I couldn't wait to see Gav's face when he saw me. I disconnected the call and waited.

« Older posts

And waited.

And waited.

What the cocking hell is the hold-up?

I crept through the lounge and into the hall. I looked up the stairs. Ah. The clothes were strewn everywhere, and the bags lay next to them, the bottoms completely split.

My phone vibrated. Text from Gav.

NICE TRY, SUCKA

Damn. Outsmarted by a chimp. I thought about just leaving them there, until Doris nearly broke her neck on a pair of Gav's crusty kecks on the landing.

In the end, I scooped the clothes up and shoved all I could into the washing machine.

This house has defeated me yet again.

In a way, it was kind of a relief when Natalie and I took Doris to the Silver Club at Morningside.

We were greeted by the organizer, who sat Doris in a chair next to this old bloke with an impressive moustache. He probably uses as much wax in it as Pete Cotterill does in his hair.

'Good evening, shipmates,' he said. 'My name is Reginald Arthur Stanforth, but everyone here calls me the Colonel.'

For a second, I thought it was Harry in an old bloke mask. I resisted the temptation to try and pull his face off.

'Colonel?' I said. 'Why's that?'

'Because I used to be a colonel in the navy, boy,' he said.

'Oh right.'

Anyway, he introduced us to all the regulars: Donald, Flo, Ethel, Blind Trevor. (I didn't ask why they called him that. He had a white stick and everything.)

Now, I'm only going to admit this here, but it was a really fun night. There was bingo, music, they even got an old Nintendo Wii out and had them playing games on that.

On the way home, all Doris could talk about was the Colonel.

'Ooh, he's a handsome gentleman,' she said. 'He reminded me of Cliff Richard, but with a moustache.'

'I think someone has a crush on someone!' I said.

Doris went all red. 'Stop it, you. I shall have you know I'm not a floozy.'

Walked Natalie home afterwards. Desmond came to the door and she just stormed past him. I stood there and I didn't know what else to do, so I waved.

'Hello, Mr Tuft,' I said. 'Nice evening, isn't it?'

'Is it?' he said.

'I, um, I don't know,' I said. 'I mean, I suppose for September it is quite reasonable, but when you compare it to the summer, it's rather chilly. As you may have noticed, I'm wearing a light jacket. Always best to be cautious, I think. Of course, my mum's always telling me that I don't have enough meat on my bones, so maybe that's why I feel the cold. I can't imagine you having the same problem.'

Wait a second, said Hank. *Did he really just call his girl-friend's dad a lardass?*

'I didn't mean that!' I said, laughing really loud and high. 'I just mean you're a much more well-covered individual than me. Which is a good thing. Sign of a happy life, that's what Doris always says. Mind you, she says a lot of wacky stuff. Once she said there was a chicken hiding in the bathroom, but no amount of searching could uncover it.'

'I hear you haven't sorted your work experience yet,' said Desmond.

I tried to calm myself down and stop my eye twitching. Jim told me he might be able to have me working with him, but he wasn't certain about his insurance.

'N-no, I suppose I haven't,' I said.

'Why is that?' he said. 'After all, you did have all summer to sort something out.'

Don't say, 'Because I was too busy getting to second base with your daughter.' Don't say, 'Because I was too busy getting to second base with your daughter.' Don't say, 'Because I was too busy getting to second base with your daughter.'

'I, uh, I don't know.'

Desmond sighed and stepped out of the house. 'Listen,' he said. 'It's a tough world out there, and if you want to thrive, you have to be professional, and you have to be organized. Especially if you're serious about my daughter. You are serious, aren't you?'

'Um, yes,' I said. 'Very serious.'

'Good,' he said. 'Because Natalie is destined for great things and I don't need her being held back by shiftless idiots.'

'Um, no, I'm not that,' I said. 'If anything, I'm shift . . . ful.'

'Then I may be able to help you,' he said. 'I mean, when Seb was your age, I had him doing his work experience with me, and that's how he became my protégé.'

'So, I could do my work experience with you?' I said.

Desmond laughed. 'Good Lord, no,' he said. 'But I know a chap who's always looking for help and I know for a fact you can start on Monday.'

'Thanks, Mr Tuft, but I was probably just going to go with my stepda—'

« Older posts

'It would be to your advantage to accept my offer, Joe,' said Desmond.

He stared into my eyes. Maybe this was my chance to show him what I'm made of, to show him that I'm better than that stupid Seb.

'Thank you, Mr Tuft,' I said. 'I'll do it.'

'Excellent,' he said, handing me a card. 'Be at that address at seven o'clock Monday morning and ask for Dingley.'

'Thank you, Mr Tuft, but do you mind me asking what the job is?'

'Goodnight, Joe,' he said, and went back inside, closing the door behind him.

I wonder why he wouldn't tell me what the job is. That's a bit weird, isn't it? Maybe he just didn't hear me when I asked. Yeah, that's what it was. This is going to be fine.

10 p.m.

OMG! When I did the washing earlier, I must have put my red undies in with all Gav's school shirts! **BAAAA HAHAHAAAA!** They're all <u>pink</u>!

He keeps chasing me around the house but I have the speed and agility advantage and he knows he's fighting a losing battle. And what's best is, he can't not go into school or wear non-uniform because of his bond! I swear on Picard, nothing can ruin my good mood now.

I have never felt pain like this.

My face feels like it's being squeezed by a giant ape.

I'd been trying to think of a way to get out of having this brace put on, but I couldn't do it. Where my mum's concerned, not even one of Harry's strategies would stand a chance.

I keep going to the mirror and looking at my teeth. They're hideous. Gav didn't help either, pointing at me and laughing.

He's just pleased the attention is finally off him. Everyone was talking about his shirt at school. Rich Crossley from 11c actually dared to call him Pinky to his face. I mean, he probably shouldn't have, because he spent the rest of break being held upside down by his ankles, but still.

« Older posts

'TIN GRII-IIN,' Gav chanted at me. 'TIIIN GRIIII-IIIIIN!'

I wanted to shout back at him, but moving my mouth in any way was agony.

'You wouldn't say that to Lil Hustla,' I muttered, nodding at a poster on our wall of a rapper with completely metal teeth.

'Too right I wouldn't,' said Gav. 'Cos Lil Hustla's grill is pure diamonds, you get me? Yours is like chicken wire.'

I glanced at it again in the mirror. Cocking hell, he was right.

'Oh God, I'm going to have to leave the country, aren't I?' I said.

'Nah, don't be like that, man,' said Gav.

He looked genuinely sorry. I turned to walk out, but then he continued. 'I mean, for one thing, there's no way you'd get through the metal detectors at the airport.'

Then, as if things couldn't get any worse, Natalie turned up!

Don't worry, Joe, said Norman. *If she really likes you, a brace is hardly going to put her off.*

I don't know, man, said Hank. *This chick is kinda out of your league as it is. This could be a tipping point.*

'Hi, Joe!' said Natalie. 'Just thought I'd pop in.'

She leaned in to give me a kiss, but I jerked my head back quick, keeping my lips pressed tight shut.

'What's the matter?' she said.

'Mmm hmm.'

Page 57 of 352 »

Natalie frowned and smiled at the same time. 'What's this about? Why won't you open your mouth?'

I stretched my lips over my teeth. 'I am opening it,' I said. 'Look. Nothing out of the ordinary here.'

She laughed. 'No, not at all. Other than the fact that you look like a tortoise.'

'Tortoish?' I said. 'That ish a shcandaloush accushation.'

'Oh for Pete's sake, Joe, stop being such a wazzock and show Natalie your bloody brace,' Mum called from the other room. I swear she has the hearing of a bat.

'Brace?' Natalie smiled. 'When did this happen?'

I sighed and put my face back to normal. The metal was digging into the inside of my lips anyway. 'Today,' I said. 'It'sh terrible.'

Natalie put her hands on her hips. 'Give us a smile, then.'

'There'sh nothing to shmile about,' I said.

She raised her eyebrows.

'Fine,' I said and gave her a really quick smile.

'Oh, it's not that bad,' she said, giggling.

I sighed. 'Are you going to dump me?'

She gave me a kiss. It was nice but hurt like a beast.

'Does that answer your question?'

'Yesh.'

« Older posts

Thursday 13th September

Insults heard today at school:

Metal mouth

Brace face

Tinsel teeth

Robochops.

That last one was Harry's.

Other kids came in wearing pink shirts today. This school makes me sick. It's like they choose the stupidest possible person as their leader. Imagine if real democracy worked like that.

5.30 p.m.

Pain wearing off slightly. Tried to teach myself to pronounce the letter S again. Jim walked in on me reciting, 'She sells sea shells on the sea shore,' over and over again into the bathroom mirror. He turned around and walked off, muttering something about being 'the only person in this house who isn't a headcase'.

Friday 14th September

I've been thinking about Desmond. If I became an entrepreneur like him, would he approve of me? Maybe I should go on that *Dragons' Den* show and pitch them my series of twenty-first-century emoticons.

The way I see it is, there aren't enough emoticons to get across the full spectrum of feelings and emotions we experience in the modern age. :) :(and ;) simply no longer cut it. So I've formulated these new ones:

: (:)	Braces
: ~)	Crooked nose man receives good news
: (}	Big chinned man receives bad news
:	Happy ninja
:	Sad ninja
OP	Cheeky Cyclops

6 p.m.

Just checked the website. Apparently, you have to be eighteen to go on that show. Never mind. My emoticons are good enough to succeed on their own without one of those so-called 'dragons' getting their cut. Yes, all the emoticon cash will be mine.

8 p.m.

Natalie is worried about my work experience next week. Apparently, Desmond keeps refusing to tell her what it is, only saying that it will be a 'test of my abilities'.

I keep trying to tell her I love tests.

Monday 17th September

BUT NOT THIS ONE.

« Older posts

I arrived at the address Desmond gave me at quarter to seven:

Tammerstone Council WDU, Shanks Street

Given how flashy Desmond is, it wasn't quite what I was expecting. It was a run-down-looking garage-type building in an abandoned industrial estate. I was wearing my best trousers and shirt, and my shoes had been polished, first by me, and then by Doris, so I knew I was looking sharp.

I knocked on the door and waited. And waited. After about three years it opened and what appeared in the door-way almost made me turn and run.

I actually thought it was a zombie. His skin was as grey as it is possible to be while still being alive, and random tufts of hair stuck out from his otherwise completely bald head. The name tag on his tattered hi-vis vest said 'Dingley'.

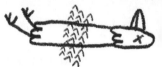

'What?' he said.

'Good morning, my name is Joe Cowley, and I'm here to begin my work experience placement.' I held out my hand.

He nodded, wiped his snotty nose then shook my hand in what must go straight in at number one in the top five most disgusting moments of my life.

He led me inside the filthy garage of Hades and grunted at some overalls hanging up on a hook. I'm no forensics expert, but these garments looked like they'd last been washed around about the time the *Titanic* sank.

'Hurry up and get dressed,' he said in a voice that sounded like he gargled sandpaper. 'We've got a lot to get done.'

I put the unholy stinking overalls on and awaited further instruction. Why the hell would Desmond send me here?

Dingley nodded at a clapped-out old truck. 'Get in.'

I did as I was told, and soon we were away. Dingley lit up a cigarette and immediately started hacking his lungs up.

'So what are we doing?' I said, wafting the smoke away from my face. 'What's the, um . . . what's the plan?'

Dingley peered at me sideways. 'Ain't he told you?'

'No,' I said. 'No, he hasn't.'

'Dingley, what are you laughing at?'

Tuesday 18th September

'He had you picking up ROADKILL?' Natalie yelled.

« Older posts

Harry and Ad laughed so much, they had to hold onto each other. The other diners in Griddler's looked narked off.

'Oh yes, this is hilarious,' I said. 'Well, let's see how funny you find this: I came home after work today and Doris asked me what was in my hair. I looked in the mirror and what do you know? Badger brains.'

This did not stop the laughs as effectively as I'd hoped. In fact, it made them worse.

'Oh God, old son,' Harry panted. 'I think I'm going to die.'

'I can't believe Desmond would do that,' said Natalie. 'He is such a knob.'

I rubbed my eyes and tried to cleanse myself of the memory of a day of scooping up splattered animals, chucking them in the back of the truck, then loading them into an incinerator. God, why couldn't I have got out of work experience like Gav? Oh, that's right, because I'm not a menace to society. This stinking life is so unfair.

'Look, just don't go tomorrow, Joe,' said Natalie. 'They can't make you.'

'No,' I said, 'I have to stick it out. This is a test. If I complete it successfully, your dad will approve of me.'

'Joe, Desmond doesn't approve of anyone,' said Natalie. 'That's just the way he is.'

'He approves of Seb,' I said.

She just shrugged and picked at her sandwich. Needless to say, I wasn't eating.

'Anyway, enough about me,' I said. 'How are you all getting on?'

'Grand,' said Harry, who was working at a bookshop. 'They let me restock the Military History section today. I was in heaven, old boy.'

'Yeah, and at the Co-op they got me to count the tins of beans,' said Ad. 'I couldn't believe they trusted me with such an important job. How about you, Nat?'

'I'm enjoying my week so far,' said Natalie. 'That Colonel is quite a character. But still, I won't be able to concentrate now I know what you're going through, Joe.'

'I'll get through it,' I said. 'I promise.'

Thursday 20th September

'That's it, I quit!'

'You can't,' said Dingley, with a laugh that sounded like bubbling tar.

'Oh, I can,' I said. 'I wouldn't chop a dead deer in half with a spade if I was being paid a thousand pounds, let alone for nothing!'

'Kids these days,' he said, shaking his head. 'Not interested in learning new skills.'

He took the spade off me and did the job himself. I will never be able to watch *Bambi* again. I made him take me back to the depot, where I got changed, then ran home and jumped straight into the shower.

« Older posts

No matter how hot the water is, it will never wash these past few days off.

Friday 21st September

I was woken up at ten by my phone ringing.

'Good morning, Joe,' said Desmond.

I actually did a little scream. 'Good morning, Mr Tuft.'

'Dingley tells me you haven't completed your week's work experience with him, is that correct?'

Say he's lying, said Hank. *Tell him he must have been huffing turps or something.*

Hank, Joe is at home when he should be at work, how is lying going to help this situation?

'Yes, sir, that is correct, sir.'

There was a pause on the line. 'Well, I must say I'm disappointed,' he said. 'I mean, I knew you weren't business-minded but I at least thought you'd have some work ethic.'

'I do have work ethic, I mean, right now I am working on a brand new range of emoticons,' I said. 'It's just, you know, scraping dead things off the road . . . '

'Everyone has to start somewhere, Joe,' he said. 'Just like I did as a humble fitter. And I'm afraid you've failed before you've even begun.'

'But, Mr Tuft, sir, I—'

He hung up.

This can't be good.

Monday 24th September

Miss Tyler, the General Studies teacher, kind of chewed my arse for not completing my work experience, but when I told her what it was, she passed me anyway. She is a strict vegan, and any kind of animal cruelty makes her go all queasy, even if they are already dead.

I mentioned my emoticons idea but she didn't seem too impressed. Apparently, there aren't enough cheeky Cyclopes out there for it to be viable. We'll see. I bet Edison had doubters when he invented the light bulb.

Mr Pratt called an assembly to say that the trend for pink shirts has to stop immediately. It definitely will because Mum bought Gav some new white ones and took the old pink ones down to the charity shop. It's unbelievable. If Gav came to school dressed as a clown, the whole place would be awash with Cocos by lunch.

9 p.m.

We took Doris to her club tonight. Everyone at the home welcomed Natalie back like an old friend. We had a game of bingo which the Colonel won. What was the grand prize? A hundred quid? A yacht? No. It was a tin of biscuits. And he didn't even keep them, he just gave them to Doris. She swooned so much, anyone would think it was a dozen roses. She gave me and Natalie a biscuit each, but they were a bit stale so I fed mine to Blind Trevor's dog.

« Older posts

As I walked Natalie home, I spotted a squished hedgehog on the side of the road and it gave me horrendous flashbacks.

'I should have done it,' I said to her. 'Just one more day.'

'Don't be stupid,' said Natalie. 'He should never have sent you there. One day you are going to be a brilliant illustrator, not someone who scrapes carcasses off tarmac.'

'I still feel like I have to prove something to your dad, though,' I said.

Natalie stopped and stood in front of me. 'For the last time, I do not care what he thinks of you, OK? Now just forget it.'

I've tried to forget it, but I can't.

I have to show him I'm worthy of his daughter. And that I can be a successful businessman.

I have to take the *SOUND EXPERIENCE* to victory.

Tuesday 25th September

'So have you heard back from Bangaz?' I asked Harry on the way to school.

'Negative,' he said.

'But I thought you were great DJ . . . thingies,' I said.

Harry ripped a twig off a bush. 'Bangaz wouldn't know quality if it smashed them in the sack.'

'Never mind, eh?' said Ad. 'There's always next year.'

'No,' I said, surprising myself with my anger. 'There must have been some mistake.'

The gold Jag pulled alongside us again. Cocking hell, is he a stalker or something?

'Hey, guys,' said Seb, tapping the side of the car to the beat of whatever cack music he was blasting. 'Got your audition yet?'

We didn't say anything.

'Oh, that's a shame,' said Seb, grinning like he didn't mean it. 'Guess you'll have to stick to deafening headmasters from now on, eh?'

'Deafness would be a sweet release if I had to listen to whatever it is you're peddling,' said Harry.

Seb shrugged, that infuriating grin still slapped across his face. 'Whatever, lads. And to think, when I win the prize, I was going to invite you to Buzzfest as my guests.'

'Really?' said Ad.

'Nah,' he said, before driving off.

My eye twitched while Hank hammered controls.

'I am going to get you an audition,' I said, my mouth moving while my brain wondered what the hell it was doing. 'Don't you worry.'

'How?' said Harry. 'I didn't know you had connections at Bangaz Radio.'

'I don't,' I said. 'But I'll do it.'

6 p.m.

I'm sitting in the lounge trying to think of a way to get the

« Older posts

SOUND EXPERIENCE an audition. Think, man, think. What would Captain Picard do?

At least the house is quiet. Ish. Mum has fallen asleep on the settee. There's a documentary about Simon Cowell on TV. Forget Picard, I need to think like him.

SIMON COWELL

PICARD

6.45 p.m.

I think I have an idea.

But it won't work.

Will it?

8 p.m.

Subject: AUDITION!!!!!

Before now, I never took you seriously when you called me your manager, but I'm starting to think I might actually be good at it. Do you know why?

BECAUSE I JUST GOT YOU AN AUDITION FOR THE COCKING BUZZFEST COMPETITION!!!!

I know, I'm the daddy.

It's next Saturday at Scutty's in town (the same night as Little Lord Bumface), so let's get rehearsing so we can blow his tiny mind.

Yours arse-kickingly,

Joe 'the guv'nor' Cowley

PS: I may have told Bangaz a little white lie to get you in. It's no biggy, but I'll fill you in tomorrow.

Wednesday 26th September

'YOU TOLD THEM WHAT?' Harry screamed.

I'd waited until lunchtime to give them the details. I thought it would be better when we were all together.

'I'm not sure I like this, mate,' said Ad.

'Are you mad?' said Natalie.

'Look, everyone needs to chill,' I said, freezing in horror at the realization that I was starting to talk like my dad.

'CHILL?' said Harry, his voice a furious whisper. 'Bloody chill? You told Bangaz Radio that we're the world's first DJ duo who are also a gay couple!'

'Are you saying there's something wrong with being gay, Harry?' I said.

He opened his mouth, then closed it. 'Of course I'm not,' he said. 'It's just . . . the idea of touching Ad's gentleman quite frankly turns my stomach.'

« Older posts

'Hey, it's a DJ competition, not a heavy petting . . . jamboree,' I said. 'They're not going to expect you to kiss.'

'What possessed you to tell them that, Joe?' said Natalie. 'Of all the things you could have said.'

I leaned forward and lowered my voice.

'These days you need an angle,' I said. 'Bangaz said your demo was good, but when you were up against acts with an angle, you fell down the pecking order. Take Seb. He's the son of an MP. That's why they picked him before you. You needed something to help you stand out.'

They still looked doubtful.

'Look at *The X Factor*,' I said. 'Loads of talented singers audition for that. But do you know which ones get on telly? The ones with the dead granny, or the drug addiction, or the depressed goldfish. The ones with an angle.'

I leaned back and popped a smiley face potato waffle into my mouth.

'I can almost see your point now, old son,' said Harry.

'Me as well,' said Ad. 'Except I don't remember anyone on *The X Factor* with a sad fish.'

I turned to Natalie. 'What do you think?'

She shrugged. 'If it means you guys get a chance, it's worth a go, right?'

Harry and Ad looked at each other, then quickly looked away.

'Look, how long have we been going on about Buzzfest?'

I said. 'Ages. This could be our golden opportunity. And you've met DJ Filthyballs. We can't let him win.'

Natalie smiled. 'I'd love to see his face if you won. And Desmond's.'

I held her hand under the table.

'So, are we in, boys?' I put mine and Natalie's hands in the middle of the table.

I looked at them sitting across from me. *Cocking hell. This is how it feels to be Harry.*

'All right,' said Ad, adding his hand to the pile. 'I'm in.'

'Harry?'

He took a deep puff on his empty pipe.

'Fair enough, old son,' he said, slapping his hand down. 'Consider me part of the alliance.'

I grinned like a moron. This is going to be brilliant.

Thursday 27th September

I thought about telling Seb about the *SOUND EXPERIENCE'S* big turnaround but decided against it. The element of surprise will be delicious.

7.30 p.m.

Found out who his dad is. Henry Mangrove MP (Conservative). I've found his Wikipedia page and added:

He has a son called Seb who is a right knobber.

I'm like a cyber-terrorist or something.

« Older posts

10 p.m.

The Wiki police have uncovered my sabotage. It now says:

He has a son called Seb who is a right knobber (citation needed).

Friday 28th September

Bangaz have sent an email out to all the contestants in the heat. So much for the surprise. Ah well, at least Seb will have plenty of time to cower in fear of our awesomeness.

Anyway, Natalie's coming over in a bit, so I'll be signing off.

9 p.m.

I remember a time when the most embarrassing thing that ever happened to me was when I accidentally called an old lady a 'thieving cow' over a loudspeaker in a meat van.

Me and Natalie were lying on my bedroom floor, doing History homework. We got to a tough bit about Hitler's domestic policy and started kissing.

I should point out that the snogging was completely unrelated to the subject matter. Nazi Germany is not one of my turn-ons.

Anyway, we had a nice sesh going, and it got to the point when we were ready to break it off.

But we couldn't.

I looked into Natalie's eyes. She was so close, my vision

went weird and she looked like a Cyclops. I hoped she wasn't just being cheeky. But if she was, I would have at least had an ideal emoticon for the situation.

'Uhh?' I said.

'Uhh!' was her reply.

I went to pull away, but she cried out:

'Aaargh, why li!'

'Uh?'

'Why li!'

It was then I realized what had happened. Her lip piercing had somehow got caught in my braces.

I tried not to panic but I'd never had someone attached to my face before.

We got up slowly and sideways-walked over to my mirror, knocking over a glass of lemonade and a lamp in the process.

I tried to look in the mirror, but I had to push Natalie's hair out of my face first. Even then, it was unclear how this had happened. It looked well and truly stuck.

'Uh, ry iss,' said Natalie. She grabbed her lip and started guiding it around the wire, but that just got it stuck even more.

'Uhhh.' We tried going the other way, with me moving in the opposite direction. It still didn't work.

This was when I really started panicking. What if we were stuck like that forever? I mean, I like Natalie and everything, but that would be going too far. I even imagined what our life would be like if we couldn't be separated.

« Older posts

We'd have to give ourselves a name. Like Jatalie. Or Noe.

'Oh oo ee oo?' I said. TRANSLATION: What do we do?

'I oh oh!' said Natalie. TRANSLATION: I don't know!

We tried everything to free ourselves, but nothing worked. Natalie couldn't take her piercing out because her lip was twisted around and the ring had somehow got all bent. Maybe we really were stuck. Then the door opened.

'Oh my days, blud, you're at least s'posed to like, move around and that,' said Gav.

We shuffled around to face him. That was when he saw the problem. I'd like to say he immediately sprang into action, helping us free ourselves and swearing never to mention it to anyone. But I'd be lying.

'This is going straight on Facebook,' he said, after taking about six photos on his phone.

'Oh uh oh, oo uhhing ihhhea,' I said. TOO RUDE TO TRANSLATE.

'Aight.' Gav wiped tears of laughter from his eyes. 'I s'pose I best help you geeks out.'

'Ahh hyou,' I said.

'HELEN!' he called down the stairs.

MUM? MUM? Jumping Jesus on a pogo stick.

Sometimes I wonder if there is a universe outside these four walls, said Hank.

'What's up?' said Mum, clomping up the stairs. 'If you've blocked the toilet again, there's going to be hell to pay.'

She came into our room and stood next to Gav. Then she started laughing. Great. The only thing that makes her laugh is THIS.

She stepped in, still laughing, and tried to separate us. But she couldn't do it.

'God, it's like a bloody switchboard in there,' she said.

She pulled her phone out and for a horrible second, I thought she was going to take some photos as well, but what she actually did was even worse.

'Joe Cowley and Natalie Tuft,' the receptionist called out. 'Dr Priss is ready to see you now.'

Everyone in the waiting room was staring at us. They weren't even being subtle about it, either.

'Mummy, why are they stuck together?' I heard this little kid ask.

'Because they're very naughty,' she said. Stuck up cow.

« Older posts

'Well, well, well,' said Priss. 'What do we have here?'

What kind of question was that? He knew exactly what he had here. He got his little torch out and shone it into our mouths.

'Remarkable,' he said. 'In all my years . . .'

He moved away and I heard what sounded like a phone being dialled.

'Hey, Watkins, get in here, you have to see this,' he said. 'Yes, definitely bring your students.'

So after about fifteen minutes of being stared at by eight different people, Priss finally got some pliers out, did some delicate snipping and we were free. Then he replaced the wire in my tooth cage of doom and sat us down for a lecture.

'With this much metalwork involved, a catastrophe like this was bound to happen,' he said. 'From now on, take it easy. Closed-mouth only, until you're ready to be responsible.'

By the time I got home, that photo of us had been shared on Facebook over two hundred times. That website is nothing but a catalogue of all the humiliating things that have happened to me.

Saturday 29th September

Trying to forget about yesterday by getting into my role as manager. Maybe I'll make a career of it and become more Cowell-like. I might go down Primark and bulk-buy some black T-shirts.

And then, when I'm a billionaire music mogul, I will buy and sell Seb's lousy DJ business and use the money to wipe my rich arse, and Desmond will be BEGGING to fit the bogs in my mansion, where I no longer have to share a bedroom with the swamp monster.

I started the day with *SOUND EXPERIENCE* rehearsals in Ad's garage. The smell of meat from his dad's butcher overalls made me feel a bit queasy, but I got used to it after a while.

They had all their equipment set up on an old pasting table: little boxes that make noises like drums and weird little bleeps and bloops, along with a laptop and a set of decks.

I'll be honest now. Even though I am a kick-ass music manager, I don't really know much about music. Definitely not this type of music. I can't even tell if it's good or not. But Natalie says it is, so I'll trust her judgement.

« Older posts

'All this rehearsing is fine,' said Harry, during a break. 'But we need gigs so we're not rusty for the audition. We haven't done a set since the prom.'

'Leave it with me,' I said. 'I'll sort you out.'

Are you sure? said Norman. *Perhaps you should think before you go making wild proclamations.*

Can it, Norm, said Hank, a cigar clamped between his teeth. *We don't need wet blankets like you in the music biz.*

I tried googling clubs to see if they did try-outs but came up with nothing. I kept looking though, the thought of Desmond's smug face spurring me on. If I don't do this, he's going to forever be trying to replace me with Seb.

That's when it occurred to me. I could go to Desmond for help. Show him I'm making an effort.

'Oh, it's you,' said Charlie, answering the door. 'I didn't think you'd be back.'

'Well, maybe I'm a resilient go-getter,' I said. 'You make sure you tell your dad that, too.'

Charlie said nothing and let me in.

I psyched myself up and entered the lounge. Desmond was in the same spot as before, staring at the BlackBerry again.

I cleared my throat. He didn't flinch.

'Um, Mr Tuft.'

He peered at me over his glasses as if I were a Jehovah's Witness trying to sell him a timeshare.

'Ah,' he said. 'Hello, John.'

'It's uh, Joe, actually.'

'Pardon?'

'Never mind.'

'Natalie's in the garden, distracting the world's slowest gardener,' he said.

'Actually, it's you I want to speak to,' I said.

He put the BlackBerry down and took his glasses off.

'What do you need to speak to me about? I'm a busy man,' said Desmond.

'Well, this is the thing,' I said. 'I kind of have a favour to ask you.'

His mouth went all tight. Like a cat's bum sucking a lemon.

'No, not a favour,' I said. 'A business proposition.'

He sighed. 'Go on.'

'You know I mentioned my friends are DJs?'

He shrugged.

'Well anyway, they're short on gigs at the moment, and I know you're a well-connected businessman who must know some people who might be able to help them get their name out there? If you wouldn't mind. Sir.'

He stroked his chin. 'You want me—the owner of Tuft's Toilet Company, with the highest reputation for quality WCs in the Midlands region and beyond—to risk my reputation on a couple of unknowns?'

« Older posts

'I know it's a big ask,' I said. 'But I promise they won't let you down.'

He studied me like a lab specimen.

'It's just, I was thinking about what you said the other day, about my work ethic, and I want to prove to you that I love to work, and that I can be business-minded.'

Desmond tapped his fingers on his chin. 'All right, Jack,' he said. 'You've intrigued me. It just so happens that I'm good pals with Kevin Paul, the best corporate DJ in the country. Does our Christmas do every year.'

'OK,' I said.

'Turns out he owes me a favour,' he said. 'And as I'm in a generous mood, I'll see if he can sort your boys out.'

'Oh, that's brilliant,' I said. 'Thanks, Mr Tuft.'

He cut me off with a raised hand. 'Don't thank me yet. Because if these so-called clients of yours don't do the job, it'll look bad on me. And if I look bad, I'm likely to become unhappy, do you understand?'

'O-of course. That's spiffing,' I said.

Spiffing? said Hank. *You know what, I was wrong. Stick to 'great'.*

'Right,' said Desmond. 'Anyway, let's consider this a test of your managerial ability, shall we? Use this as an opportunity to prove your worth.'

I know what he really meant by that. This is about showing him I'm good enough for Natalie.

'OK,' I said. 'Thanks for the opportunity.'

He winked at me. 'You're welcome, Jason. I'll be in touch with the details asap.'

I went out into the garden to find Natalie talking to Clifton next to a hedge giraffe.

'Hey, Joe.' Natalie turned and hugged me. 'What are you doing here?'

'Just a bit of business with your dad,' I said.

'Have you come to headhunt me, son?' said Clifton, with a smile. 'Because I'm not cheap, you know.'

'No, I think you'd run out of stuff to do after our two hanging baskets.'

'What business is this?' said Natalie, looking spooked.

'Your dad is going to sort a warm-up gig for the Sound Experience,' I said. 'You know, maybe he's not so bad after all.'

Clifton and Natalie raised their eyebrows at each other.

'What?' I said.

Sunday 30th September

My last Sunday before Dad gets back from Ibiza. Should I feel bad for making the most of it? Ah, balls to it.

Anyway, that doesn't matter, because Desmond has come through and got us a gig! Natalie called with the details. It's Thursday at the Tammerstone Social Club starting at five-thirty.

« Older posts

'I'm not sure about this, Joe,' said Natalie. 'Desmond's acting weird about it. More weird than normal.'

'It's fine,' I said. 'Your dad's a businessman. I'm a businessman. We all want the best possible outcome from this.'

'Jesus, Joe,' she said. 'You're starting to sound like one of those douches from the *Young Apprentice*.'

I'm not. Am I?

Monday 1st October

Intensive rehearsals with the Sound Experience. No time to write.

Tuesday 2nd October

More rehearsals.

Attempted first open-mouthed kiss with Natalie since the incident. Went fine, and the danger made it a bit more exciting.

Wednesday 3rd October

'Ad, you were late with that breakbeat,' I interrupted 'Kamikaze Attack' for the fifth time.

'Come on, old boy,' said Harry. 'You don't even know what a breakbeat is.'

'All I'm saying is, that beat you were playing had not broken in a satisfactory manner,' I said. 'Now, let's go through it again.'

'But my hands hurt, Joe,' said Ad.

'Dammit, Ad,' I said. 'If you won't break the beats, I'll come over there and break them myself.'

'Go on, then,' he said.

I stood there for a second.

'All right then, we'll take five,' I said.

Natalie is still worried about this gig tomorrow. I keep telling her there's nothing to worry about.

Thursday 4th October

What can I say, other than THIS MEANS WAR.

Before I left home tonight, I found an old suit I inherited

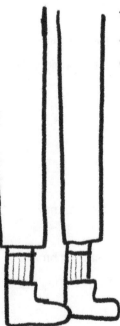

from my cousin, Liam. Men's Domain says a good way to get ahead in your career is to dress smartly.

I stood in front of Mum's full-length mirror. I looked OK, even though my trousers stopped a few centimetres above my ankles. Reaction downstairs was mixed:

Doris: 'Oh, aren't you smart?'

Gav: 'You look like a perv, blud.'

Jim: 'Has it shrunk in the wash, or what? '

Mum: 'My baby is growing up. Waaaaah!'

I met Harry, Ad, and Natalie at the club.

'Mr Bean, ahoy!' said Harry.

'Right, game faces on, people,' I said, ignoring his HILARIOUS remark. 'Consider this a dress rehearsal for Saturday night.'

While the *SOUND EXPERIENCE* set up, me and Natalie sat at a table at the back of the stage.

'Why are you wearing that?' she said.

'To look professional,' I said.

'Why do you need to look professional?' she said. 'What's wrong with your usual look?'

'I didn't know I had a look,' I said. 'Unless you consider a *Star Trek* T-shirt and jeans the height of fashion.'

'Well, I like it,' she said.

The *SOUND EXPERIENCE* did a quick soundcheck and we were ready to go. Harry put some subdued techno music on to welcome the party people in.

My eye started twitching. *Here we go.*

The door at the other side of the room opened. *Wait a minute, I recognize him.*

SEB?

I stood up.

'What are you doing here?'

He laughed. 'Just come to check out the competition.'

But how did he know?

I exchanged a look with Natalie. *That's* how.

'I knew this was a set-up,' said Natalie. 'God, I HATE Desmond.'

I was about to try and reason with her and say it could have been a coincidence when the party people filed in.

All dressed in black.

'Bloody hell,' said Harry.

'I know!' said Ad. 'It's as if they've been to a funeral or something.'

We all stared at him until he twigged.

'Oh bum!'

'Nice gig you've got us here, MANAGER,' said Harry. 'At least YOU'RE dressed for the occasion.'

Natalie looked like she was about to punch something.

'Look, we can't afford to panic,' I said. 'Men's Domain says that to succeed in business, you have to adapt to change. Ad, stick on some seventies classics.'

Ad nodded and fumbled with the laptop.

The room began to fill with mourners. Seb stood at the back, barely able to suppress his giggles. Then his giggles turned into a full-on laugh when the first seventies classic blasted out:

'Going Underground'.

It was the first time I've ever run away from an angry mob of mourners whilst lugging heavy audio equipment, and I don't plan on doing it again.

« Older posts

While we waited for Ad's dad to pick us up, Natalie phoned Desmond.

'How could you do this?' she shrieked. 'You set us up. What the hell is your problem?'

My hands shook. Ad was hunched over a drain as if he was about to spew.

'Yes, I do know who I'm talking to . . . Oh, you're such a . . .'

She growled and thrust the phone at me. 'He wants to speak to you.'

'H-hello?'

'Evening, Jake,' he said. 'My daughter seems to be under the impression that I was unfair in offering your friends this opportunity. Is that an opinion you share?'

I took a breath as my pulse thudded in my ears. 'Well, I do think you could perhaps have mentioned that it was a funeral. Just like you could have mentioned I was supposed to be scooping fox guts.'

'I told you it was a private party and that it would be a test of your managerial skills,' he said. 'If you couldn't make the appropriate enquiries, I'm afraid your abilities leave something to be desired. This was yet another chance to prove your worth, and I'm afraid you've failed.'

Calm down, Joe, said Norman. *Don't antagonize this man.*

Screw that! said Hank. *If I were you, I'd antagonize my boot right up his ass.*

'Well how about this, *Desmond*,' I said. 'When the Sound Experience win the Buzzfest contest and beat that pet labradoodle of yours, then you'll see what I'm worth.'

I hung up. Natalie stared at me for a second then gave me the best kiss ever. We didn't even care about the risk of linkage.

'I find you so irresistible right now,' she said.

'Um, cool.'

I looked at Harry and Ad. They were paler than a *Twilight* fancy dress party.

'Are you ready for Saturday night, boys?' I said.

'Are you kidding me?' said Harry. 'I never want to go near these decks again. Especially whilst pretending to be Ad's boyfriend.'

'Yeah,' said Ad. 'And, I don't want to offend you or nothing, but this whole thing has kind of turned you into a knob.'

'If by "a knob" you mean "super-determined", then yes, I am a huge knob,' I said. 'The biggest.'

« Older posts

The Jag pulled up again.

'"Going Underground"?' said Seb. 'Classic, lads, classic.'

'Ah, sit on a cactus, Seb,' said Natalie.

He grinned as if she'd told him he was a top bloke.

I looked around for something heavy to drop on his bonnet.

'Anyway, if you losers are going to let this put you off, there'll be less competition for me,' he said. 'Not that you'd have stood a chance, anyway.'

I noticed Harry chewing extra hard on his pipe.

'Catch you later, guys,' said Seb. 'And, Nats, if you ever get fed up of hanging out with the odd squad, you can always hit me up.'

He pulled away, laughing and blasting his crap music.

'All right, mate,' said Ad. 'I'm in.'

'I'm in too, soldier,' said Harry. 'I'll be Ad's wife if it means silencing that buffoon.'

Brilliant.

Friday 5th October

After school, Natalie asked me to meet her in the park and to bring my suit. I thought it was a bit weird, but whatever. When I got there, she took the suit off me and chucked it in the clothes recycling bin.

'What did you do that for?' I shrieked.

'One, it doesn't fit. Two, you look like an idiot,' she said.

'But that was the only business attire I owned!' I said.

'Ah well,' she said. 'Think of it this way, donating it will help someone less fortunate than you . . . to look like a knob.'

8.30 p.m.

Just got off the phone with Dad. He and Svetlana got back from Ibiza late last night. Apparently, the whole place had a 'wicked fresh vibe'. What's worse is, he's promised to take me out there when I'm eighteen. And I promised that if he did, I'd jump out of the emergency exit at thirty thousand feet. Don't think he heard me.

Saturday 6th October

Here we go. The day of the audition. I feel sick.

About five minutes ago I had a phone call from a number I didn't recognize.

'This Joe?'

'Hello, Sebastian,' I said. 'If you or your sugar daddy have any more gigs for us, you can cram them up your balloon knot.'

'Shut up,' he said, his fake as hell charming voice gone completely. 'I saw what you did to my dad's Wiki page.'

'Come on, he's a politician,' I said. 'There must be millions of people waiting to give him abuse.'

Yeaaah, boy! Hank yelled.

'I'm going to get you for that,' he said. 'And I'm going to start by beating those monkey boys of yours.'

Then he hung up.

The *SOUND EXPERIENCE* are not monkey boys. They are monkey men.

8 p.m.

So nervous. I'm going to blog through the night to give my hands something to do. Scutty's is open early for the auditions. I thought it would be just performers and judges, but they've let the public in. And they're selling drinks half price. What could possibly go wrong?

Oh God, a drunk bloke has just swaggered over to me, pointed at my T-shirt and yelled, 'CAPTAIN KIRK!' right in my face. I was going to explain the many ways Kirk is inferior to Picard, but he burped and walked off. I'll have to let this one go.

We've had the running order—there are six acts and two will go through to the semi-final. The last two on tonight are the *SOUND EXPERIENCE*, then DJ Filthybeatz. Good. He'll look like a chump trying to follow us.

8.10 p.m.

Getting twitchy now. There must be about a hundred in. Ad's just been to the toilet to throw up and says his glasses fell in the bowl. Despite his assurances that he's swilled them thoroughly, I'm not letting him get too close.

8.15 p.m.

DJ Filthypants still not here. Maybe he's too scared to show his face.

8.20 p.m.

Ten minutes to show time. Just took the boys and Natalie out into the corridor for a pep talk.

'I know it's scary,' I said. 'But you can do this. I may not have been that supportive of you guys in the past, but I've seen the light. You can be world-beaters. You just have to believe in yourselves.'

'Cripes,' said Harry. 'What Disney film did you nick that from?'

'Fair point,' I said. 'Well let me put it to you this way. Seb is the Luftwaffe coming across the sea to destroy our air defences. Are we going to let him?'

'No fear!' said Harry.

'There's the Battle of Britain spirit!' I said.

'But I'm really scared,' said Ad.

'I've heard that it helps if you imagine the audience naked,' I said.

Ad's eyes suddenly went wide.

'Except Natalie,' I said. 'That's not allowed.'

'But I'm doing it now, Joe, I can't stop.'

I jumped on him and covered his eyes, then I remembered where his glasses had been and went and washed my hands.

« Older posts

8.30 p.m.

Seb has finally turned up. With his entourage. Worf's ridges. There's two girls in little dresses and two of the most enormous slabs of man meat I have ever seen. They make the Blenkinsops look like Jedward. Seb keeps staring at me as if he's going to start something. Oh cock. I probably shouldn't have fiddled with his dad's Wiki.

8.45 p.m.

We're underway. The MC (some bloke called Mental Mickey) ran on stage and was all, 'Oi, oi! Are we ready to 'ave it?' The crowd went wild, and Ad went a darker shade of green.

The first act was called DJ Fuzzyfuzz, or Fuzzylumpkins, or something like that. He sounded OK to me, but Harry assured me that he was 'a rank amateur'.

9 p.m.

So far so bad. The second act, DJ Push and MC Pull, are terrible. Even I can hear that.

Seb is still staring at me. Maybe I should mouth, 'Do you fancy me, or something?' at him? No. He might send the Axis of Evil over to punch me in the neck.

9.10 p.m.

Push and Pull have got a big light show, which throws different coloured lights over the crowd. This is doing my retinas no good whatsoever. God, that girl Seb's with is giving me evils. How much is he paying her to do that? The more I see of her face though, the more familiar she looks. Wait a minute.

Oh balls.

9.15 p.m.

Lisa? My ex? LISA?!

They can tell I've realized because they've got identical smug smirks on their faces. Oh, and now they're kissing. Great.

9.20 p.m.

'Is that your ex with Seb?' said Natalie.

'Um, yeah, no, maybe, I hadn't noticed,' I said.

'Yeah right,' she said. 'You know he's doing that just to get at you, don't you?'

I shrugged. 'I suppose so.'

Natalie put her arms around me and kissed me. Quite

« Older posts

hard, to be honest. My lips hurt now. Is this going to turn into some kind of kiss-off? Because if it is, I am prepared to do my duty.

9.30 p.m.

OMG, it's nearly time for the *SOUND EXPERIENCE*. They're on stage setting up now. If Ad projectile vomits into the crowd I will literally die.

I give them a thumbs up. I mouth, 'Battle of Britain spirit,' at Harry and he clamps his pipe between his teeth and salutes.

Natalie grips my hand tight. Here we go.

9.40 p.m.

OK, they're on and they're sounding great. I think. People are dancing like mad and the floor is full. One slight snag might have been Mental Mickey's intro:

'And now, let's get ready for the next contestants—they're loud, they're proud, and they're OUT. They're the competition's only gay couple—give a massive Scutty's welcome to the Sound Experience!'

You should have seen that tool, Seb, laughing. He'll be laughing out the other side of his face when he LOSES. I'm sure I saw Lisa saying, 'I knew it,' to him.

'They're amazing, aren't they?' Natalie shouts at me over the pounding. 'Brutal and . . . real.'

I nod, but I have no idea what she's talking about. We go to the raised area overlooking the dance floor. After so many disastrous gigs in front of confused Year Sevens and even more confused OAPs it's great to see Harry and Ad finally find their audience.

Cocking hell, speaking of audience, there's this really embarrassing middle-aged bloke perv-dancing with this young woman. He's wearing a bright pink T-shirt. And now he's looking at me. Oh. Oh no.

9.50 p.m.

'Hey, son!' Dad yelled as he came over. 'Your guys are totally rocking the joint.'

I pinched the bridge of my nose. Why can't I have a normal dad who only ever uses the word 'joint' when he's making stuff out of wood?

He pointed at Natalie with a glow stick. 'Is this your chica?'

'Hi!' Natalie yelled back. 'Yes, I am Joe's chica.'

'Far out, man,' he said. 'Anyway, I'd better get back to the floor, can't keep my lady waiting.' He nodded at Svetlana, looking bored and checking her phone.

'So that's your dad then?' said Natalie, when he'd gone.

'Yep,' I said.

'No wonder we're both so messed up,' she said.

« Older posts

10 p.m.

The *SOUND EXPERIENCE* came off the stage to a massive round of applause. The look on Harry's face was priceless. I hugged him, then Ad, who promptly puked down my back. Lovely.

10.20 p.m.

By the time I'd got all the chunks off my jacket, DJ Filthypants had already started.

And he was crap!

I mean sure, everyone was dancing and cheering, but that's just because they were still high from the *SOUND EXPERIENCE'S* set.

You should have seen him up there, with his **RIDICU- LOUS** hair. And sunglasses. At night. INDOORS.

Lisa and the other girls were at the front of the dance floor, dancing and whooping, and his two bouncers stood either side of the stage with their arms folded. Presumably, in case everyone tried to rush the stage to stop him inflicting any more of his knobwash music on them.

10.35 p.m.

Dad just danced over to us.

'This kid's amazing!' he screamed. 'He's dropping phat beats in the hizzouse!'

I cornered Harry and asked if that was true.

He nodded with a grim look on his face. 'As much as it pains me to say it, he is quite good.'

10.40 p.m.

Jesus bum-flapping Christ. Seb's got a light show.

There's laser beams, laser stars, a load of lasers shaped like a globe. He even projected hearts around the room when he played this crappy, soppy chipmunk-style love song.

'And his dad's an MP,' said Harry. 'If I were a taxpayer, I'd be outraged.'

10.45 p.m.

It's over. The crowd is going crazy. I still say it's thanks to us warming them up for him, but whatever. Now his bouncers are escorting him through the crowd. If he was any further up his own arse he'd be crawling out through his mouth.

Mental Mickey has come back on and said that voting slips are available at the front of the stage.

IT'S A PUBLIC VOTE? If the pink shirt episode taught me anything it's that the public can't be trusted. Time to do some canvassing. Against the son of an MP. Eep.

11 p.m.

OK, all votes are in. That was intense. The first person I spoke to was Dad.

« Older posts

'I trust you'll do the right thing,' I said.

'Well, that last dude was pretty fresh, son,' he said.

I glared at him until he put his cross next to the SOUND EXPERIENCE.

What followed was ten minutes of trying to win the votes of drunken idiots.

'All right, kid,' said a bloke swaying on the spot. 'I'll vote for your boys, but only if you sing for me.'

If I wasn't so committed to the cause I would not have belted out a verse of 'Comfortably Numb' in the middle of the dance floor, but when you're in the music biz, you gotta do what you gotta do.

I glanced over to the other side of the dance floor and saw Seb chatting up some girls with his minders.

'Oh yah, music is totally my outlet, yah.'

Sounds like he's talking out of his outlet.

Me and Natalie approached a couple who still hadn't voted yet, but then so did Seb.

'Hey, guys,' said Seb. 'Thinking of voting for DJ Filthybeatz?'

'Or the Sound Experience?' I said.

They looked confused.

'Come on, you shouldn't throw your vote away on these amateurs,' said Seb.

Norman tried to restrain Hank. He didn't succeed.

'Amateurs?' I said. 'Ask yourself, do you really want

to encourage the type of person who wears sunglasses indoors?'

'Hey, how do you know he's not blind?' said the bloke.

'Good point,' I said, flicking a V right in front of Seb's face. 'Hey, how many fingers am I holding up?'

He glanced at his minders. 'Rupert, Benedict.'

They advanced on me and we beat a hasty retreat.

11.15 p.m.

'OK, you mad bunch of mentalists,' Mental Mickey yelled. 'It has been very close, but we have a winner.'

Harry chewed hard on his pipe. Ad sat on the floor with his head between his knees. I glanced over at the arse corner. Lisa had her arm around Seb. Pfft. What do I care?

'In first place, winning the hundred pound prize and going to the semi-final is . . . '

He paused. I gripped Natalie's hand.

'DJ Filthybeatz!'

Seb's moron corner exploded with cheers.

Lisa held up her hand in the shape of an L on her forehead, except it was backwards, so it was more like a J. I had to hold Natalie back.

'And in second place, and also earning a place in the semi is . . . the Sound Experience!'

YES! We've done it. It would have been nice to beat Lord Ebenezer Bum Hole, but whatever, the dream is still alive.

« Older posts

When we got outside, Ad puked again. How could he have anything left inside him? His stomach is like the TARDIS.

Seb and his crew came out behind us.

'Nice try, gay boys,' he said.

'Hey, we're not—' said Harry, before stopping himself. 'I mean, up yours, you homophobe.'

Seb and Lisa cackled.

'Don't listen to him, guys,' said Natalie, eyeballing Lisa. 'If two people ever deserved each other it's them.'

Lisa turned on Natalie. 'Oh yeah, come on then . . .'

The two giants stepped in and carried Lisa away.

'Aw, man,' said Ad. 'We could have seen a girl fight.'

'I don't fight like a girl,' said Natalie. 'Believe me.'

Sunday 7th October

Had to spend ALL DAY with Dad today, when all I wanted to do was prepare for the semi-final. He suggested having some coloured crystals put in my braces. Because I clearly don't get enough wedgies.

'I tell you what, son,' he said, sipping something he called a mojito, 'that chica of yours is *on point*. The emo look is so in right now.'

'She's not on point,' I said. 'She's looked like that as long as I've known her.'

'Cool beans,' he said. 'So she's a trendsetter.'

Svetlana rolled her eyes and drained the rest of her vodka.

rat dog

Had hummus and steamed vegetables for dinner. It was bum. I sneakily fed most of mine to Hercules the rat dog. He's bound to get big-time squits now. Rather him than me.

Strategy meeting after school tomorrow. Can't wait.

Monday 8th October

MINUTES OF *SOUND EXPERIENCE* STRATEGY MEETING

    LOCATION: AD'S GARAGE

    MEMBERS PRESENT:

    JOE COWLEY—MANAGER/ROADIE

    NATALIE TUFT—CO-MANAGER

    HARRY HODGELEY—TALENT

    AD LAWRENCE—TALENT

    MALCOLM LAWRENCE—BLOKE (NB: MALCOLM ONLY CONTRIBUTED INTERMITTENTLY, WHEN COMING IN TO LOOK FOR A PLUNGER)

4.30 p.m. Meeting begins by discussing ways of improving the *SOUND EXPERIENCE* and making them better than DJ Filthyarse.

4.35 p.m. HH suggests pressing issues are lack of light show, muscle/security, and AL's rampant nausea. ML says AL has always been the same for nervous puking and suggests travel sickness pills. JC recalls that the force of it was incredible—like a geyser.

4.40 p.m. AL expresses concern at growing rumours at school about his and HH's relationship. JC points out that

« Older posts

at present, the rumours are just that, and no proof exists, so really, it's still just a few idiots calling them gay, which is no different from before.

4.45 p.m. NT expresses concern at the involvement of Lisa Hall in the Filthybeatz camp, calling her an 'uberbitch'. This view finds no objections.

4.50 p.m. JC, in his capacity as manager, promises to resolve issues and procure a light show and muscle for the semi-final. AL is entrusted with getting his own travel sickness pills, but JC worries that he might accidentally take sleeping pills or laxatives, so promises to obtain the medication, too.

4.55 p.m. AL begins game of Would You Rather?

4.57 p.m. After careful deliberation, HH decides he would rather pee every time he stands up than poo every time he sits down.

4.58 p.m. AL agrees.

4.59 p.m. NT disagrees.

5.00 p.m. JC refuses to be drawn on such a discussion.

5.01 p.m. ML wonders aloud what he did wrong to produce such a sicko of a child.

5.05 p.m. AL opens bag of M&M's and is freaked out to find one of them has a W on it.

5.30 p.m. Everyone gives up trying to explain it to AL.
END OF MEETING

Took Doris to her club afterwards. They were doing drawing today. We joined in, but I wasn't interested in sketching a fruit bowl, so I drew one of Seb being eaten by a shark.

Tuesday 9th October

Hey, Joe.' Pete Cotterill stopped me in the corridor. 'Is it true that your two mates are lovers?'

'No comment,' I said, sweeping past him into the form room, where Harry and Ad were under siege by a mob.

'Is it true?'

« Older posts

'Are you two together, or what?'

Ad cowered in the corner, pretending not to see them, while Harry tried to face them down.

'You people are worse than the Gestapo!' he said. 'And if you don't cease hostile action with immediate effect, I shall have no choice but to retaliate.'

That speech didn't work.

Come on, man, said Hank. *You're supposed to be their manager. You have to fix this.*

'HEY!' I yelled.

Everyone turned around.

'Leave them alone, right now,' I said. 'We will not be addressing any rumours being bandied around school. We just want to concentrate on our music. Now, if you'll excuse us.'

They stared at me for a second. Then someone said, 'OK,' and they all walked away.

See? said Hank. *This is what happens when you man up. People respect you.*

I smiled, thinking to myself that I must be gaining a fearsome reputation as a musical impresario. Then I turned around and saw Gav standing behind me. Ah.

Still, I think this has solved one of our problems.

'So let me understand this,' said Gav at lunch. 'You want me to be the bodyguard for your little band?'

'We're not a band, we're an electro-techno-dystopian-dubstep outfit,' said Harry.

Gav just glowered and Harry went quickly back to his spag bol.

'Well, whatever,' said Gav. 'What do I get out of all this?'

'I'll field this one, guys,' I said. 'You, Gavin, get the chance to be part of something huge at the ground level. You get to be the enforcer for the best damn electro-techno . . . Lego . . . thing this country has ever seen.'

He sniffed. 'Nah, can't be arsed,' he said. 'Just got Tech Ops for the Xbox, innit?'

I looked at the guys. They wouldn't make eye contact.

'Come on, Gav,' I said. 'If nothing else, it'll get you out of the house for a bit. You can't be enjoying it in that hellhole any more than I am. I mean, just this morning your nan tried to put a pair of her pants in the toaster.'

'I don't know, man,' said Gav. 'I mean no offence, yeah? But hanging with you lot ain't gonna do me no favours.'

I was starting to give up hope. Until Seb and Lisa stopped by.

'Hey, homos,' said Seb.

'What'd you say?' said Gav.

'Shut up, Gav,' said Lisa. 'I got fed up with boys like you, so I got a real man, OK?'

Gav laughed. 'A real man don't take more time over his hair than a girl,' he said. 'And he's wasting his time 'cause

« Older posts

I've seen better looking bum hair than that.'

'So you go around looking at bum hair?' said Seb with that posh-boy donkey laugh. 'Chav.'

Gav jumped out of his seat. 'You best run.'

Mr Pratt on the next table stood up too. 'Gavin James, if you don't sit down right now, you'll be violating your bond and will be suspended.'

Gav huffed and sat back down. 'Just watch yourself, yeah?' he said to Seb.

'Oh, I'm so scared,' said Seb. 'Come on, babes, we've spent enough time with the losers.'

They walked away laughing. Gav's face had gone bright red.

'That was our competition,' I said.

Gav nodded. 'All right, I'll do it.'

That's our muscle sorted. I don't think Seb knows what he's just started.

Wednesday 10th October

Foods that are NOT suitable for braces:
  Chewing gum
  Mars Bars
  Toffees.

Basically, just imagine you have false teeth like Doris. Yes, Joe Cowley, you are quite the catch.

Thursday 11th October

We all sat together at lunch for a quick strategy meeting. I started by asking how it was going.

'Wicked,' said Ad. 'Since the G-man came on board, we've hardly had any trouble.'

'You're really trying to get that nickname off the ground, aren't you, Gav?' I said.

Gav nodded and crammed a fistful of chips into his gob.

'There's just one thing,' said Harry. 'We still need a light show.'

He's right. I knew it wouldn't do to just match Seb's effects, we needed to go bigger and better. But how could we do that with no money? A top-of-the-range effects unit would set us back hundreds. I looked around the room for inspiration. And then I saw it.

Greeny.

Master of special effects. Creator of the hologram ghost that make Gav cack his pants and want to leave my house and run to his mum in Scotland. Half-idiot, half-genius.

'What do you lot want?' he said as we sat around him. He was tucking into what looked like his second sticky toffee pudding.

'I come with a business proposition,' I said.

He slammed his spoon down. 'Yeah well, you can stick it. Last time you gave me one of them, I end up getting slapped by a granny.'

« Older posts

My heart froze. I'd just remembered that Gav didn't know Greeny was behind the hologram ghost.

'S'aight,' said Gav. 'I knew it must have been one of his. You plums ain't clever enough to do anything like that.'

'May I just go on the record as being rather perturbed by this?' said Harry. 'I mean, no disrespect, but we're letting people into our organization who used to be our tormentors.'

I sighed. 'Look, they let Klingons into the Federation, didn't they? And besides, Greeny's days of tormenting are behind him. Aren't they, Greeny?'

'I literally didn't understand any of that sentence,' said Greeny. 'Anyway, what's this propulsion thing you're on about?'

I explained to him about the *SOUND EXPERIENCE* and the competition.

'I don't know,' said Greeny. 'I mean, I swore I'd never work with Gav again.'

'They always come back,' said Gav, nodding like some kind of Mafia guy.

We tried to convince Greeny with the promise of money, fame, and a slot at *BUZZFEST*, but he still wouldn't be swayed.

'We want to beat Seb,' said Natalie. 'And we think with your help, we can do it.'

'Seb?' said Greeny. 'The sixth-former with the gold Jag?'

'Yeah.'

'Well, why didn't you say so? I'm in.'

Turns out they've got history. Every now and then, Seb's dad, the MP, and a load of other saddos picket Greeny's dad's film studio for 'corrupting moral decency' with titles like *Werewolf Strippers* and *Vampires with Big Knockers*.

So now the ⅂OUND EXPERIENCE team is fully assembled—a group of wildly different individuals, united by a shared hatred of one massive, throbbing knobhead.

ME

GAV

GREENY

AD

HARRY

NATALIE

Friday 12th October

We have a date for the semi! It's on Friday 26th October at Club Hydro in Birmingham. That gives us two weeks to prepare. Only one act from that goes through to the final, so we need to up our game. We're having rehearsals this weekend with Greeny, so he can decide what effects to use.

After school, Natalie had a go at converting Doris to the wonders of emo music as a change from Cliff Richard. She reckoned at their core, they're not that different.

« Older posts

You ripped out my soul,
And buried it down in the deep.
Now I'm standing outside your window,
Watching as you sleep.

Imagine Cliff Richard singing that. Terrifying.

We watched *Star Trek*: *First Contact* after that, but I couldn't concentrate. My mind was buzzing with ideas to make the SOUND EXPERIENCE better and better.

'I've never seen you so enthusiastic about anything,' said Natalie. 'You really want to win this, don't you?'

'Course I do,' I said. 'I can't have your dad thinking you're going out with a loser.'

'How many times?' she growled. 'I do not care what he thinks. I know you're not a loser and that's all that matters.'

'I know but—'

'Trying to please him will make you end up like him,' said Natalie. 'Trust me.'

Saturday 13th October

Ad's birthday today. I bought him a cup with a ball on a string attached. He says it's his favourite present because it's so challenging.

Even though it's his birthday, and his nan from Newcastle had come down to see him, we still had rehearsals in his garage. With our new members, it's getting a bit cramped, but there was a good atmosphere, with every-one working together.

I sat and listened and even though it all sounds like a washing machine having a nervous breakdown to me, I'm certain I detected signs of improvement. Greeny took notes, drawing diagrams and recording the songs on his iPad whilst somehow eating a Twix. Plus, I think I saw Gav's head nodding slightly, but I can't be sure.

As is traditional, we went to the park for Ad's birthday. Normally, it's just the three of us, but now we have an extended family.

Ad kept going on about how many girls he was going to get at *BUZZFEST* when they win.

'How will that work?' said Greeny. 'Everyone's going to know you as the gay couple.'

'Oh yeah,' said Ad.

'Looks like it's just inflatable ones for you, old son,' said Harry.

'Hey, I ain't got an inflatable girlfriend,' said Ad.

'You did, but you had to let her down gently,' I said.

I thought that deserved more than the slow handclap it received.

The only worrying moment was when Ad decided to climb a tree in the dark to see if he could—and I quote—'catch an owl'.

« Older posts

'Why do you want an owl, old bean?' said Harry.

'So I can get it to deliver messages for me, like the one off Barry Potter,' he said.

'Ad, get down from there right now,' I shouted up the tree. I had visions of him falling down and hurting himself. That would be a disaster with the semi-final coming up.

'Damn, blud, you sound like his mum,' said Gav.

'The G-man's right,' said Ad.

'And you can stop calling him that,' I said. 'Look, just get down, because if you fall and hurt yourself, we're all bollocksed.'

'Quite right, old son,' said Harry. 'I'll go up and fetch him if you like?'

'No!'

Anyway, he managed to get down without major injury. I nearly had a coronary, though.

'When did you stop being fun, anyway, Joe?' said Ad.

'Good question,' said Natalie.

Sunday 14th October

After Dad's, went to Ad's for rehearsal. Amazingly, Greeny had already developed effects for 'Kamikaze Attack', creating a giant virtual laser tank that shoots laser rockets.

Gav said that this effect was 'sick' and we were all in agreement. Ad's nan, who came in to say goodbye, wasn't though.

Anyway, Natalie seemed a bit off with me the whole time. I had no idea why. Then, when I pulled out a *Financial Times* I bought from Mr Singh's, she went berserk. I bought it because it's what business guys are supposed to read.

'What do you think you're doing?' she said.

'Nothing much,' I replied. 'Just checking the fttseh. You know, options and that.'

'You know it's pronounced footsie don't you, old bean?' said Harry.

'Whatever.'

I was actually looking for the comics, but there weren't any. What kind of a crappy paper was this, anyway?

'Just stop it, OK?' she said.

I glanced at the others, and I could tell they were pretending not to listen, but were actually listening so hard, their ears were in danger of falling off.

'Stop what?'

'This whole . . . ' She waved her hand in my general direction. 'Desmond thing.'

'Desmond thing?'

'You know what I'm talking about,' she said. 'I'm not going to let this happen again.'

'What do you mean, "again"?'

'Nothing, just,' she sighed. 'I need to go for a walk.'

There was an awkward silence after Natalie left. I thought about going after her, but it probably wouldn't have been a good idea.

'And there was me about to buy her a subscription to the *FT*,' said Harry.

Natalie seemed calmer when she got back and gave me a hug, then threw my newspaper in the bin. 'I just don't want you to change, OK?' she said.

I assume she's talking about my personality, because if she means pants, that's nasty.

Tuesday 16th October

Things are starting to come together for the semi. The effects are looking great, the music is sounding good (probably) and Natalie has stopped accusing me of being her dad's Mini-Me.

'We do still have one problem, old son,' said Harry, probably noticing me getting too comfortable. 'It says we're supposed to bring someone over the age of eighteen.'

'OK,' I said. 'Can't Ad's dad come in?'

'Think about it, old boy,' said Harry. 'Do we really want our parents knowing we're pretending to be a couple?'

'Ah,' I said. 'Don't worry. I'll think of someone.'

Who?

Doris?

By the way, I totally caught her and the Colonel holding hands tonight. I can't decide whether it's quite sweet or a bit disgusting.

Thursday 18th October

Arranged to have a date night with Natalie tonight. I think we both agreed that we'd been spending too much time with the *SOUND EXPERIENCE* and needed some time alone.

Trouble is, my house is still about as peaceful as an abattoir, and Natalie's house is about as welcoming as . . . well, as an abattoir. So we're going to the cinema to watch a film of Natalie's choice: *Night of the Tortured Demons*. Sounds like a laugh riot.

10.30 p.m.

I called at Natalie's on the way to the cinema. Charlie answered the door AGAIN. Is he the only one who can do it or something?

'Oh. Hello,' he said.

'Hello, Charlie,' I said. 'Is that sister of yours ready?'

'As I lack X-ray vision, I don't know if that sister of mine is ready or not,' he said. 'But what I do know is Desmond won't be pleased to see you.'

« Older posts

Before I could ask why, the man himself appeared behind him.

'What are you doing here?' he said.

'Me and Natalie are going to the cinema.'

'Oh really?' he said. 'Not distracting her from her studies with one of your practice sessions?'

Oh, bite me, you freaking jerk, said Hank.

'No. Night off tonight,' I said.

'Just as well,' he said. 'Waste of time if you ask me. Seb won't be beaten easily. He's born to win.'

I sighed. 'Look, Desmond.'

He eyeballed me as if I'd just called him Lieutenant Bumjuice.

'Mr Tuft,' I said. 'I really like your daughter. And, regardless of what you think, I know she likes me. So I just think it would be nice for you to, perhaps, be a bit more support- ive, or something? I mean, I don't know, it might help you and Natalie get along better.'

He seemed to grow about fifteen feet tall. He blew out through his nose like a bull. He looked around and stepped outside, closing the door behind him.

'I don't know who you think you're talking to, you snot-nosed little scrote,' he said.

That's ridiculous. Scrotes don't even have noses.

'But you have no right giving me advice about how best to deal with my daughter. I've learned some things about you, and I'm not happy about them.'

Things? He hadn't found out about me weeing the bed on the Year Six camping trip had he? I was eleven!

'And I won't be supporting you either, because I've moulded Seb into a strong, productive young man, who was my protégé before you arrived on the scene, and will be around long after you've sodded off back to your council estate.'

'But I don't live on a—'

He silenced me with a raised finger. 'I wasn't happy about Natalie having to attend that ghastly so-called school of yours, but unfortunately there was no alternative. And seeing her fraternizing with the likes of you is like seeing my worst nightmare come true.'

My mouth dropped open. 'You . . . you can't stop us seeing each other.'

'Oh, I can,' he said. 'But for now that isn't the course of action I'm taking. Natalie may be many things, but she is not stupid. I have faith that one day she will grow up, and realize she should stick with her own people.'

Norman had to chain Hank to a pipe to restrain him.

« Older posts

Desmond squeezed my shoulder, hard. 'And another thing, if my daughter hears about this conversation, I will stop her from seeing you. And there'll be nothing you can do about it,' he said. 'Do we understand each other?'

I nodded, my eye twitch going to warp ten.

'Good.'

The door opened, and Natalie stood there, eyeballing us suspiciously.

'What's going on?'

'Oh nothing,' said Desmond, squeezing my shoulder harder. 'Just having a chat about business. Bit of friendly banter, that's all. Isn't that right, Joe?'

I nodded again like a gimp.

'Right,' she said, not looking convinced. 'Since when do you banter, Desmond?'

Desmond grumbled something under his breath, then barked, 'I want you back for nine thirty sharp.' He went back inside and slammed the door.

'What did he really say to you?' said Natalie, holding my hand as we walked away.

'Oh, nothing,' I said. 'As he said, it was just friendly banter.'

My head was buzzing all through the film. I couldn't even get into the snogging as well as I normally do. I think Natalie knew something was up, but there was no way I could tell her. I can't stand the idea of us being apart. And Desmond is such a slimy worm, he'll find a way to do it.

When I got home, I found Mum eating pickled onions with chocolate on the settee, and I actually smiled. My parents may be weird, but at least they're not evil.

Saturday 20th October

More *SOUND EXPERIENCE* rehearsals. The music and light show are coming together nicely. I never thought I'd see Harry and Ad getting on with Greeny. It's amazing what uniting against a knobhead can do. Maybe they should send him to the Middle East to sort everything out there.

Greeny said Henry Mangrove had organized another protest outside his dad's studio. Ad suggested we go down there and pelt them with piss balloons, but when I pointed out that would definitely get us arrested, he went off it. I had a much safer idea.

Welcome to the homepage of Henry Mangrove MP

Greetings, scum! I am Henry 'the Knob Polisher' Mangrove—Conservative Member of Parliament for Tammerstone.

I have voted for spending cuts, public sector job losses, and against same-sex marriage. This is because gay people make me feel all funny in my trousers.

When I'm not being a complete arseladder in Westminster, I enjoy spending time at my constituency home in Tammerstone, with my douchey son, Sebastian Pubehead, and my wife, who is actually a rare kind of haddock. My hobbies include golf, shooting the poor, and playing the tuba with my bum hole.

I'd like to say this was all my work, but it was actually a team effort. Greeny managed to hack into it on my laptop. It'll be interesting to see how long it stays up.

Monday 22nd October

The Colonel told us some tales about his sea-faring days

tonight. He's had some real adventures, including fighting pirates! I know! And the way he speaks is so authoritative as well. If he told me to drop and give him twenty, I would do it. In fact, I would probably give him thirty, just to be on the safe side.

All this talk of life and careers got us chatting about the future on the way home.

'Well, obviously I'm going to be a therapist,' said Natalie. 'And in my spare time I am going to run my own record label.'

'Oh, are you?' I said. 'I thought you weren't into business and stuff like that?'

'Music's different though, isn't it?' she said. 'It's not a block of loos or a plastic doll. It's love. It's life.'

I agreed even though I wasn't entirely sure what she was talking about. 'So how would your company work?' I said.

She swung my hand backwards and forwards. 'Art before profit—that'll be the ethos. And I'll be in charge of signing up the bands, and you will do the arty stuff and design the sleeves.'

'Oh, so I'm involved in your plans?' I said.

'Course you are,' she said. 'Why wouldn't you be?'

'I don't know,' I said. 'I just didn't realize you felt that way about me.'

She jumped in front of me and kissed me on the end of my nose. 'You're a knob, Joe Cowley,' she said.

« Older posts

Tuesday 23rd October

You know, in some schools, they have these 'Hall of Fame' type things for kids who excel in PE. I don't know why that is, I mean, you'd never see one of those for Maths geeks, would you? And if you ask me, knowing what the cocking hell Pythagoras' theorem is all about is way more impressive than being able to kick a ball further than anyone else.

Anyway, if they ever did a PE Hall of Fame at Woodlet, I would literally be the last person on there. In fact, I think that cone I was replaced with the other week would stand a better chance.

Here's what happened today: Boocock decided that we were doing football. Everyone cheered except me. I hate football, and have done ever since Gav two footed me back in Year Seven and bruised my kneecap. The thing was, I wasn't even playing—I was the ref.

I hoped that I'd be able to get out of it because I forgot my football boots, but Boocock just smirked and said the words that felt like a sadistic stretch on the torture rack.

'Don't worry, Cowley. You can have . . . THE SPARES!'

The spares? Crappity crap! How could I have forgotten about the cocking spares? The spares are a pair of boots so old and stinky, they were probably first worn by God's dad.

Plus, they're two sizes too big for me. I looked like the world's most disappointing clown.

Boocock lined us up for penalties practice. The way he sees it, if kids start learning penalties early, the England football team won't keep getting knocked out of tournaments. Yeah right. As if any of us would ever make the England team. Greeny gets out of breath running after the ice cream van, for crying out loud.

'OK then, you bunch of brain-dead zombies,' Boocock barked. 'You will each have a chance to put a peno past me—the Cat.'

Everyone groaned. Boocock has always fancied himself as a top goalie, just because he played a season for Tammerstone Tigers back in 1586, or whenever.

I made sure to stick myself at the back of the queue. I'd managed to sneak my phone out in my pocket, and had been craftily checking my emails every few seconds. Bangaz were sending out the line-up for our semi and I was desperate to know whether we would be facing off against Seb. My heart would jump every time I saw I had a new email, only for it to be:

GROW 3 INCHES OVERNIGHT GUARANTEED!

No thanks, I'm happy with my height.

All of this meant I wasn't really paying attention to the penalties—all I knew was that no one had scored past Boocock yet. He kept putting people off by wobbling his legs

« Older posts

around and making noises like a moose being strangled. Then, when they missed, he'd say stuff like, 'YUSSS, NO ONE BEATS THE CAT!'

I refreshed my inbox again.

An email!

From Bangaz!

Turns out we're in a different semi to Seb. Shame. It would have been a chance to dump him out of the competition for good. Seriously. The boys are just getting better and better.

'COWLEY!'

Oh bum.

'What the hell are you doing on your phone?'

'Um, it was um, an emergency,' I said.

Everyone laughed. Except Boocock, who marched over and snatched my phone away.

'Oh, there's going to be an emergency by the time I've finished with you.'

'Come on, Mr Boocock, you can't do that!'

'Oh, I think I can.' He went back to the goal and chucked my phone in the corner. 'I'm going to keep this is my drawer for the rest of term, how does that sound?'

I facepalmed. The idea of Boocock reading mine and Natalie's texts or seeing a picture of me dressed as Captain Picard was too much.

'Tell you what,' I said, letting Hank take control. 'How about we make a wager?'

Boocock smoothed his moustache. 'A wager, you say?'

I nodded. 'If you save my penalty, you keep my phone. If I score, I get it back.'

Everyone laughed again.

Boocock's beady eyes darted around. 'OK, Cowley,' he said. 'You've got a deal.'

I turned to Gav, who was busy flicking clumps of dirt at Squirgy Kallow. 'Any advice?'

'Yeah, man, hard and low.'

I don't know why I was asking him, his wasn't even on target.

I picked up the ball and wiped it down my front. I have no idea why I did that, it's just something I've seen footballers do when Jim has matches on at home. I placed it on the spot, which was actually a big circle of squelchy mud.

I tried to assess the situation logically. The goal was big, and Boocock couldn't possibly fill all of it, even when he was flapping around like an agitated emu. I ignored Gav's advice and picked a spot in the top right corner. Then, to add a bit of intrigue, I glanced at the opposite corner. I thought it would throw Boocock off the scent.

I took a long run-up. I knew this would need both power and accuracy, like the weapons on the *ENTERPRISE*. Deep breath.

« Older posts

Firing photon torpedoes in five . . . four . . . three . . . two . . .

I ran up and swung my foot at the ball as hard as I could. It went quick, so I had the power part at least. I held my breath as I watched it scythe through the air in slow motion. Rising . . . rising . . . rising . . .

Straight into Boocock's arms. Damn.

My head dropped. I'd lost my phone. That thing had everything on it: music, those texts from Natalie that I read in my bunk at night and make me feel all weird. All gone. Then I noticed something weird about my foot. My boot wasn't on it.

I looked up just in time to see the two sizes too big spare kick Boocock straight in the goolies.

He dropped the ball and hit the ground, holding his crotch. He was making weird noises like before, but they sounded a bit higher.

Seeing the golden opportunity, I ran at the goal, smacked the ball into the back of the net and grabbed my phone.

Thank God for the spares.

Anyway, because I had potentially wiped out future generations of Boococks, I was sent to see Mr Pratt at lunch. I never thought I'd be sent to the head's office. That kind of thing is for people like Gav. I made sure I had my excuses ready.

'It wasn't my fault,' I said. 'It was those spares. I'm only a size eight, and he gave me a ten! I realize you don't have the best resources at your disposal, Mr Pratt, but keeping such hefty spare boots was an accident waiting to happen.'

Pratt frowned, which had the effect of smashing his two huge eyebrows together to create one monstrous caterpillar in the middle of his forehead. We were sitting on these really low down chairs by the window in his office.

'This isn't the first time you've been involved in an incident with Mr Boocock, is it, Joe?'

Oh come on, said Hank. *He shouldn't be taking past incidents into account. These things should work on a case-by-case basis. Besides, there is a world of difference between ribs and gonads, am I right, Norm?*

How about you just apologize, Joe? said Norman.

Before I could say anything else, the door opened.

'Don't mind me, Mr P.'

Oh, spit in my face and call me Locutus of Borg. Seb? Really?

'Ah, good afternoon, Sebastian, the work is on my desk over there,' said Pratt.

« Older posts

'Not interrupting anything, am I?' said Seb.

'Oh no, just a pupil kicking a member of staff in the nether regions, you know, everyday stuff.'

They both laughed as Seb went over to the desk and sat down. Fantastic. I started gnawing at the inside of my cheek.

'Sebastian is here doing some voluntary work to help with his university application,' said Pratt. 'You know, it wouldn't be a bad idea for you to learn from him.'

I glanced over Pratt's shoulder and saw Seb flipping middle fingers at me.

'No thanks, I think I'll be fine,' I said.

I silently eyeballed Seb, trying to send him horrendous abuse by the power of telepathy.

'Your lack of motivation worries me, Joe,' said Pratt.

He blathered on about some other crap, but I wasn't really listening, because Seb was holding up a piece of paper with '*I AM SO TELLING DESMOND ABOUT THIS*' written on it.

'Oh, just you freakin' try it.'

Wait, did he just say that out loud? said Hank. *I think he's channelled me. Shucks, I'm honoured.*

'Excuse me?' said Mr Pratt. 'Who do you think you are talking to?'

'May I say something?' said Seb, quickly hiding the paper.

'Of course, Sebastian.'

'As a student of Psychology, with an A grade at AS level,

I believe the problem here may lie with who he is associating with.'

God, if he was any slimier he'd be able to slide up a window like a slug. At least then I could shrivel him with salt.

'Well, I know he lives with Gavin James but there's not a great deal I can do about that,' said Pratt.

'No, I mean his girlfriend,' said Seb. 'I think she may be distracting him from his studies. I mean, that must have been why he had his phone with him.'

Pratt nodded, as if he was actually considering it. What kind of teacher is he, anyway?

Seb grinned at me. He knew exactly what he was doing. My eye twitch cranked into life with a vengeance. Then I had an idea.

'Actually, Mr Pratt,' I said. 'The only reason I had my phone on me was because my mum is heavily pregnant and could go into labour at any moment.'

She's not due until mid-December but he didn't have to know that.

'Can you prove it?' said Pratt.

'Sir, if you want to drag my ridiculously pregnant and thus ridiculously insane mother down here to show you her ridiculous bump, then you're a braver man than I am,' I said.

Pratt sighed. 'Fine. I'm going to let you off with a warning, this time. But any more incidents like this and you will be suspended.'

I shrugged, at least relieved to be keeping my phone.

Seb showed me out into the corridor.

'Nicely done, Sebastian,' I said. 'You know, you couldn't be more obvious if you tried.'

He laughed. 'I have no idea what Natalie sees in you, you talentless little freak.'

'And I suppose you're really talented,' I said. 'At, you know, wearing stupid sunglasses and kissing Pratt's arse.'

'Good one,' he said. 'You got me there.'

'Oh, I'll get you,' I said. 'When we win our semi this Saturday and go to the final, I'll be top dog. That stupid knob Desmond won't care about you.'

Seb smiled. 'Thanks,' he said.

'For what?'

'For telling me when your semi is,' he said. 'Oh, and calling Desmond a knob. I'll be letting him know about that, too.'

It's weird how one pair of football boots can wreck your entire day. I'd laugh if I wasn't so sure I'd weep.

Thursday 25th October

The day before the semi. I couldn't finish my cereal this morning because I was so nervous. Well, that and the smell of Mum's bacon and raspberry syrup was making me queasy.

They went for the final scan yesterday. Mum is still saying she doesn't want to know the sex of the twins, but I can tell Jim does.

Anyway, Mum showed me the photo, and started getting all emotional.

'Isn't it wonderful, Joe?' she said. 'The miracle of life.'

I squinted at it. It was like one of those magic eye things. I thought if I stared at it long enough I'd be able to make out a picture of a boat or something.

'It's . . . great,' I said.

She smiled, so I think I got away with it.

Doris is excited too, because soon Ivy will have some friends to play with. I mean, really?

8 p.m.

Lisa walked past me and Natalie in the corridor and said, 'All right, weirdos. Still trying to beat Seb?'

This was the first bit of abuse I'd had all day. It was probably something to do with the infamy I gained from the Boocock incident. By the time it had got around school, the version of events was that Boocock was picking on me, so I smacked him in the knob with a hockey stick, stole his phone, and sent a text to his wife saying he's leaving her for Mr Groggit, the eighty-year-old caretaker.

'You silly cow,' said Natalie to Lisa. 'Can't you see he's using you? Just like you were using Joe.'

Lisa opened her mouth to say something, then just stormed off.

'Wow,' I said. 'That was brilliant.'

Natalie smiled. 'Gav's not your muscle, I am.'

We had one last band meeting after school. Performance-wise, everything was flawless, but Natalie pointed something out that none of us had thought of.

'You need a look.'

'A look?' said Harry, running his hand down the lapel of his tweed cardigan. 'What's wrong with our look now?'

'Well, you haven't got one,' she said. 'And every great group has a look.'

'What are you saying?' said Ad. 'Like, we need costumes or something?'

'Exactly,' she said.

'Well, where are we going to get them?'

'Hello,' said Greeny.

We headed over to Greeny's to have a look through his dad's collection of film costumes. Ad quickly found a skimpy bra.

'No way,' he said. 'Is this the bra Leonora wore in *Lingerie Gangsters*?'

'Yeah, but you can't wear that though.'

'Your dad made *Lingerie Gangsters*?' said Gav. 'Man, that is sick.'

Greeny smiled. It's very rare Gav says anything nice about Greeny. Or anyone.

Ad held the bra up to his chest. 'Man, if I had boobs for one day, the things I would do.'

'What would you do, Ad?' I said.

'Look at myself in the mirror, mainly,' he said. 'After that, I'd probably just use them as a place to store pencils.'

Natalie nearly spat out her drink. 'They're not all they're cracked up to be,' she said.

'No, they ain't,' said Greeny.

'How about this?' Harry pulled a werewolf costume out of a chest.

'Nah, werewolves ain't cool,' said Ad.

'This is a werewolf?' said Harry. 'I thought it was supposed to be your mum.'

Gav high-fived him. 'Burn.'

'Now this is what I'm talking about.' Natalie's voice came from behind this giant wardrobe. We went over to investigate and found her holding up these two tatty, brown, blood-stained jackets.

'Wicked,' said Ad.

« Older posts

'Oh yeah,' said Greeny. 'These were used in the film *Frankenslappers*.'

'Beautiful,' said Harry.

'They fit your style perfectly,' said Natalie. 'Scary, brutal, and . . . slightly stupid.'

Friday 26th October

Well, my Boocock kicking fame was short-lived. Pete Cotterill has gone around telling everyone that it was just the boot flying off and that I was so upset about hurting the teacher that I cried. Now everyone is calling me the Grim Weeper.

Greeny brought the coats in at break time. He's designed this brilliant *SOUND EXPERIENCE* logo and printed it onto the backs.

'That is very impressive,' said Harry. 'But we have forgotten one minor detail.'

I searched my memory banks but came away empty-handed.

'We still need a chaperone.'

'Oh.'

'I thought you were taking care of this, old boy,' he said.

'I am,' I said. 'It's just, there's been a lot of stuff going on . . .'

'I know, but when you're the commander you have to be able to deal with it.'

I took an aggressive slurp of my juice carton. I know Harry's used to being in charge, but now it's my turn. I got my phone out. This was a last resort. He always is. But at least he already knows about the gay gimmick.

'Hey, son,' said Dad. 'What's shaking? I'm kicking it at the office at the mo, but I've always got time to pow-wow with my number one playa.'

Every molecule in my body cringed.

'Right,' I said. 'Thing is, I need to ask you a favour.'

There was a moment of silence. 'Shoot, *el hombre*.'

'Well, the Sound Experience have their semi-final tonight, and I was wondering if you could chaperone us.'

'Man, that would be *rinsing*,' he said. 'I'd love to. Just give me the time and place.'

I gave the guys the thumbs up. 'We have to be there for seven to set up, and it's at Hydro in Birmingham.'

There was another silence. 'Hy-Hydro?'

'Yes,' I said. 'What's the matter?'

'That may be a *problemo*,' he said.

'*Problemo*?'

'Well, the thing is, my man,' he said. 'I may be, um, barred, from that particular joint.'

'You're barred from a nightclub?' I said.

'Afraid so,' he said. 'Don't ask why.'

'But . . . what about Svetlana?' I said, clutching at the greasiest of straws.

« Older posts

'She can't do it, either,' he said.

'She's under eighteen, isn't she?' I said. 'I knew it.'

'No,' he said. 'She's twenty-three, like I keep telling you. No, Svet can't go because . . . well, she's barred as well.'

'But why is she—' I stopped myself before I could ask the question. Something told me I didn't want to know the answer.

'Never mind,' I said.

'Look, I'll happily drive you all there in Svet's Mitsubishi, but I can't go in. Hey, why don't you ask your mum, or whatshisname?'

'No, I can't ask them—for one thing, Mum is insane, and two . . . it's complicated.'

'I'm sorry, dude,' he said.

'We'll take the lift,' I said. 'I'll just have to find another adult.'

I hung up.

'So,' said Ad. 'How did it go?'

I sighed. 'Don't any of you know any adults?'

'None that I don't mind thinking I'm shtupping with Ad,' said Harry. 'I just can't believe you didn't sort this earlier, old bean.'

I rubbed my eyes. I had no ideas. Then Natalie grabbed me.

'I've just thought of someone, we'll find him at lunchtime.'

'Afternoon, folks,' said Clifton. 'Why aren't you at school?'

'Lunch break,' said Natalie. 'Why are you plastering? Desmond only pays you to garden, you know.'

'I know,' he said. 'But your father said it needed doing, so . . . '

'Cheapskate,' she said. 'Anyway, we have a favour of our own to ask you.'

'A nightclub?' Clifton's eyes bulged out. 'I can't go to a nightclub. What will my wife say?'

'Please, Clifton,' she said. 'You're our only hope. And we really want to win this competition.'

He sighed and scratched the back of his head. 'I don't know . . . '

'If you come I won't tell my dad about you reading,' said Natalie in a sing-song voice.

Clifton smiled and folded his arms. 'This girl is going to go far,' he said. 'Always knows what to say to back a man into the corner. I'd be careful if I were you, son.'

So it's settled. Dad's driving us and Clifton's coming in. Clifton made us promise that Desmond will never find out about this.

We got back to school after lunch and told the other guys the good news.

'Well done, soldier,' said Harry. 'Just try not to leave it so late next time, OK?'

Grr.

« Older posts

6.45 p.m.

That was exciting. Desmond insisted that Natalie wasn't allowed out tonight because she's supposed to be studying for a test, so she had to sneak out. I crept around the back and watched as she climbed out of the window and shimmied down the trellis. Natalie wasn't worried about them noticing she'd gone.

'I've spent entire weekends in my room without them checking on me. I could have a drugs lab in there and they'd have no idea.'

Now there's a thought for a money-making scheme. No, I've seen *Breaking Bad*. Plus, I'm crap at chemistry.

7.15 p.m.

Harry and Ad are setting up now while Clifton goes to the bar. The journey over here was so embarrassing. We all crammed into Svetlana's car with the gear, while Clifton sat in the front with Dad.

When Dad found out Clifton was from Jamaica, he put on a Bob Marley album.

'Great man,' said Dad. 'Prophet. You a fan?'

'He's all right,' said Clifton. 'Prefer Jimmy Cliff myself. Toots, the Folkes Brothers.'

'Oh,' said Dad. He seemed a bit deflated. 'Who's your favourite artist of all time, then?'

'Easy,' said Clifton. 'The Beach Boys.'

Dad didn't say much after that.

8.15 p.m.

The $SOUND$ $EXPERIENCE$ are on last. Headliners. As it should be.

8.17 p.m.

O, M, and indeed G. I've just realized I forgot to get Ad's sickness pills. This club is twice the size of Scutty's. That means he'll produce double the puke. It'll be like the closing scenes of *Titanic*, but more disgusting.

8.30 p.m.

Harry and Ad have their costumes on and Natalie has somehow convinced them to wear eyeliner, which she's applied herself.

Gav is acting as 'muscle', which seems to mainly involve standing around ogling women.

PUKE WATCH: None yet, but we can't afford to be complacent.

8.40 p.m.

The first act are on. How the hell did they get through their heat? They sound like a robot taking a dump. I look at Clifton and notice he has cotton wool in his ears. I wish I'd thought of that.

« Older posts

8.45 p.m.

Just went to the bar with Ad. He ordered water. The barman asked if he wanted ice. He replied, 'Yeah, but melted.'

I noticed the glass shaking in his hand. I tried to reassure him, but he couldn't hear me over THE WORST SOUND ANYONE HAS EVER MADE, EVER.

Still no puke.

9 p.m.

The next act is on. Some bloke called Lethal Injection. He sounds pretty bad, too. When these people hear us, their minds will be blown.

9.10 p.m.

There's a group of girls standing near me and Natalie.

Greeny just went over and said, 'Hi, I'm with the band.'

And one of them said, 'What, the gastric band?' He's now consoling himself with a bag of Quavers.

PUKE WATCH: False alarm. Just a dry heave.

9.15 p.m.

Natalie asked me how I was feeling. I said I was nervous. She said, 'Don't be, our boys are going to smash it.' She always knows what to say to make me feel better.

Clifton is now reading *Crime and Punishment* by torchlight.

9.25 p.m.

The *SOUND EXPERIENCE* are about to take to the stage. Greeny is going up with them, to operate the effects. He's wearing a matching coat. They look great. We give them the thumbs up.

For God's sake, Ad, don't puke.

9.30 p.m.

OK, they're up and they are rocking it. If that is the correct terminology. Anyway, even if they sounded cack, people would be too amazed by Greeny's effects to notice. So far, he has sent futuristic robo-plane holograms flying into the crowd, along with robo warriors with laser guns, and big laser words spelling out 'ATTACK'.

The group of girls next to us are going wild.

'Oh my God, it's that fat kid who was trying to chat you up.'

'He's a genius!'

He's loving it, pressing the controls and blasting the crowd with finger pistols. Ad's keeping time, too, despite the fact that he looks like he's about to collapse. Harry is puffing furiously on his pipe and Gav is standing by the stairs leading up to the stage, looking mean. I give Natalie's hand a squeeze. I'm so proud of my family.

10.30 p.m.

Balls. Balls. Balls.

« Older posts

Anyway, we're through, that's the main thing. Through to the final in London on the second of December. I know! I can't get too excited right now though, I'm still panicking about what happened.

The *SOUND EXPERIENCE* were getting towards the end of their set. The crowd were going crazy, with hologram zombies marching out at them, and the loud beats blaring. Then I noticed Natalie's grip on my hand get tighter.

'Oh, crap,' she said.

I looked across the club and saw Seb.

I wasn't too surprised to see him there after I blabbed the date to him on Tuesday, but I wasn't planning to tell Natalie about that.

'Here to see a real show?' I said.

'No, not him,' she said. 'Look.'

I squinted through Greeny's thick dry ice and I think my heart actually stopped.

'W-what's your dad doing here?'

It took me about two seconds to figure out who must have tipped him off.

Natalie grabbed my face. 'We all have to hide!'

Desmond looked like he was scoping the place out. If he found us, there'd surely be trouble.

'CLIFTON!'

He didn't look up, so Natalie shook him. He looked like he was about to have a coronary.

'We need to move!' Natalie screamed over the music.

He gestured at the wool in his ears and shrugged. Natalie yanked one out.

'You need to move, NOW.'

I helped him to his feet and started leading him towards the exit. I thought if I could get him out of the club, we'd be safe. We turned the corner and found the exit blocked by Seb's two bodyguards.

'Oh Jesus Christ.'

Natalie ran into the women's toilets. There's no way Desmond would go in there.

'What's the matter, Joseph?' said Clifton. 'Why are you dragging me around the place? My dancing days are behind me.'

I turned to face him and didn't know what to say.

'Let's . . . let's go to the toilet,' I said, and dragged him into the bathroom.

'What for?' he said. 'I agreed to chaperone you, not hold your thing!'

My mind chattered a million miles a minute. Norman and Hank talked over each other. The door opened behind me. Before I could think, I threw a cubicle door open and ran inside, dragging Clifton with me.

'What are you doing, you crazy fool?' said Clifton. 'Let me out this instant.'

I scrambled in front of the door and blocked him in.

'I will not be falsely imprisoned!' he yelled.

I gestured for him to keep quiet. 'The thing is, Clifton,' I whispered. 'Desmond has just got here.'

Clifton's mouth dropped open. 'Tuft is here? Why?'

'I don't know,' I said. 'But it is bad news.'

'You're not kidding.'

'Look,' I whispered. 'You'll have to stay in here until it's over. When we're sure the coast is clear, you can make a run for it.'

Clifton puffed out his cheeks. 'I knew this was a bad idea.'

'I'm sorry, Clifton,' I said. 'But this is all going to be fine. Just stay in here and read your book and it'll be over soon.'

I thought if I said it out loud I could make myself believe it. Clifton sat down on the toilet and re-opened his book. I squeezed out of the cubicle and he locked it behind me.

'Hello, Joe.'

Even Norman screamed.

'Hello, Mr Tuft,' I said. 'Nice night, isn't it? For going to the . . . toilet.'

His face twisted into a crooked smile. 'Certainly is. In fact, I think I'll use this one.'

My guts churned as he shook the door. 'This is locked,' he said. 'But how can that be when I just saw you coming out of there?'

'D-did you?' I said. 'Are you sure?'

He nodded, that smile still on his face.

Just try and direct him into another cubicle, Joe, said Norman.

Forget that, said Hank. *Kick his ass out of here. He's a wuss, even you could take him.*

'Who's in there, Joe?'

My mouth flapped open and shut. Desmond's eyes burned into mine. 'It's my friend,' I said. 'He's not very well and I was just checking on him.'

Nicely done, said Norman.

« Older posts

'Who is he?' said Desmond. 'Because those other friends of yours have only just come off stage.'

'It's my friend . . . Jerry,' I said. 'Isn't that right, Jerry?'

Don't talk to him, you freakin' moron!

Clifton mumbled something unintelligible.

'See? I told you he's poorly.'

My eye started twitching.

'He seemed OK a minute ago,' said Desmond. 'In fact, his voice sounded familiar. Like a Jamaican.'

Seriously, man, said Hank. *Smash his head into the condom machine, steal his wallet, and run away to Mexico with his daughter.*

'Yes, my friend Jerry is Jamaican,' I said. 'Jamaican Jerry, that's what we call him. And not in a racist way. He likes being called that.'

Desmond leaned across me and banged on the cubicle door. 'Jerry . . . oh, Jerry,' he called in a sing-song voice. 'Why don't you come out so we can see you?'

Clifton mumbled something.

'Come on, JERRY, you don't want to keep me waiting, do you?'

'Please, Mr Tuft,' I said. 'J-just leave him alone. He's agoraphobic.'

Desmond laughed. 'It just keeps getting better and better. OUT, JERRY. NOW.'

My eye twitch kicked in with a vengeance. I was out of

BLAAAAAH

ideas. We were all doomed.

The main door swung open behind us and cracked against the tiles. 'Out of my way!'

Desmond spun around, but before he could move, Ad had spewed all over his expensive-looking suede shoes. I knew there was a reason why I didn't buy those pills!

'You bloody idiot!' Desmond stormed over to the other side of the bathroom and started rinsing his shoes under the tap.

'We won, Joe,' said Ad, wiping his mouth with the back of his hand. 'We're going to the final!'

'That's great, Ad,' I said, then smacked the cubicle door. 'Jerry,' I whispered. 'It's safe to come out, but you'll need to run.'

Clifton opened the door a crack and peeped out. 'You sure?' he said.

I checked Desmond, who was still cleaning the contents of Ad's stomach off his loafers and swearing. 'Yes,' I said. 'In three . . . two . . . one.'

Clifton made a run for it. He skidded in Ad's vom, then nearly knocked over two people walking in, but he got away. Just.

Desmond turned around and put his shoes back on. The last time I'd seen someone with

« Older posts

a face like that was when Svetlana found Hercules making sweet love to her best mink coat.

'Where did Jerry go?' he said.

'Who's Jerry?' said Ad. I gave him a quick dig in the ribs to shut him up.

Desmond pointed at him. 'I'll be sending you the bill for this damage. Now where is he?'

I looked around. Then I saw one of the lads who Clifton nearly knocked over by the dryers. He had dreadlocks. Surely that would work.

'Here he is,' I said, grabbing him around the shoulder. 'Wha g'wan mi bredren?'

He glared at me, then said in a posh voice, 'Are you taking the piss or something?'

Desmond stared me out. 'There's something not right here,' he said. 'And I'm going to get to the bottom of it.'

He huffed and squelched out of the door. I hoped Clifton had been able to make a getaway.

'Who was that then, Joe?' said Ad.

'That was Natalie's dad,' I said.

'Ah right,' he said. 'Must be her mum with the purple hair then.'

'Are you going to let go of me or am I going to have to call security?' said 'Jamaican Jerry'.

When we got outside, Gav, Greeny, and Harry were loading the gear into Dad's car.

'Hey, son,' Dad said from the front. 'I would come and help, but I think that bouncer recognizes me.'

I turned and saw a giant bloke eyeballing my dad from the front door.

'Why are you banned from here, anyway?' I said.

Dad avoided eye contact. 'Maybe I'll tell you when you're older.'

I got my phone out and called Natalie.

'Where are you?' I said.

She sounded breathless. 'I'm at the Maccy's around the corner with Clifton. I had to climb out of the toilet window.'

'Did anyone see either of you?'

'I don't think so,' she said. 'I hope not.'

'Me too.'

'Hey, Joe, you're supposed to be our roadie as well as our manager, remember?' said Harry, nodding at the gear still to be loaded in.

When I'm a millionaire, I'll have people to do this for me. And I'll have lackeys to put up with Harry's crap, too.

After we'd picked Natalie and Clifton up, there was a weird mood in the car. I think it was partly jubilation at winning the semi and the two hundred and fifty quid, and partly sheer terror at the near miss.

« Older posts

'So how was it, guys?' said Dad. 'Did you drop it like it's hot?'

'It has been no good for my blood pressure,' said Clifton.

'Well, dudes and dudettes,' said Dad. 'If you need someone to ride with you to the LDN, I'm your dawg. I love to partay in the smizzoke when I get the chizzance, you dig?'

'I'm not sure I do, actually, old son,' said Harry. 'But you are absolutely welcome to join us, if that's what you're saying.'

I gave Harry the evils. I know Dad is realistically the only person who could take us, but that doesn't make it any nicer. I decided to try and get back into manager mode.

'Has, erm, everybody got everything?' I said. 'Haven't left anything at the club?'

'No.'

'No.'

'No, old boy.'

'I have.'

I leaned forward and looked at Clifton. 'You have?'

He nodded.

'Do you want to go back and get it, Clifton?' said Dad.

'No, it's OK,' he said. 'It's nothing.'

Hmm.

Saturday 27th October

Good news. Natalie managed to climb back into her bedroom before Desmond got home. It was close, though. He didn't say anything to her either, so maybe we got away with it.

Received a congratulations email from Bangaz this morning. It turns out ours was the last semi and all the finalists are now in place. And—big cocking surprise—Seb is one of them. I reckon he must have paid the judges or something.

Went down to breakfast to find Doris playing her Cliff Richard album in the kitchen. If am to survive with my sanity in this house, I'm going to need some industrial-strength earplugs.

'Remember this one, son?' she said to Jim. 'I used to bounce you on my knee to this and you'd giggle and giggle.'

'How could I forget?' said Jim. 'I was twenty-seven at the time.'

Doris laughed at this like it was the funniest joke in the world.

My phone beeped. Text from Natalie:

This is weird. Dad wants you to come round tonight. Says it's to discuss competition. Don't like this one bit. X

What is there to discuss? He obviously hates me. Unless he wants to broker a peace deal, like the Treaty of Algeron in *STAR TREK*? I was intrigued. I spread jam on my toast and considered my options.

« Older posts

'OK, people,' I said to the Sound Experience gang at Griddler's. 'Excellent work last night.'

Ad nodded, his mouth full of cheeseburger. 'We totally smashed it.'

'And we've got two hundred and fifty quid,' said Harry. 'Whatever happens, that's the Buzzfest fund nearly full.'

'Interesting,' I said. 'But don't you think we should perhaps reinvest that money?'

Natalie gave me a weird look. 'You're reminding me of my dad again.'

'You know how to charm the ladies, old boy,' said Harry.

'What I'm trying to say is,' I said, leaning in, 'maybe we could use that money to buy some better equipment.'

'What's wrong with our equipment?' Harry put his fork down.

'Nothing's wrong with it,' I said. 'But Seb has seen us now. Twice. He knows what we do and he's going to prepare to beat us. As we speak, he'll be amassing better gear than us, I guarantee it.'

Harry took his pipe out. 'So you're saying this is kind of like an arms race?'

I spiked a chip with my fork and pointed at him with it. 'Exactly,' I said, glad that he was beginning to see it in his terms.

'OK,' he said. 'Well, I saw a high-end sampler and 808 set in town. We could get it for a hundred quid if we traded in our old gear.'

I took a bite of the chip. It was too hot, but I didn't want to look like a wimp when I was being managerial, so I had to tough it out. 'Terrific,' I said, the roof of my mouth burned to a crisp. 'And how about you, Greeny, could you get a hold of some more special effects stuff with the rest?'

Greeny's face lit up. 'Mate, I could get a unit that will make your eyes bleed with its sheer wickedness.'

I looked around the table. Everyone seemed to be on board. Except Ad.

'Everything all right, mate?' I said.

'I dunno,' he said. 'It's just, we've got the money now. What if we don't win? We'll be back where we started.'

Don't be such a sissy, four eyes! yelled Hank.

'We're going to win,' I said. 'With this new stuff, there's no way we can lose. You two are going to make their ears bleed, Greeny is going to make their eyes bleed. That place is going to be a bloodbath.'

Ad shrugged. 'If you say so.'

'How quick can you guys get the gear?' I said.

'Today,' said Harry. Greeny nodded.

We walked into town afterwards and got our new stuff. Harry and Ad went back to Ad's garage to try it out. I would have loved to have gone with

« Older posts

them but we've got to go to Natalie's later. Possibly for a peace treaty. Harry told me not to be Neville Chamberlain but to be Churchill-like. Ad was confused because he thought Churchill was the insurance dog off the telly.

11 p.m.

No. That did not just happen.

Yes it did, you freakin' moron.

We arrived at Natalie's to find Desmond lurking in the hall.

'You're late,' he said.

'Actually, you told us to be here for six and it's six now, so we're not late at all,' said Natalie.

'If Joe was any kind of professional, he'd know to arrive at least ten minutes early for appointments,' he said. 'Anyway, let's get on with it, shall we?'

He opened the living room door and nodded for us to enter. Natalie rolled her eyes and went in first.

'Clifton,' she said. 'What are you doing here?'

Clifton smiled weakly and gave a little shrug. He was sitting on the sofa, next to Catherine.

'What's going on?' Natalie turned on Desmond, her fists clenched.

'Just sit down, Natalie,' said her mum. 'Let's not prolong this.'

'Prolong what? What are you talking about?'

Desmond gave her a look and she sat down next to Clifton. I took the other seat. Desmond stood in front of us and made a pyramid with his fingers. They didn't have the TV on or anything. Silence.

Don't worry too much, Joe, said Norman. *It could be a peace treaty, like you said.*

Then why's Jamaican Jerry here? said Hank. *Be ready for a fight, my man.*

'I think you know why we're here,' said Desmond.

'No, actually, we don't, so why don't you just get on with it?' said Natalie.

'Very well,' said Desmond. 'Clifton, did you, or did you not, take my daughter and Joe to a nightclub last night?'

Clifton went to speak, but Natalie cut in. 'No, that's not true,' she said. 'Don't say anything, Clifton, he has no evidence. Besides, I was in my room all night.'

Desmond smiled. 'Seb saw you,' he said.

'That won't stand up in a court of law,' said Natalie. 'Besides, you can't take what that slimy idiot has to say seriously.'

Desmond looked outraged. 'Sebastian is not an idiot.'

« Older posts

'Slimy though,' said Natalie.

'Anyway, enough with this nonsense,' said Desmond. 'It seems I do actually have some evidence.'

I glanced at Clifton, then at Natalie. My eye started twitching.

Desmond picked up a remote and switched the TV on. The screen flickered into life to show a wobbly mobile phone video. To begin with it was too dark to see what was happening. Then something purple glimmered in the corner. Natalie. With me and Clifton.

'Pretty damning, wouldn't you say?' said Desmond.

'That could have been anyone,' said Natalie.

I started gnawing at a loose piece of skin on my finger.

'All right then, well how about this little item I found in that nightclub bathroom?' Desmond reached into a drawer in a sideboard and pulled out a thick book. I could feel Clifton crumple in his seat.

'*Crime and Punishment*,' Desmond said to himself. 'How apt.'

'Yeah, so what?' said Natalie. 'Haven't you ever seen a book before?'

Desmond opened the front cover and read something.

To Clifton. Happy birthday to the best gardener ever. Love, Natalie.

Natalie sighed and shook her head.

'This is very serious,' said Desmond.

Cocking hell.

'Clifton,' he said. 'While I would be well within my rights to dismiss you, I have decided to be lenient on this occasion.'

Clifton puffed out his cheeks.

'You are suspended indefinitely,' he said. 'On half pay.'

'What?' Natalie cried. 'You can't be bloody serious.'

'I am deadly serious,' said Desmond. 'And mind your language. I see this boy has had quite the influence on you.'

She folded her arms and swore under her breath.

'Now, there is the small matter of what to do with you,' he said.

'Do your worst, DESMOND', said Natalie.

He made that stupid finger pyramid again. 'I obviously can't trust you, can I?' he said. 'You sneaked out of the house against my wishes and made our gardener go with you to a nightclub.'

'We needed a chaperone,' said Natalie. 'So what if it was Clifton?'

'Because you were supposed to be at home studying.'

'Ah, who cares?' said Natalie.

'Natalie, we raised you better than this,' said Catherine.

'Did you? You're so obsessed with special little Charlie, I doubt you'd notice if I grew HORNS!'

'That's it,' said Desmond. 'We've allowed this to go on long enough. You are to have no further contact with Joe.'

'What?' we cried in unison.

« Older posts

'You can't stop us,' said Natalie.

'How about this, then?' said Desmond. 'If I hear about you two being anywhere near each other, I will fire the gardener.'

'What?' cried Clifton.

'Please, Clifton, you're on thin ice as it is,' said Desmond.

'Desmond,' said Catherine.

'We have to be strong on this,' he said. 'We know all about this hooligan's activities.'

'Activities?' I said. 'What are you talking about?'

'Don't try and play innocent with me,' said Desmond.

Ah, suck on my ass through a straw, old man, said Hank. *This boy hasn't done anything bad. He's too much of a goddamn wuss!*

That's not strictly true, Hank, said Norman. *What about when he hacked that website?*

Ah crap.

'Now, I'll be having your phone, please, Natalie,' said Desmond.

Natalie started crying. 'Why are you doing this?' she said. 'Why can't you just let me be happy?'

'Phone. Now.'

Natalie dried her eyes with the back of her hand, and threw her phone on the floor.

'You're not helping matters, dear,' said Desmond, bending over to pick it up.

My breath started getting shorter.

'You know, I wouldn't be so angry if you hadn't lied to me last night, Joe,' said Desmond. 'It really speaks to your character that you would do that. Especially when you seemed so sincere about wanting to impress me.'

'Look, Mr Tuft,' I said. 'I'm sorry, I really am, but I never meant to lie. I just didn't want Clifton to get into trouble. And it really wasn't my idea for my friend to vomit on your shoes, either.'

Desmond's face went from smug to sucking on lemons.

'The thing is, I'm not that bad a person,' I said. 'And I really like Natalie. And I would never hurt her. Ever. Please don't do this.'

Desmond stared at me. If this were a film, his icy exterior would break at witnessing my feelings for his daughter and he would give us his blessing. But this isn't a film.

'Sorry, it's too late,' he said. 'You've led my daughter astray for long enough and I won't allow it to continue a moment longer.'

My head felt like it was going to burst when I got outside. I had no idea what to do. Without knowing how I got there, I found myself at Ad's. They were mid-rehearsal.

'Bloody hell, old boy, you're perspiring more than Greeny was after he ate that pack of pasties,' said Harry. 'No offence.'

'Nah, to be fair I did have some chronic pie sweats,' said Greeny.

« Older posts

I tried to suck some oxygen back into my lungs. 'It's a disaster,' I said. 'Natalie's dad found out about what happened at the club and he's stopped us seeing each other. And he'll sack Clifton if we do.'

'Ah bum, what are we gonna do?' said Ad.

'I don't know,' I said. 'Maybe we should withdraw from the competition? That might make him less angry. I mean, we wouldn't be interfering with Seb, and Natalie wouldn't be involved in it any more.'

'You have to be pulling my plonker,' said Harry.

'Yeah, man,' said Gav.

'Surely the old chap can find alternative employment?' said Harry.

I kicked a fold-up chair over. 'Even if he could, that's not all,' I said. 'He says he'll go to the police about us hacking that website.'

No one spoke for a few seconds.

'They ain't gonna know that was us,' said Ad.

'Yeah,' Gav joined in.

'Actually,' said Greeny. 'They can trace the IP of anyone who edits them.'

'He's got us,' I said. 'No matter what we do.'

Gav stepped forward and put his giant hand on my shoulder. 'You want me to knock him out for you?'

'That would be nice, but it won't solve anything,' I said.

Everyone looked at each other. There was silence.

'But neither will quitting,' said Harry. 'Plus, we've spent our money now and we're back to where we started. The new gear is top drawer, by the way.'

'Well, can't we just take it back?' I said. 'Get a refund?'

'They won't do refunds,' said Harry. 'Only exchanges. And besides, that isn't the point.'

'Well what is the point?' I said.

Harry cocked his head to one side and took his pipe out of his top pocket. 'Do you really want to let him win?'

'Of course I don't,' I said. 'But what else can I do?'

'You underestimate your old friend,' said Harry. 'I'll think of something.'

'What?' I said. 'What can you possibly do to get us out of this one?'

'I'll think of something,' he said again. 'I always do.'

'Will it work though?' I said.

He smiled. 'When have you ever known my strategies to fail?'

'Well, there was that time the two of you tried to manufacture your own line of aftershave in your shed, but the barrel exploded all over us.'

'Yeah,' said Ad. 'People were calling us the three musky queers for months after that.'

'A youthful mistake,' said Harry. 'This one will not fail. I just need some time to work it out.'

'I don't know,' I said.

'Look.' Harry looked around and stepped close to me. 'The thing I've always admired about you, old son, is that you don't allow yourself to be defeated by bullies. Are you about to start now?'

Goddamn it, he's right, said Hank. *I've always liked that pipe guy.*

I sighed. 'No.'

Harry smiled with his pipe clamped between his teeth. 'Gather round, troops.'

Gav, Ad, and Greeny joined the huddle.

'You heard what Private Cowley said, one of our comrades is being held by the enemy,' said Harry. 'Now are we going to let that happen?'

'NO!'

'We never leave a man, or woman, behind,' he continued. 'And the enemy's laughable attempt to get us to surrender will not work. Am I right, Private Green?'

'NO SURRENDER!' Greeny yelled.

'Private James?'

'NO SURRENDER!'

'Private Lawrence?'

'NO SURRENDER!'

'Private Cowley?'

They all stared at me. I supposed this was my only hope.

'No surrender,' I said.

Sunday 28th October

I feel sick. I sent Natalie emails but have heard nothing back. How can he be stopping her from communicating with me? There has to be some kind of law against this.

Went for a walk in the park to see if it would help me think things through. I stood by the lake and watched the swans. The male one was pursuing the female all over the lake, but every time he got close, she'd move. Eventually, she just flew away altogether. The male swan swam to the side of the lake and stood on his own. I gave him a sympathetic nod. That was me, once.

I should point out I meant that metaphorically. I have never chased a swan around a lake with amorous intentions.

Monday 29th October

First day of half term. This is killing me to death. At least at school, I'll be able to see her.

Had to take Doris to her club alone. Natalie couldn't go because I was there. Everyone asked where she was. I told the Colonel that Natalie's dad wouldn't let her come out, and he said he sounded like a 'rotter'. He doesn't know the cocking half of it.

I asked Doris if she'd ever experienced anything like this.

'Yes, actually, Joseph,' she said. 'When I was courting Teddy Smith, my father said he was the wrong sort, and I wasn't to see him ever again.'

« Older posts

'And what happened?' I said. 'Did you see him anyway and live happily ever after?'

'Oh, no. He said, "Well sod you then," and started courting my best friend, Elsie,' she said.

'Thanks, Doris,' I said. 'I feel much better now.'

Wednesday 31st October

After spending most of the morning staring at the ceiling, I got a phone call from Harry.

'I've had an idea, old son,' he said.

Now there's a sentence that has launched a thousand disasters.

'We're going to try and get to Natalie,' he said.

I sat up and started listening properly.

'Go on,' I said.

11.30 p.m.

'That is the best costume you could find?' said Harry.

'Well, it's all I could come up with at such short notice,' I said. 'I would have borrowed one off Greeny if he wasn't on holiday.'

'Yeah, but Prince William?' said Harry.

'It's the only mask we've got,' I said. 'It's Jim's.'

'Why the cape though?' said Harry.

'I don't know,' I said. 'Maybe I'm a vampire Prince William, OK? Anyway, what have you two got?'

Harry pulled a hockey mask out of his bag. 'I'm Jason from *Friday the 13th*,' he said.

'How about you, Ad?'

'Check it,' he said, pulling a black cloak and a white mask out. 'I'm Scream.'

'He's not called Scream,' I said. 'That's just the name of the film.'

'Yeah, he is,' said Ad. 'That's how the film gets its name. Like *Jaws*—that's named after the shark.'

'Sharks don't have names, Ad,' I said. 'And if they did, what if it was called like . . . Colin, or something? They're not going to call a film about a killer shark Colin, are they?'

'Don't be stupid,' said Ad. 'Whoever heard of a shark called Colin?'

« Older posts

I facepalmed. 'Right, are we ready, then?'

Harry put his mask on. 'Oh yes.'

As we were leaving the house, Jim saw us and started creasing up.

'What are you laughing at?' Mum called from the living room.

'Nothing,' said Jim. 'It's just Prince William, Jason, and Scream about to hit the town.'

'Aaaaaaah,' said Ad, pointing a victorious finger. 'Told you he was called Scream.'

Goddamn it.

As we got to the end of Natalie's drive, I started to panic. If this went wrong, it would be a disaster. Clifton would lose his job and I'd be in the clink for cyber sabotage, and possibly kidnap. Still, we had to at least try.

'Look.' I pointed to a sign nailed to a tree.

STRICTLY NO TRICK-OR-TREATERS

'What a Kilroy,' said Scream.

'Killjoy, old son, killjoy,' said Jason. 'Anyway, it doesn't matter because Scream and I are unholy killing machines that can't read because we know only death and destruction.'

'What about me?' I said. 'Why can't I read?'

'Because you've always had servants to do it for you, but now you're a vampire, none of them will come close enough,' said Jason. 'Right, enough of this tomfoolery, it's time to begin OPERATION DAMSEL IN DISTRESS.'

My breathing got heavier, making the plastic inside of the mask go all nasty and damp. I watched from behind a bush as Scream and Jason rang the doorbell. After a while, Catherine answered.

'Trick or treat!'

'We've put a sign up saying we don't want any trick-or-treaters—can't you read?'

'Madam, with the state of our education system, it's a wonder I can even dress myself,' said Jason.

This got her going on one of her rants about our school, so I took the opportunity to ghost around the back of the hedge and make my way into the back garden.

As soon as I got around there, I searched for a ladder. None. Not even lying down around the side of the house like where Jim keeps his. This was going to be trickier than I thought, and Jason and Scream could only keep them distracted for so long.

I picked up a pebble and lobbed it towards the window. Unfortunately, I'm a terrible shot, so it just pinged harmlessly off the latticing on the wall.

The window was hard to make out in the darkness, but I tried again. This time, it looked like it was heading in the

« Older posts

right direction, but it didn't make a sound like a pebble hitting a window, it was more like an ouch.

For a horrible second, I thought Natalie had opened the window and I had hit her in the face. Then this happened:

'Oi! I know you're out there. We have CCTV you know!'

Desmond!

I let out a little yelp then belted back around the front, where Scream and Jason were running away. Damn it. I went to join them, but a shadowy figure blocked my way. He must have jumped down the cocking stairs.

I turned around and ran back into the garden, trying to hide in the darkness.

'Give yourself up, Joe,' Desmond yelled.

My breathing was raspy and it felt like my heart was kicking several shades of crap out of my ribcage. His footsteps got closer.

I threw myself to the floor and rolled behind a hedge. I held my breath as he ran past.

How the cocking hell am I going to get out of this?

Well, you can't go back the way you came or you'll run the risk of being seen, said Norman, trying to deactivate the alarm system in my brain.

Jump out of there, kick his ass into that pond, and hold him under until the bubbles stop! Hank screamed.

'Where are you, Joe?' Desmond shouted. 'I'm calling the police!'

I could see the cell door closing on me. I had to do something. I searched for a way out. And then I saw it. A small gap in the bottom of the fence. Desmond sounded like he was coming back, so I crawled towards it, and pulled myself through onto the other side. The grass was wet and I shivered when the wind hit me.

I was in the next-door-neighbour's garden, but at least I was out of trouble.

For about three seconds.

The first time I was aware of the dog was when I felt my trousers go tight. I turned around and saw it. My God. I'm used to Hercules chewing on me, but this beast was eight times bigger than him. It growled and massive wads of spit flew as it shook its head.

I wanted to cry out, but if I did, Desmond would find me. The dog came away with a chunk of cloth in its mouth, so I made a run for it. I got about two metres before the hound from hell got my other trouser leg.

This is it, Norm, said Hank. *This is how we die. We're going to be dog turds within the hour.*

In a way, I'm not surprised it's ended like this, said Norman. *It's been a pleasure working with you, my friend.*

I wish I could say the same, said Hank.

I pulled my leg away, but that seemed to make the dog angrier and its massive teeth inched closer to my leg.

I peered through the darkness and saw the front gate

was open. If I could get away from the dog, I reckoned I could make it. But there was no way this dog was going to let go of me. Or rather, my trousers.

That's when I had the idea. I didn't like it, but it was probably my survival instinct kicking in. I unbuckled my belt and kicked off my shoes.

Here we go.

I flew across the garden, the wet grass soaking my socks and the freezing wind whipping my bare legs. *Oh God, why did I put on such a threadbare pair of pants this morning?*

I heard the dog gaining ground behind me. If it got me this time, it'd be my flesh coming away in its jaws, not denim.

I jumped through the open gate and slammed it shut behind me. The dog slammed into it and started scraping at the wood and howling.

It was only then that the gravity of the situation hit me. I was stranded on the other side of town. With no trousers on. Dressed like a vampire Prince William.

What was worse was I didn't bring my phone so I couldn't even call Harry and Ad and ask them to bring me some replacement trousers. And even if I had, it would have been in my trousers, clamped in the jaws of the hound of the cocking Baskervilles.

Damn. What the hell do I do now?

I don't know, man, said Hank. *Even for you, this is weird.*

Perhaps you could wrap the cape around your waist? said Norman.

Now, there was an idea. I mean, it would look like I was wearing a skirt, but that had to be better than half the town seeing me in my yellow Y-fronts.

I started to undo my cape when a noise at the end of the drive distracted me.

'Oi, I can see you!'

Ballsacks!

I hopped over a little wall and ran out of the street. Desmond was right behind me, making a grab for my cape. I weaved in and out of dustbins, trying to lose him. If he caught me I'd be done for cybercrime and trespass. And maybe indecent exposure.

I heard him stumble, which allowed me to gain a little headway. I dodged around a bin, then pushed it over. Desmond tried to hurdle it, but caught his foot on it and hit the rubbish-covered ground with a smack.

Before he had chance to get back up, I ducked down a dirt track and hopped over a fence onto the canal towpath. Going down there is risky at the best of times without being dressed like a pervy vampire prince, but I had no choice.

I thought about taking my mask off, but then stopped. Yes, this was embarrassing, but at least no one would know it was me. I calculated that if I ran I could be home within ten minutes.

« Older posts

My feet killed because of all the stones but I couldn't stop. I'd worry about being crippled when I got home. Just ten minutes.

Shouts echoed from the tunnel up ahead. Damn. I thought about getting off and taking the road way, but then I realized it would lead me to one of the busiest streets in town. I know it was Halloween, but no way did I want to be seen in my pants by everyone.

The wind kicked up. It was so cold, I'm pretty sure everything downstairs had retreated inside me. At least, that was my excuse.

The shouts got louder.

It's all right, Joe, just keep running, said Norman. *If you don't stop, they can't get you.*

My footsteps echoed down the tunnel. I could hear voices, but I couldn't see anyone. Then, just as I got to the end, two figures stepped out in front of me.

Don't stop!

I picked up the pace and put my arms out. The two men had their backs to me. I pushed them out of the way. One of them teetered over slowly, and landed in the canal.

Crap! What have I done?

Against my better judgement, I stopped.

The man grabbed the edge and looked up at me. His eyes went huge.

'Jesus!'

I turned around and the other man was running away. Why the hell were they so scared of me? Oh yeah, the costume. They must have thought they were tripping balls.

I heard a little voice.

'Thank you.'

'Huh?'

The other bloke climbed out of the canal and ran the same way as the other one.

'Thank you.'

A little old lady stood on the bank clutching her handbag.

'Thank you, Your Majesty.'

God, she thought I'd saved her from being mugged! I felt like Batman!

'No need to thank me, citizen,' I said. 'Remember to stay safe, and avoid canal towpaths from now on!'

'I will,' she said. 'But can I ask you your name?'

'My name?' I said. 'My name . . . is the Prince of Pants!'

I'd like to say I got home without being seen, but that wasn't true. Thank God for the mask. I let myself into the house and crept upstairs without being rumbled by Mum or Jim. Then I took my mask off and went into my room.

'Heyyyy,' said Gav. 'So they gave you a job at the gay disco after all, bruv. Congrats, innit?'

Bruce Wayne never had to put up with comments like that from Alfred.

4 a.m.

Can't sleep. What if Desmond finds out I'm the Prince of Pants?

4.05 a.m.

No, it's not as if those trousers have my name in them.

4.10 a.m.

OH MY GOD. Were they the pair with my name in them?

4.15 a.m.

No, it's OK. I've found the named trousers. Cocking hell, I'm such a dork.

4.20 a.m.

I miss Natalie.

Thursday 1st November

Miserable. Going to have my braces tightened at three o'clock.

3.30 p.m.

Even more miserable.

4 p.m.

Called Harry and told him about what happened last night. I think he's actually going to die laughing.

5 p.m.

Mrs Brewer's cat is stuck up a tree. I'm looking at my Prince of Pants costume in my wardrobe.

5.10 p.m.

No. The Prince of Pants is the hero Tammerstone deserves, but not the one it needs right now. Plus, I'm scared of heights. And cats.

Friday 2nd November

Had a thought. What if Desmond calls the police and tells them I was at his house dressed as the Prince of Pants? I have to dispose of the evidence.

6 p.m.

I put the costume in the bin to begin with, but that's the first place the police would search, so I wrapped it in a bin liner and chucked it in the dog poo bin at the park.

7.30 p.m.

I keep looking at pictures of me and Natalie together. I wish I didn't have such a lopsided face. I cover myself up with my hand and just look at her.

7.45 p.m.

Gav walked in and caught me cuddling an old stuffed bear I had when I was little, and now he's started calling me 'Paddington shagger'.

Sunday 4th November

Keep ringing Harry to see if he has any more ideas. He said he needs time to assess the next move. I hope he can come up with something.

Dad offered to take me for a haircut to cheer me up. Apparently, I don't have enough shine and bounce, which is something that needs to be addressed on a follicular level.

I asked him if we'd be going to his hairdresser. He said yes, so I declined.

Monday 5th November

'Remember, remember, the fifth of November.' Well, I'm not likely to forget it in a hurry because today has been the WORST. I woke up to find Doris had baked my Maths homework into an upside-down cake.

Me, Harry, and Ad walked into school to find Natalie waiting for us by our lockers.

I really wanted to stop, but Chloe and Ellie were hanging around nearby and I couldn't risk them telling Lisa and Lisa telling Seb. So I had to ignore her.

Took Doris to the club tonight. Everyone's really missing Natalie. The worst part was during the organ recital, when Blind Trevor asked me to dance. I tried telling him I'm not a lady, but it turns out Blind Trevor is also a bit deaf, so I had to do a waltz with him.

This is a new low, said Hank.

When I sat down, Ad called and asked if I wanted to go around his because his parents had gone out and he'd managed to get hold of some fireworks. I said no, because I quite like having skin.

On the way home, some little kids asked me for a penny for their Guy. It looked a bit like Seb so I gave them a quid.

Me and Gav went to Uncle Johnny's. Syd has taken a vow of silence. Good.

« Older posts

Tuesday 6th November

Boocock didn't say a thing to me today. He didn't call me a zombie, or make me demonstrate slide tackles with Bruiser Blenkinsop, he didn't even make me run laps. At the end of the lesson, I went to pass him my bib back and he flinched. Cocking hell, I think he's scared of me.

Harry still hasn't come up with a way of sorting this mess out. I wish he'd hurry up because this is driving me mad. Everywhere I go, I feel like I'm being watched, by Seb, or Lisa, or one of their minions. They're all waiting for us to slip up. It sucks.

Me and Natalie are in the same class in History, and we can't sit together any more, so I got Harry to be our go-between. He didn't mind because we were doing the Second World War and he knows more than Mr Beaker about it anyway.

I started by passing him a note:

Miss you.

A minute later, and her reply was pressed into my hand under the table.

I miss you too. I hate my dad so much.

Mr Beaker looked at us, so I sneakily pushed the note under my textbook. When he turned his back I took it out again.

We're going to find a way to sort this. I promise.

Good. Love you. X

GAH!

My heart rate rocketed. The already stuffy room suddenly got unbearably hot.

Take your time, Joe, said Norman. *This is a big step.*

Take your time? Hank cried. *Sure, that's just what this situation calls for: hesitancy.*

I glanced over at Natalie. Those red patches flared up on her cheeks as she took notes in her book.

Really?

Hank slow-clapped. *Bra-freakin'-vo.*

Yes, really. X
Me?

You.
You love me?

Yes. X

Bloody hell, old son, this is excruciating. If you don't say you love her back, I'm going to do it myself.

I love you too.

Cool. ☺

Oh, and Harry, you're not supposed to be reading these messages, let alone writing them.

Right you are, old bean.

Oh my God. Someone loves me. Me? There's something not right about that. No one's ever loved me before. Well, I suppose Mum and Dad do, but that doesn't count, does it?

« Older posts

Not really. How do I feel about this? I don't even know.

When I got home, I lay on my bunk with the note and ripped off all the depressing bits about her dad, so just the love bit was left. It would have been proper romantic if Gav hadn't walked in, let a ripper of a fart go, then turned and run to the bathroom, shouting, 'I knew that was a risky one.'

8.30 p.m.

Oh you have to be cocking kidding me. I just picked up Jim's copy of the *Tammerstone Times* and saw this:

ELDERLY WOMAN SAVED BY MASKED VIGILANTE

A Tammerstone woman has told of how she was rescued from an attempted mugging by a bizarre superhero.

Edith Battenberg-Staltzman, 75, was accosted by two men on the canal towpath near Giswick Lock on Wednesday evening. They were about to run away with her handbag, but were chased off by a man in a Prince William mask, a vampire cape, and yellow Y-fronts.

'It was rather queer,' said the widow. 'He referred to himself as the Prince of Pants.'

Mrs Battenberg-Staltzman is offering a £300 reward to the mysterious hero, if he can prove it was him.

I could have made three hundred quid if I'd kept hold of that costume!

9 p.m.

Maybe it's still in the dog poo bin . . .

9.15 p.m.

No. Even if it is still in there, there's no way I can go public as the Prince of Pants. Desmond will know it's me, and then I'll need my reward for bail money. What a terrible life this is.

9.30 p.m.

I'd better tear that story out of the paper. If Jim sees it he's bound to put two and two together. I just hope he wasn't planning on using that mask any time soon.

Wednesday 7th November

'What's the matter, old boy?' asked Harry on the way to school. 'You look like your nan's died by choking on your winning lottery ticket.'

'It's Nat, innit, mate?' said Ad.

I nodded.

'Yeah, I can always tell,' he said. 'I've been having woman troubles myself.'

Me and Harry gave each other a look.

'Really, old son?' said Harry.

Ad nodded. 'Candy's left Babestation.'

Harry raised his eyebrows at me and clapped Ad on the shoulder. 'Well, at least you have your memories.'

« Older posts

Ad nodded sadly.

'Anyway, soldier,' said Harry. 'Now we've dealt with Ad's issue, let's hear yours.'

'Have you thought of another way of rescuing Natalie yet?' I said.

Harry plucked a leaf off a bush and rolled it in his hands. 'These things take time,' he said. 'But I am formulating some possible solutions.'

'What are they?'

'You certainly are eager,' said Harry. 'But then, I suppose you're tired of having to, you know, take Captain Picard to warp speed by yourself.'

It took me a couple of seconds to figure that one out.

'You make me sick,' I said. 'And anyway, we don't do that.'

'Could have fooled me, old boy,' he said. 'Ooh, Joe, I love you.'

I pushed him on the shoulder. 'Shut up, Harry.'

'Uh, yeah, that's, that's interesting,' he said, doing an impression of me that sounded nothing like me. 'I, um, love you too. I think.'

He and Ad laughed it up for ages. Ad laughed so hard he wobbled over someone's front wall into a rose bed.

'That's not funny,' I said.

'It is a bit though, mate,' said Ad, picking thorns out of his skin.

'Fine,' I said. 'Anyway, tell me about your ideas.'

Harry wiped the tears from his eyes and tried to compose himself. 'Right,' he said. 'The first one is high risk, but would be a good long-term plan if executed successfully. The second is even higher risk, and would only be short term.'

'What do you mean, short term?' I said.

'Well, it would be temporary, but it would allow you enough time to, you know, play park-the-spitfire-in-the-hangar.'

'HANGAR?' I yelled. 'And, I told you, we don't do that!'

'Yes, I believe that like I believe Ad saw the Prime Minister in Poundstretcher.'

'I did see the Prime Minister in Poundstretcher!' said Ad.

'How did you know he was the Prime Minister?' said Harry.

'He was wearing a suit, weren't he?' said Ad.

'You know when you were born, did the midwife drop you on your head?' said Harry.

'Anyway, enough,' I said. 'Tell me about these plans.'

Can you give me Clifton's number?

I passed the paper to Harry, who slipped it to Natalie. I watched as she sneakily wrote his home number on the paper. When Harry passed it back, I folded it and stuck it in my top pocket.

How are you?

The reply came back quick.

« Older posts

Crap. The idiot has even cut off the internet connection in the house. Why do you want to talk to Clifton?

I need to discuss options with him.

OK . . . I really want to see you. You know, properly.

I'm working on it.

As is my helpful, intelligent, and devilishly handsome best pal, Harry.

Harry, stop reading these!

Sorry, old boy.

Natalie's next note sent a jolt of electricity up my spine. Not literally, she hadn't booby-trapped it or anything.

I've had an idea. In your next lesson, at exactly 11.15, ask if you can go to the toilet. Then meet me at your locker. It will only be five minutes, but it's better than nothing.

Five minutes is more than enough for Joe.

HARRY!

'Barry gets on a train at Tammerstone at 8 a.m., travelling at eighty miles per hour towards London. Ranjit boards another train leaving London for Tammerstone at the same time, but travelling at sixty miles per hour. Assuming the distance between the two is one hundred and twenty miles, at what time do the trains pass?'

Mr Shenko looked out at the class. Everyone tried to avoid eye contact. Harry put his hand up.

'Judging by the state of the British rail system, sometime next Tuesday,' he said.

'Please, Harry,' said Mr Shenko. 'Let's keep it about the Maths, OK? Remember what I always say, leave your issues at the door, so the Maths can have the floor.'

Ugh. I looked at my watch. Thirteen minutes past. I really didn't want to put my hand up, but it looked like I had no choice.

'Yes, Joe?'

'Can I go to the toilet, please?'

There was a sprinkling of laughter. 'He probably needs to go and puke,' said Pete Cotterill.

After the amount Ad had projectiled recently, it is a crime that I'm still known as the vomity one.

'Do you have to go now, Joe?' said Mr Shenko. 'If you need the loo, for pity's sake, don't go in Maths, go in the break.'

'I, I know, but I can't wait,' I said. 'I'm, you know, desperate.'

'OK, if you must,' he said. 'But have a stab at the question first. You know what I say, if you don't know the answer, take a chancer. Who knows? It might advance ya.'

I puffed my cheeks out. Fourteen minutes past. I stood up and headed for the door. 'Ten o'clock,' I said, then walked out. As I ran upstairs, I couldn't help but wonder if I was right.

I smashed the door open and headed down the corridor. I could hear voices.

'Why have you followed me here, anyway?'

'I need the toilet, just like you.'

Oh God. Lisa.

'Yeah, right,' said Natalie. 'You're stalking me.'

'I'm no stalker,' said Lisa. 'And if I was, I wouldn't stalk a sad witch like you.'

'You're doing this for Seb, to make sure I'm not meeting Joe, aren't you?'

'None of your business.'

I crept closer and hid around the corner. If Lisa spotted me, that would be it.

'Oh, Lisa,' said Natalie. 'You stupid girl, can't you see he's using you?'

'Shut up, freak,' said Lisa. 'I don't get used.'

'You're normally the one that does the using, I know, but he's got you, here,' said Natalie.

'Pfft, you're just bitter 'cause Seb chucked you.'

Icicles of doom pierced my heart. Did that really happen?

'You don't know what you're talking about,' said Natalie.

'Don't I?'

I could hear Natalie sigh. 'Are you going to leave me alone, or what?'

Silence.

'You're going to get yours one day,' said Natalie.

I listened to them walk away. God, this is bad.

Um, excuse me, said Hank. *What's all this about Seb dumping Natalie?*

Don't concern yourself, Joe, said a frazzled-looking Norman. You know what Lisa's like.

Yeah, but what about when her parents said they want her to like him AGAIN?

I tried to silence the control room as I trudged back to class. I remember her telling me the only boy she'd ever kissed was this smelly Frenchie called Guillaume. She wouldn't lie to me, would she? The obvious way to find out what's happening would be to ask her, but I can't even do that. This is bad.

9 p.m.

I went out the back and got my phone out. Time to activate Harry's first scheme.

'Hello, is that Clifton?'

'Yes,' he said after a pause. 'Who is this?'

'It's Joe.'

'I don't know anybody by that name, sorry you must have the wrong number, thank you, goodbye.'

He hung up.

I took a deep breath and considered my options. He's not going to answer the phone. Maybe he'll answer the door? I remembered where he lived from when we dropped him off in Dad's car. I knew sorting Clifton out

« Older posts

wouldn't solve this whole mess, but at least it would be one less thing to worry about. My criminal secrets would have to wait for another day.

I dragged my bike out of the shed and started along my road. I pedalled so hard, my calves burned.

I took a moment to get my breath back when I got there and knocked on Clifton's door. It opened and Clifton stood there with a look of panic on his face.

'Can't you take a hint, boy?' he whispered, looking up and down the street. 'Stay away!'

'Please, Clifton,' I said. 'I need to talk to you, it's important.'

He scoped the street out again. 'All right,' he said. 'Get in the car.' He leaned back into the house. 'Just popping to Sainsbury's, love.'

I got into his car. He followed and started the engine. Without a word, he threw it into reverse and gunned it out of the drive. There was a loud bang, followed by metallic scraping.

'What was that?' Clifton looked scared to death.

I peered at the twisted wreckage on the pavement. 'That was my bike.'

'Ah,' he said. 'Sorry about that, Joseph.'

He didn't speak again until we were on the other side of town. 'So,' he said. 'What did you want to see me about?'

'Just wondering how you were,' I said. 'Been feeling a bit guilty, you know.'

'A bit guilty?' he said. 'I stand to lose my job over this.'

'I'm sorry,' I said. 'And we are being extra careful, by the way. There's no way we'll be seen together.'

'Oh, well now I feel much better,' he said. It's weird to hear an old bloke doing sarcasm.

'Look,' I said. 'Do you really need this job? I mean, can't you find something else?'

'At my age?' he said. 'They'd take one look at me and say no thanks. There's no use for an old man like me in this world.'

Damn. I'd never thought of that. He really does need this job.

'You'll get your job back,' I said. 'I promise.'

He sighed. 'I hope so. You know, I haven't told my wife about it.'

'Why not?'

'Ah, she'll just worry, and I could do without that,' he said. 'I've been taking myself off in the morning and coming back, pretending I've been at work. And I don't like lying, Joseph.'

I nodded and looked at the CDs in the pocket on his car door. All Beach Boys.

'There was one other thing I wanted to ask you, Clifton,' I said.

He gave me a quick sideways look. 'Oh yes?'

'I know you and Natalie have always been close,' I said.

He nodded.

« Older posts

'Did she and that Seb ever have a, you know, thing?'

'A thing? I don't know anything about that,' he said. 'It's true, I have seen a lot of the boy at the house, but I don't know anything about a thing. And even if I did, young man, I don't think Natalie would thank me for telling you her business.'

I rubbed my eyes.

'For what it's worth though,' said Clifton. 'I don't like the boy. He's a nasty piece of work. Reminds me of Tuft himself.'

He dropped me off a little way from home, just to be safe.

9 p.m.

Oh for crying out loud . . .

Tammerstone Times Online
PRINCE OF PANTS INTRIGUE HITS FEVER PITCH

Tammerstone bookies are taking bets on the secret identity of masked vigilante, the Prince of Pants, after his reward money doubled in size.

Local businessman Desmond Tuft, 53, has pledged another £300 to the man behind the mask.

'I believe that heroism of this sort should be richly rewarded,' said Mr Tuft. 'And I am as curious as anyone to know who this person is.'

Damn you, Desmond.

Thursday 8th November

I didn't get much sleep last night. All this crazy crap that's happening is making me forget about my homework. Had to get up super early to do Maths, despite the fact that at that time of the morning, if someone told me $1 + 1 = 37$, I'd believe them.

I felt slightly more reassured about Natalie and Seb after speaking to Clifton, but I still couldn't shake my suspicions. I had to speak to her, or rather, get Harry to send a message for me.

'Bloody hell, old boy, if I was charging the same prices as the Royal Mail, I'd be a millionaire,' he said. He seemed quite narked that scheme one wasn't exactly a massive success.

'As your esteemed manager, these are the kind of favours I will occasionally ask,' I said.

'Oh, speaking of which . . . ' Harry pulled a piece of paper out of his bag. 'I've had the paperwork for the final through. They're putting us up in a hotel. Shall I put Natalie down?'

'Course you should,' I said. 'Because she is going to be there, no matter what.'

'All right, soldier, but you two aren't allowed to share a room. As the wife of a vicar, I don't believe in sharing a bed before matrimony.'

'For the last time, we aren't doing . . . that,' I said.

« Older posts

'Methinks the lady doth protest too much,' said Harry.

'Nah, she ain't protesting enough,' said Ad.

I wrote a note in History.

How are you?

Thinking of committing some serious patricide. Tried talking to Catherine, but she doesn't care. I think she's given up on me and has moved on to Charlie. How about you? X

Not bad.

My pen hovered over the page, but I didn't write what I wanted to write.

Everything OK?

Yep.

Come on, what's the matter? I can see your eye twitching.

I took a deep breath.

What's the deal with you and Jeb? Were the two of you ever a, you know, thing?

Natalie stared at the note for a long time. Those red patches came up again, faintly. She picked up her pen and began to write.

'Sir!'

'Yes, Lisa.'

'Natalie Tuft and Joe Cowley are passing notes to each other and it's distracting me from my learning.'

Hank stood up and kicked his chair over. *You meddling—*

Hank, please remain gentlemanly at all times, said Norman.

'Yes, I thought something had been occurring over there,' said Mr Beaker. 'Right, Natalie, you sit over there in that corner, and Joe can sit in the opposite corner.'

For crying out loud.

I gathered my things and sat next to crazy Jason Downey.

'I don't like new people,' he mumbled.

I looked over and saw Lisa eyeballing me. This can't be enough to grass us in for, can it?

After the lesson, I found her by her locker.

'Lisa, we weren't passing notes,' I said.

'Uh, yeah you were,' she said. 'I totally saw both of you.'

'Fine, but don't tell Seb,' I said.

She slammed her locker door shut. 'And why not? I tell my baby everything.'

Baby? Give me a cocking break.

'Look, if you do, a bloke's going to lose his job, OK?' I said. 'And bad things might happen to me.'

'As if that's my problem.'

'I-I'll do anything,' I said. 'Just don't tell him.'

Her blue eyes sparkled. I remember a time when they used to make me go all wobbly. They don't any more. Not at all. Not one little bit.

« Older posts

'Fine,' she said. 'I want you to tell everyone that I dumped you and not the other way around.'

'But that's not even true!' I said.

'Does it matter what's true?' she said. 'I'm fed up of people thinking I'm not good enough for someone like you.'

'OK,' I said. 'If it's so important to you, I'll do it.'

She smiled. 'Good. You can start at my form room after lunch. I'll write you a little speech.'

I blew out through my lips. 'OK, if it'll keep you from telling.'

'Oh, it'll keep me from telling about this,' she said. 'But not anything else. I've still got my eye on you.'

At lunch, we sat in our group. Everyone except Natalie.

'You should see the effects I've got lined up for London,' said Greeny. 'It's going to totally blow their balls off.'

'I concur,' said Harry. 'No balls will remain intact after our set. What we need though is a warm-up gig. Preferably not at a funeral. Do you reckon you could sort us out, Joe?'

'I kind of have other things on my mind at the moment,' I said.

'Come on, old boy,' he said. 'Are you a manager or a mouse . . . ager?'

I rubbed my temples. 'Maybe I'll be able to find you something,' I said. 'Anyway, how's it coming with scheme two?'

'It's coming,' said Harry. 'Just a few bugs to work out before we engage, but trust me, it's going to be spectacular.'

'Ah wicked, are you getting flying monkeys, like I said?' said Ad.

Harry put down his knife and fork and held his face in his hands.

'Yes, Ad,' he said. 'I'm getting flying monkeys.'

Ad nodded and went back to his lasagne.

I stood in front of the board in Lisa's form room. She quietened the class down and told them I had something to say. My stomach twisted into a knot.

'What's this about, Puke?' yelled Pete Cotterill. 'You coming out?'

Jordan Foster laughed. 'Yeah . . . out.'

I cleared my throat and squinted at the piece of paper.

'Hello, everyone. Even though you all think I dumped Lisa, that totes isn't true,' I began. God, the least she could have done was made it sound like me.

'The truth is, she chucked me. I wasn't sure why this was, but it turns out the only reason she went out with me in the first place was because her dodgy GHDs she got from down the market fritzed while she was straightening her hair, and it sent some well weird electric shocks to her brain and made her go mental for a bit.'

« Older posts

Everyone stared at me. Lisa stood at the back, smiling.

'So, yeah, as I was saying, I'm a freak and the only reason that rumour started about me dumping the well gorge Lisa was 'cause that silly bint Leah Burton was well jel 'cause I snogged Gav before she did.'

'You snogged Gav?' said Pete Cotterill. 'Knew it.'

I shrugged and walked out. Job done. Lisa followed me.

'Oi,' she said. 'You messed the ending up.'

'No, I read it exactly as you wrote it,' I said.

'Yeah but you knew what I meant.'

I sighed. 'It's done now though, isn't it?'

She folded her arms and studied me through narrowed eyes.

'All right,' she said. 'But only 'cause I'm feeling so happy right now.'

'Good for you.'

'Yep,' she said, before I could walk away. 'So happy with my *man*.'

'Great,' I said. 'And I'm so happy with my . . . nan, so, you know, big whoop.'

'You've always been weird, haven't you?' said Lisa.

'Yep,' I said. 'And what's wrong with that?'

She tutted. 'I don't know why you're bothering with this competition anyway, there's no way Seb can lose.'

'Why do you even care?' I said.

'Because he loves me,' she said. 'He tells me all the time.'

'Of course he does,' I said.

Gah, this sucks. I can't even exchange notes with Natalie now. This is like *Romeo and Juliet*, except I don't talk in poems like Mr Shenko, and I'm not intending to top myself. Yet.

Friday 9th November

Oh God, maybe I need to reconsider that last statement.

I was feeling sorry for myself last night and tried to find that note from Natalie where she told me she loved me. I couldn't find it. It was gone. My first thought was Doris. Just the other week I couldn't find my Biology book and I found her using it to scrape bird poo off the kitchen window.

I crept into her room and looked around. I didn't find Natalie's note, but I did find three of my shirts, a pair of Gav's trousers, Jim's claw hammer, and eight spoons.

Anyway, the note was nowhere to be seen. I went back into my room.

« Older posts

'Ga-av?'

'S'up?'

'Have you seen my . . . note?'

He took his finger out of his nose and grinned. 'You mean that love letter?'

My eye twitched. 'Yes.'

'Yeah, I saw that, it was bare jokes, man,' he said. 'Ooh, what? Me? Oh cocking hell. HA HA HAAA!'

Why does everyone think they can do an impression of me?

'Have you done anything with it?' I said.

'Nah, man, I put it back down on the drawers,' he said. 'I mean, I took a photo of it first though. Pure comedy.'

I checked the drawers again. Still not there. I even dragged them away from the wall and checked it hadn't fallen down the back.

A horrible cold feeling swamped my brain. In that moment, I knew where it was.

Jim stopped me as I walked through the living room.

'Wouldn't go in there if I were you, Joe,' he said. 'She's a bit emotional.'

'What else is new?' I said.

'All right, but don't say you weren't warned,' he said, then turned the football up loud.

I poked my head around the kitchen door.

'Hi, Mum.' I spoke gently, as if I were trying to talk her down off a ledge. 'Everything OK?'

She sat at the table with her back to me. She turned around and all her mascara was running down her face. She looked like one of those emo blokes on Natalie's bedroom wall. I didn't tell her that though.

'Oh, son,' she said, smiling. 'Come here. Come and sit with your mother.'

I crept in quietly, being careful not to make any sudden moves that might anger her.

I sat down and saw the note on the table. My ears felt like they were literally on fire.

Man, is this embarrassing, said Hank. *Your mom finding your love letter. What a rookie mistake.*

Don't listen to him, Joe, said Norman, then turned to Hank as if I couldn't hear him. *You're right though. OUCH!*

'Oh God,' I said.

Mum smiled and stroked my face. 'My baby boy is growing up.'

I gulped. 'Yep.'

She picked up the note. 'I found this in your bedroom when I was tidying,' she said. 'I'm sorry, I know I shouldn't have been looking. But then I saw the L word and . . .'

She started snivelling. If a sinkhole opened up beneath me right then and sucked me into the Earth's crust, I probably wouldn't have minded.

'I just can't believe how quickly you're becoming a man!'

« Older posts

She started flapping at her face and blowing. I had no idea what to do.

'Um, yes,' I said. I put an awkward hand on her shoulder. 'Can I get you something? A drink? Something to eat? A sedative?'

'Do you know all the details?' she said. 'You know, about the birds and the bees?'

I covered my face with my hands and groaned. I had heard enough of the birds and the bees through her bedroom door, thank you very much.

'You could say that,' I said. "Between you and Dad, I think I'm covered.'

'Good,' she said. 'Not that you should be doing that at your age but . . . '

'OK!' I yelled. 'Please, just stop saying words. We're not doing . . . that anyway.'

Mum looked as if she didn't really believe me. 'As long as you stay safe,' she said.

'Safe as houses,' I said. 'Could I have my note back, please?'

Mum looked at the note, then nodded. I quickly folded it and stowed it deep in my pocket. Anyway, if it's anyone who needs a talk about contraception it's old Preggers McGee here, not me.

'Haven't seen Nat for ages,' said Mum. 'Is everything OK? She hasn't dumped you has she?'

'NO!' I said. 'And how come you assumed she'd be dumping me, anyway?'

'I didn't mean anything by it,' said Mum. 'I just think she's a lovely girl. I must admit the first time I saw her I thought, *Woah,* hair like a pencil troll! But she is wonderful.'

'Yeah,' I said. 'She is.'

'And I'm glad you're still together because you're a great couple,' she said. 'And you deserve to be happy, son. And I love you.'

I took a deep breath and tried to remember a time when my mum wasn't insane.

She ran her hands over her bump. 'And that won't change when the twins arrive, you know that don't you?'

'Really, Mum, I'm not going to be jealous.'

She smiled and rubbed her face, smearing the mascara. 'So how come Nat hasn't been around lately?'

I shrugged. 'Just some problem with her dad. No biggy.'

Mum gave me her patented deadly look, as if she knew

« Older posts

I was holding out on her. Damn, pregnancy hasn't affected her ability to see through my crap. I wish it did.

'What's the problem?' she said. 'You can tell me, I won't interfere.'

'MUM, PLEASE DON'T DO THIS!' I yelled as I chased her through the lounge.

She stormed out of the house and got into her car. I jumped in after her. 'You said you wouldn't interfere!' I said.

'Yeah, well that's before I found out this man thinks his daughter is too good for my boy,' she said. 'Is there anything behind me?'

'Um, no,' I said.

'Good.' She threw it into reverse and screeched out of the drive, throwing me up against the window with the force.

Why can't you keep your goddamn mouth shut, numb-nuts? said Hank.

I didn't tell her about my criminal activity, at least.

We pulled into Natalie's drive, sending gravel flying against Desmond's Jag.

'I'm begging you, Mum,' I said. 'Do not do this.'

'I'm just going to have a word with him,' she said. 'A friendly chat.'

She smiled at me, but was still breathing like a racked-off bull. She hammered the door.

Please don't be in, please don't be in, please don't be in.

'Hello?'

Oh cock!

'Mr Tuft, I presume?' said Mum.

'Yes?'

I stepped out of the shadows and mouthed 'I tried to stop her.'

'WHERE DO YOU GET OFF, TREATING MY BOY LIKE THIS?'

So much for a friendly chat.

'Excuse me?'

'Keeping them apart?' she said. 'You're a piece of work, mate.'

I pinched the bridge of my nose. I thought maybe I ate a dodgy burger and this was all a fever dream from the food poisoning.

I'm afraid not, said Norman. *While that burger was indeed dodgy, it has not induced psychosis on this occasion.*

Yeah, you're on your own here, little buddy, said Hank.

'Excuse me, madam,' said Desmond. 'But you have no right telling me how to run my affairs.'

Natalie appeared in the doorway behind him. 'Joe!' She tried to run out but he held her back.

'Let go of her, you miserable sod,' said Mum. 'She has rights, you know!'

Desmond laughed. 'She is my daughter, and I am responsible for her well-being,' he said. 'And if I say she shouldn't

« Older posts

be seeing that boy of yours, then I am to be obeyed.'

'Oooh,' Mum cried. 'I am to be obeyed! Listen to you—you sound like Darth pigging Vader.'

'I'm closing the door now,' he said. 'If you do not leave immediately I shall call the police. Good night.'

Mum dived forward and held the door. I tried to hold her back, but carrying these babies seems to have made her as strong as a bear on steroids.

'Listen to me, mister,' she said, low and threatening. 'My Joe is a wonderful boy, who wouldn't hurt anyone. Now you may think you're all high and mighty, with your big house, and your gardener, and your bloody . . . water features. But he is worth ten of you. Remember that.'

'Catherine,' Desmond called back into the house. 'Call the police, would you? It seems we have trespassers.'

'All right, I'm going,' said Mum. 'But you need to have a word with yourself. Because you do not want to piss me off, especially when I am this pregnant. And I am very pregnant.'

'I'm sorry, son,' said Mum on the way home. 'I just had to give that man a piece of my mind. Who does he think he is? Anyway, I hope things will get better for you from now on.'

Natalie wasn't in school today. I think things might have got worse.

Saturday 10th November

'Surely they have to go out some time,' I said to Harry.

'That's the beauty of it,' he said, adjusting his binoculars. 'Since we've been here, only one of them has left at any one time. Say what you like about them, they're efficient.'

'Cocking hell, Harry,' I said. 'They're the enemy, remember?'

'Always respect the enemy, old son,' he said. 'Even if he does own one of those little-boy-doing-a-wee fountains.'

We'd been hiding in a bush on the hill behind Natalie's house for four hours. I needed to know why she wasn't in school yesterday. I hoped my mum's outburst hadn't made Desmond do something stupid.

'Here we go,' said Harry. 'Vehicle arriving at our location.'

I grabbed the binoculars off him. I watched Seb get out of the gold Jag and swagger towards the front door.

There's no way Natalie would have ever gone out with a moron like him. No way.

'Shall we go down and key his car?' I said.

« Older posts

'Negative,' said Harry. 'As satisfying as that would be, the house is completely surrounded by CCTV cameras. Which may prove challenging when we attempt the next phase.'

'This is impossible, isn't it?' I threw the binoculars down. 'I'm never going to see her again.'

'I don't know about that, old boy,' said Harry. 'It looks like she's in her bedroom now.'

'What?' I yelled. 'Give me those back.'

I looked through them again.

'What's happening, Joe?' said Ad. 'Is she getting undressed?'

'No,' I said, squinting hard. 'She's just talking to someone.'

'Oh right,' he said. 'Well let me know if that changes, yeah?'

I used my free hand to slap him and strained my eyes to look closer.

Who is that? It's not Desmond. Or Catherine.

HOLY BALLS, IT'S SEB.

It's OK, Joe, said Norman. *This doesn't mean anything.*

No, you're right, this is all fine, said Hank. *It's only that douchebag your girl's parents love, standing in her goddamn bedroom. There's nothing amiss here.*

She stood by the window. Seb walked up closer. I couldn't tell what he was saying. Why have I never learned to lip-read? All those hours spent watching *Star Trek* and playing computer games, when I could have been learning something useful.

Natalie had her arms folded. Good. That's classic closed body language.

Or she could be trying to draw attention to her norks . . .

SHUT UP, HANK!

He got closer. Closer. Oh my God, he's leaning in for a kiss!

Time slowed down. I felt like I was in outer space, watching Earth crumble into tiny pieces.

Natalie put her hand up.

AND SLAPPED HIM!

Yeah, that's my girl! yelled Hank. *Smack the smug out of him!*

'Look at the smile on his face, Harry,' said Ad. 'She's defo undressing.'

'She's not undressing,' I said. 'This is even better.'

'What? Naked dancing?' said Ad.

'Harry, slap him for me,' I said.

'Right you are, old bean.'

'Ow! Why did you have to do it so hard?'

I watched as Seb walked out and Natalie turned and stared out of the window.

'So how are we going to do this?' I said.

'Well, soldier,' said Harry. 'Having appraised the situation, I can only say it is going to be rather testing.'

« Older posts

'But you can do it?'

Harry smiled. 'Not to honk my own bugle, but if anyone can, I can.'

He took his pipe out of his pocket and continued. 'We are being presented with a series of obstacles,' he said. 'First: we have no means of communication with our damsel in distress. Second: she is under round-the-clock surveillance. Colditz would be easier to escape from. Which brings me to the final hurdle. The CCTV.'

'So we have to get both her parents out of the house, without Natalie being able to help on the inside, and without being seen by the cameras?' I said.

'Piece of cake, isn't it?' said Harry. 'If the cake was laden with explosives.'

'So how long do you think it will take for you to think of something?' I said.

'I have some elements in place already, but I shall need at least this weekend to cogitate,' said Harry.

'OK, but we have to do it soon,' I said. 'Because I've got a feeling we haven't got much time.'

I looked back at the house. Natalie had gone from the window.

'I've had an idea,' said Ad.

We both stared at him.

'Is it piss balloons?' I said.

He shook his head. Then nodded.

'Duly noted, old son,' said Harry.

'Hey!' a shout from behind broke through the silence. 'What are you, peeping Toms or something?'

'No!' said Ad. 'He's Joe, I'm Ad, and this is Harry.'

'Run, soldiers!'

Harry took off and ran down the hill. We followed and didn't stop until we'd lost that bloke. What a country this is, where you can't even sit on a hill and spy on your own girl-friend. What did our forefathers fight and die for, anyway?

Sunday 11th November

'So,' Mum said, sitting down opposite me at breakfast, 'have you heard from Natalie yet?'

Control room, what do I do?

Tell her the truth, said Norman. *You shouldn't lie to your mother.*

Yeah right, said Hank. *If you tell her Natalie wasn't even at school on Friday, she'll flip her freakin' wig. Do you really want that crazy broad marching down there and smashing their doors down?*

'Yes,' I said. 'She text me yesterday.'

Mum grinned like a loon. 'Oh, I am so glad.'

I said nothing and tried to concentrate on my Coco Pops.

'I remember a time when you used to write me love let-ters.' Mum turned on Jim, scowling. 'Before I became a fat, hideous BEAST.'

« Older posts

Jim glanced up from his paper with a look of pure terror. He opened his mouth to speak but seemed to think better of it. Yep, I can't tell her the truth.

8 p.m.

Spent the afternoon at Dad's. The entire time was taken up with him showing me the new outfits he's bought for London. He said it's a shame we're not the same size, otherwise I could borrow his clothes. I said I'd rather borrow Mad Morris's clothes. Luckily, he wasn't listening.

Monday 12th November

Natalie wasn't at school today. Again.

Maybe she's just ill or something?

But what if he's taken her out of school? What if I never see her again?

'Come on, Joe,' said Ad at lunch, snapping me out of my daydream.

'What?'

'Would you rather do it with the ugliest, hairiest, scabbiest woman in the world, or Emma Watson, but she's got a knob?'

I pushed my plate away. 'How do you come up with these, Ad?'

'In lessons, mainly,' he said.

'Just think about it, old bean,' said Harry. 'If Ad had used all the energy he expends on Would You Rather? questions on actual learning instead, he could have been the world's greatest genius.'

'Come on, answer the question,' said Ad.

'He can't answer questions like that now,' said Harry. 'He's had so much trouser action with Natalie that he can't even conceive of doing it with anyone else.'

I slapped the table. 'For the last time, me and Natalie haven't had any . . . trouser action.'

'Would you swear on a Bible?' said Harry.

'I swore on a Bible once,' said Ad.

'Really?' I said.

'Yeah, in RE last year,' he said. 'Harry dared me to write "dickbag" on the New Testament.'

I facepalmed. 'Are we any further along with phase two?'

Harry leaned forward and clasped his hands together. 'This may be the most challenging campaign we have ever embarked upon,' he said. 'But it is feasible. I think we may be able to attempt it . . . this Wednesday.'

« Older posts

'Really?' I said.

He nodded. 'But stand down until then, old son. We can't afford to arouse any suspicion.'

He nodded across the room, where Seb and Lisa sat eyeballing us.

'So can you play it cool until then?' said Harry.

'Course I can,' I said. 'Cool is my middle name.'

'No it ain't,' said Ad. 'It's Marvin.'

The playing it cool thing was going really well. Until I was walking home from school. And the tossermobile pulled up alongside me.

'Hey, loser,' said Lisa. Even though I don't like her any more and don't even fancy her AT ALL that still hurt.

'Missing Nat?' said Seb.

'None of your business, as it happens,' I said. 'Just you concern yourself with stupid cars and crap hair. You know, your specialist subjects.'

He smiled the smuggest smile in the history of the universe. 'Nah, my specialist subject would be Natalie, and how she's so desperate to get back with me.'

'Sad bitch,' said Lisa.

Listen to me, Joe, said Hank. *Here's what I want you to do. I want you to snap his wing mirror off and force it down his throat. Sideways.*

Do NOT follow that advice, said Norman, jumping in quick.

I leaned forward, into the car. My temples thudded. 'If she's so desperate to get back with you,' I said, 'even though she was never with you in the first place, then why did she slap you the other day when you tried to kiss her?'

His eyes went massive and his mouth dropped open. Even though he didn't speak, I knew what he was thinking:

How did you know?

'WHAT?' said Lisa. 'He had better be lying, Sebastian.'

Seb slowly covered up the horror on his face and regained some of his smugness. 'Babe,' he said, turning to her and squeezing her thigh. 'As well as being a freak, he is also a massive liar. Why would I want a beast like Natalie when I've got you?'

I gripped his wing mirror and applied downwards pressure.

He turned and eyeballed me. 'One day soon, his lies are going to catch up with him.'

He wound his window up and screeched away.

Oh cocking hell. What have I done?

Tuesday 13th November

As soon as I got home, the magnitude of what I'd just admitted to Seb struck me. He must have known I was watching the house. Or had some kind of communication going with Natalie. And if he told Desmond about my boot bruising Boocock's beanbag, he'd definitely tell about that. This is going to jeopardize everything tomorrow night. Harry is going to kill me.

Later that night, I snuck outside during a particularly raucous game of pin the tail on the donkey at the club. Blind Trevor had a blindfold on, which seemed like overkill to me, but what do I know? I'd been staring at the number in my phone for the past half an hour. I could feel my pulse throbbing in my neck. I gulped, and hit call.

It rang. Once. Twice. Three times.

'Hello, Tuft residence?'

Desmond. Damn.

'Greetings, sir,' I said, in an accent that was supposed to be Chinese but sounded more like Doris after a couple of sherries. 'Might I speak to Miss Natalie, please?'

A silence followed that seemed to stretch on for hours.

'And what is this regarding?'

He's buying it! said Hank. *I can't believe the pompous old douche is actually buying it!*

'It is her subscription to *Star Trek* magazine,' I said. 'She was entered into a grand prize draw and she has won!'

Another silence.

'Look, Joe, I know this is you.'

Balls!

'Whạaa? Joe? Who Joe? My name is Ling Ning . . . Ping.'

'Just cut it out,' he said. 'Seb tells me he thinks you've been sniffing around Natalie again. Now I don't know if that's true, but if I find out it is, Clifton will be gone, I will report you to the police, and my lawyer will file a restraining order against you immediately. Quite frankly, I think I've been lenient to have refrained from doing so before now. Prince of Pants.'

'Look, Mr Tuft . . . '

'Don't "Mr Tuft" me,' he barked. 'You are on thin ice, my boy. I mean, sending your pregnant mother here to remonstrate with me, as if that will make a difference?'

'But I didn't send her there, she just . . . '

'Save it,' he said. 'I've taken steps to ensure that you will never be allowed to wreck my daughter's future, and the sooner they're done, the better.'

'Steps, what steps?' I yelled, but he'd already hung up.

I cried out in frustration and stormed back inside. I was so wrapped up in my thoughts for the rest of the night that I only just managed to dodge Doris trying to pin the tail on my forehead.

« Older posts

5 p.m.

This morning at break, Greeny was showing us the effects he was working on on his iPad. I had to admit, they were very impressive. Way better than anything that moron Seb could come up with, that's for sure.

'So when are you getting us this warm-up gig, Joe?' said Greeny.

'One thing at a time, old son,' said Harry. 'After tomorrow night, his mind maybe more focused. If you know what I mean.'

'We won't be doing that,' I said, then wondered why the hell I don't just let him think it. 'And anyway, I kind of have a confession to make.'

'What is it?' said Harry. 'Is it that you can't do it with a lady because actually you're completely smooth down there, like an Action Man?'

I buried my face in my hands. 'I may have given Seb, and subsequently Desmond, a reason to believe that we had been spying on the house.'

Ad nearly choked on his crisps.

'You did what?' said Harry. 'How?'

I sighed. 'He was provoking me, OK? Trying to get a rise.'

'Well what a bloody rise it was, old son,' he said. 'You do realize this could compromise the entire campaign?'

'I know,' I said. 'And I'm sorry . . . But that's not all.'

Harry threw himself back in his chair. 'Did you hear that, Ad? Not all! What did you do now? Blow a hole in the side of his house and just walk in and help yourself to something from the bloody fruit bowl?'

My eye started twitching. 'I called their house phone pretending to be a Chinese person called Ling Ning Ping.'

Harry nodded. 'Of course,' he said. 'Why didn't I think of that? It was staring me in the face the entire time. The key to solving this whole thing is borderline-racist prank calls.'

'Look, I'm really sorry,' I said. 'I'm weak, OK? I just needed to find out why she hasn't been at school. I just . . . needed to hear her voice.'

I stared at the floor, trying to disguise my trembling chin. There was an awkward silence.

'Does anyone want half my Twix?' said Greeny. God, he'd never normally share his chocolate.

'Are you . . .' said Ad. 'Are you crying, Joe?'

'No.' I rubbed my eyes with the ball of my palm. 'No I'm not. It's just . . . onions make my eyes water, that's all.'

'But there's no onions in here,' he said.

'You're eating Pickled Onion Monster Munch, aren't you?' I said.

He looked at the packet for a second, then crumpled it and threw it away. 'Yeah, mate. That's what it was.'

We both knew they were actually Flamin' Hot flavour, but he didn't argue. What a friend.

« Older posts

Harry seemed to soften a bit. 'Look, old boy, maybe this is partly a good thing.'

'How can any of this be good?' I said.

'Well, to be honest, an important part of the strategy for tomorrow night was for you to call them pretending to be someone else, but now I see that wouldn't have worked.' He puffed on his pipe and gazed out of the window. 'This Desmond is a quite formidable adversary.'

'Well, I don't know,' I said. 'Couldn't you do it instead?'

'Negative,' he said. 'He's going to be wary of that tactic now. The only possible way we could make it work is if someone with natural authority did it. Someone with a strong, domineering voice. Someone who is used to making men follow orders.'

'Cocking hell,' I said. 'I know the perfect person.'

6 p.m.

I sat around the table at dinner going over what I had to do. It was going to be risky, but if it paid off, it would be worth it.

'I admire your dedication, Joe,' said Jim. 'Taking mum to her club two nights in a row. It's more than I can say for her grandson.'

'I told you, man,' said Gav. 'Oldies creep me out.'

'Yes, but don't forget, it'll be you one day, Gavin,' said Mum.

'Nah,' he said. 'I ain't gonna live long enough for that. I'm going out in a blaze of glory.'

'You'll do no such thing.' Mum rubbed her bump. 'You'll have younger brothers or sisters to look after.'

Gav rolled his eyes. 'Whatevs.'

'Anyway,' said Jim, obviously trying to diffuse a potential nuclear detonation. 'How come you're going to the club tonight?'

'W-well,' I spluttered. 'You love it there, don't you, Doris? Can't keep you away, can I?'

Doris blushed. 'Ooh, I don't know about that,' she said. 'I do feel bad about leaving Ivy with you again though, my dears. Are you sure you'll be all right?'

'I think we'll cope,' said Jim.

'Yes, she was no trouble last night,' said Mum.

'Almost as if she ain't real,' said Gav.

Jim gave him a look and he went back to his chicken nuggets.

'So, Jim,' I said, keen to steer the conversation away from the subject of me taking his mother to her club for the purposes of phase two. 'How's, you know, the world of plastering?'

He looked at me weird, as if to say, 'You've never asked me about work before,' but ploughed on anyway.

'Very good thanks, Joe,' he said. 'Too good, in fact. I mean I'm glad there's plenty of work coming in, what with the babies on the way, but there's so much, I'm having to turn down perfectly good business.'

'Hmm,' I said, drifting away. 'That's fascinating.'

'What I really need,' he said. 'Is another plasterer. A grafter, with plenty of experience.'

I nodded, but I wasn't really listening. I was too busy stressing about whether I'd be able to rescue our operation.

9 p.m.

'Evening, Colonel,' I said, as we walked into Morningside. 'I've brought someone to see you.'

The Colonel's face lit up when he saw Doris. For a split second I almost got the impression of what he would have looked like as a younger bloke.

'Doris, my dear,' he said, taking her hand and kissing the back of it. 'What a pleasant surprise.'

Doris blushed and giggled like a teenage girl. I left them to it and made some tea. While I was doing it, I went through how I was going to approach this whole thing.

When I got back, the Colonel was still grinning. 'I'm just so happy you're here, my love,' he said. 'Tell me, did you come back because you couldn't bear to be away from me for another week?'

Doris giggled again. God, she's worse than I was when I met Picard.

'Well, actually, Colonel,' I said. 'I do have a bit of a favour to ask you.'

He smiled. 'Anything,' he said. 'You brought the lovely Doris here, so I am in your debt. What is it?'

I took a deep breath. 'When you were in the navy, did you ever play pranks on your comrades?'

He laughed. 'Oh yes, when I was a young officer, we did get up to some rather humorous japes.'

'Great,' I said. 'How about another one?'

Wednesday 14th November

HA!

PRINCE OF PANTS IS
LOCAL VAGRANT

The secret identity of masked vigilante the Prince of Pants has been revealed as local man Morris Crudwick, of no fixed address.

Mr Crudwick, known locally as 'Mad Morris', made himself known as the enigmatic hero by arriving at the *Tammerstone Times* offices in the Prince William mask, cape, and yellow Y-fronts.

When asked why he did what he did, he replied, 'I am on a mission from God. I will smite evildoers and bring fear to those who do not obey.'

Underneath, there's a photo of him being given a cheque for six hundred quid by that old woman and Desmond. And you should see Desmond's face—he is FUMING!

« Older posts

It would have been nice to have six hundred quid, but I suppose Mad Morris needs it more than me. And this way, I don't have to go to jail.

7 p.m.

I couldn't concentrate at school today. Two big things were playing on my mind. Number one was how everything is going to go tonight. Number two was how can Natalie still not be at school? There have to be laws against this, surely?

At break, I went down to see Nurse Snitterfield. Due to cutbacks she now has to work on reception. I tried my most charming smile. She looked at me like I'd guffed in my hand and was trying to wave it in her face.

'Hi, Nurse Snitterfield,' I said. 'Could you just check something for me?'

She snapped on a rubber glove. 'All right, but I must warn you, we're all out of lube.'

I laughed a bit too loud. 'No,' I said. 'I mean a file. Could you check if Natalie Tuft is still registered as a pupil here?'

She squinted at me over her glasses. 'And why do you want to know?'

'I-I'm her boyfriend.'

Nurse Snitterfield frowned. 'If you were her boyfriend, surely you'd know whether she came to this school.'

I scratched the back of my head. 'It's, um, complicated.'

'I bet it is, lover boy,' she said. 'But you're not having access to that information. Something about data protection and blah, blah, blah.'

I nodded and walked away. This is not good. Not good at all.

Right. It's nearly six o'clock. It's time. God, I have never been so nervous.

Thursday 15th November

Well, that happened.

It was hammering it down outside. Not exactly ideal conditions for OPERATION DAMSEL IN DISTRESS, but I wasn't about to wait for better ones.

I got to Morningside at about quarter past six. I sent texts to Harry, Ad, and Gav:

PICARD IN LOCATION ONE. DO YOU COPY?

The replies came back straight away.

Harry:

CHURCHILL AT HOMESTEAD. PAPA BEAR AND MAMA BEAR IN SITU. OVER.

Ad:

MR JOE'S MUM AT SECRET LOCATION ONE. OVER.

Gav:

GAV N GREENY OUTSIDE DAT KNOBBER SEB'S HOUSE. INNIT.

Well, I didn't expect Gav to play along with the military thing, anyway.

I went through to the Colonel's room to find him sitting in his armchair, grinning.

'Joseph!' he said. 'I can't tell you how much I've been looking forward to this. It's been so long since I've given someone a good ribbing!'

I swallowed my giggles and tried to focus on the task at hand.

'It's going to be brilliant, Colonel,' I said. 'But you must remember to play it totally seriously.'

'Absolutely,' he said. 'By the way, this fellow we're ribbing, he will be a good sport about it?'

NO!

'Oh, definitely,' I said, passing him his notes. 'Are you ready?'

He took a sip of brandy and cleared his throat. 'Ready.'

I dialled Natalie's home number, put it on loudspeaker, then placed it carefully on the Colonel's table.

It rang once. Twice. Three times. Four times.

If they don't answer, the whole thing is doomed.

'Tuft residence?'

'Hello, is that Desmond Tuft?' the Colonel said, reading from the script.

Silence.

This isn't going to work, said Hank. *I told you it wasn't going to work.*

'Yes.'

'This is Colonel Reginald Arthur Stanforth from the Royal Navy Club in Polingale. How do you do?'

'Is this you, Joe?'

'JOE?' the Colonel barked. 'What is this insolence? I've just told you who I am and yet you still ask me if I am Joe?'

'Oh, OK, sorry,' said Desmond. He sounded cowed. Good. See how he likes it.

'Anyway, the reason I'm calling is I'm afraid our club is closing down . . . '

'I'm sorry to hear that,' said Desmond.

No you're not, you callous old vampire!

'Yes, well, the march of progress and all that.' The Colonel winked at me and I gave him the thumbs up. He was doing an excellent job. 'Anyway, this news has come as something of a shock to us, as we were midway through renovations and have several unused urinals that are about to go to waste.'

« Older posts

'Really?' said Desmond. I could feel him getting sucked in. 'How much would you want for them?'

'Well,' said the Colonel. 'We wouldn't want anything. Perhaps a small donation to the British Legion might be in order, but that's all.'

I actually heard Desmond gulp. 'Great, I'll, um, send some of my men out to get them first thing tomorrow.'

'I'm afraid that will be no good,' said the Colonel. 'The doors are being locked for good tonight. You see the closure has been rather foisted upon us at short notice. Also, I do request that you bring someone with you to help carry all of this. I would offer to help myself, but I'm not as young as I used to be.'

'That's OK, I'll bring my daughter.'

The Colonel sucked in his breath. 'Do you mind me asking how old your daughter is?'

'She's . . . nearly sixteen,' he said.

'Ah, then I'm afraid she can't come in,' said the Colonel. 'I realize that she'd only be coming to help you, but the licensees are sticklers for the rules. It's the naval background, you see.'

Another silence.

It's not going to work, it's not going to work, said Hank. *I keep telling you but you won't listen!*

'Catherine! Can you come with me to pick up some toilets?'

'OK,' I heard her say in the background. 'But what about Natalie?'

'She won't be allowed in the venue,' he said. 'And there's no way she'd fit in the car with us and the bogs. I'll probably call Seb and get him to come and watch her.'

Oh my God, I can't take this any more!

'I'll be there as soon as I can,' said Desmond. 'I just have to sort out a babysitter.'

'Thank you, sir, I shall see you anon.'

The Colonel smiled at me as Desmond hung up. 'How did I do?'

'You were brilliant, Colonel,' I said. 'Thank you so much.'

He laughed. 'I haven't had this much fun since we chucked Nipper Jones's bed in the Pacific.'

I grabbed my phone back and texted Gav:

COMMENCE OPERATION NEUTRALIZE SEB IMMEDIATELY.

The reply came back:

YEH IM LETTIN HIS TYRES DOWN NOW INNIT.

He'd never make the grade at MI5.

'I've got to run now, Colonel,' I said. 'Thanks again.'

'Don't mention it,' he said. 'Always glad to be of service where love is involved.'

'Love?' I said.

'Come on, Joseph,' he said. 'You can't kid a kidder. I heard them talking about Natalie. You want her folks out of

« Older posts

the way so you can partake in a bit of tomfoolery, am I right or am I right?'

I laughed. 'Yep, you're right.'

'Then I shan't keep you a moment longer,' he said. 'Excelsior to you, my dear boy!'

I ran outside into the rain and texted Harry:

FIRST MANOEUVRE COMPLETE. OVER.

The text came back straight away:

ROGER THAT. SOME MOVEMENT IN THE HOME-STEAD. PROCEED WITH CAUTION.

I ran down the street towards Natalie's house. The rain came down faster and faster, and I was already soaked. About halfway there, a text came through from Gav:

WE DUN HIS TYRES N NOW HES TRYIN 2 GO. ITS BARE JOKES LOL.

I sent Harry a text:

OPERATION NEUTRALIZE SEB COMPLETE. PLEASE ADVISE.

I took a shortcut through the park. My lungs were burning and my legs were aching, but I couldn't stop. Not even for Mad Morris in full Prince of Pants regalia.

Text from Harry:

LOOKS LIKE PAPA AND MAMA BEAR ARE READY TO GO.

Natalie's house is on the other side of the posh part of town. I splashed on through the rain, past all the fancy supermarkets and Lars Dulphgren's Salon and Spa, until eventually I came to the hill.

It looked spooky in the dark, and climbing it when it was almost pure mud was no easy task, but something kept pushing me on. I came down the other side and flopped behind the bush next to Harry, who was still watching the scene through his night-vision binoculars. No, I don't know where he got them either.

'Papa and Mama bear leaving location together. No sign of Goldilocks or Baby bear,' he said.

I texted Ad:

MANOEUVRE TWO COMPLETE. PAPA AND MAMA BEAR EN ROUTE.

Harry turned to me as the car pulled out of the drive. 'Are you ready for manoeuvre three?'

'I think so,' I said.

Harry dug into his bag and pulled out a carrier. 'For baby bear, and for Cerberus,' he said. 'Now remember, enter the back garden through the gap in the fence, keep your hood up and do not look at the cameras, understood?'

'Got it,' I said. 'And you know, thanks. I shouldn't have doubted you.'

'Save the thanks until it's over,' said Harry. 'We've bought you a couple of hours with her, tops, so make it count.'

I nodded.

'And by your standards, you could probably have about

« Older posts

eighty goes in that time,' he said.

'You had to spoil it, didn't you?' I said.

He grinned and gripped his pipe between his teeth. 'Good luck, comrade.'

He clambered up the hill and down the other side, where his bike was chained. He was then going to join Ad at the Navy Club.

I picked up the bag and made my way down the hill towards the house. About six metres from the bottom, I lost my footing in the mud and slid all the way down on my face.

Great, said Hank. *It's the first time he's going get to see his woman in weeks and he looks like a giant turd.*

I got up, shook myself down like a dog and hopped over the small wall at the back of the neighbour's garden. I took the sausages from Ad's dad's meat van out of the bag and held them out in front of me. If that beast was going to start something, I wasn't going to leave without my trousers.

I crouched down and ran towards the fence at the side and threw myself through it. Great, so I brought sausages for nothing. I stuffed them back in the bag, then lay flat on my stomach and pulled myself along the ground like how snipers do in war films. My clothes were completely caked in mud and God knows what else.

I took my soaked phone out of my pocket and dialled the home number.

'Hello, Tuft residence?'

Charlie? Really?

'Um, hello, this is Ling Ning Ping from *Star Trek* magazine.'

'Hello, Joe.'

This is it, cried Hank. *It's over, all this hard work has been for nothing. NOTHING!*

I gulped. 'Look, Charlie, could you *please*, pretty please, put your sister on for me?'

All I could hear was the sound of the falling rain.

'I've brought you some brilliant science books.'

'So you thought you could buy my silence with a few books?' he said.

'Well, I . . . '

'And you're right, you can. Natalie!'

Thank you, thank you, thank you.

'Hello?'

'Natalie?'

'Oh my God, Joe!' she cried.

'Listen,' I said. 'I'm outside. In the back garden. I need you to do two things. Turn off the CCTV and let me in.'

'Wow, OK,' she said. 'Well, I can turn off the cameras, but I can't let you in. They've locked me in here.'

I stood up and wiped the mud from my face.

She came to her bedroom window and opened it.

'Joe!'

« Older posts

'Hi!' I waved back.

'I've missed you so much.'

'Me too,' I said. 'Do you know how I can get in?'

'My parents are going to be back any minute now,' she said.

Text from Ad:

TYRES ARE FLAT, MATE. THEY AIN'T GOING NOWHERE.

'I've got a feeling they're going to be a while yet,' I said.

'All right,' said Natalie. 'Think, think, think. Maybe I could let my hair down to you, like Rapunzel?'

'I've got a better idea,' I said. I tied the bag up at the ends and yelled, 'Catch!' as I threw it up to Natalie.

'What's this?' she said.

'Charlie's bribe.'

'What, sausages?'

'I'll explain later.'

I grabbed the wheelie bin and after about five slippery attempts, managed to climb on top of it. I made a jump from there for the flat roof, but my hands slipped and I ended up back on the floor.

I tried again, and managed to hang on. I pulled myself up, using muscles I didn't even know I had, and climbed onto the flat roof. I edged along carefully, conscious of every little creak underfoot.

Tread lightly, Joe, said Norman. *You don't want to get hurt.*

Ah well, if he falls through the ceiling, at least he's in the house, said Hank. *And what a story to tell the grandkids!*

I noticed the trellis next to Natalie's window. I thought that maybe if it could hold my weight, I'd be able to get in that way.

I gripped the trellis and stuck my foot in. The gap was just about wide enough. It was only as I took my first step that I remembered that I am terrified of heights.

You'll be fine, Joe, said Norman. *Just don't look down.*

Don't say that! said Hank. *Because the first thing he's going to do is . . .*

'AARGH!'

See? said Hank.

The only thing that kept me going was seeing Natalie waiting at the window. I climbed higher and higher, until I was level with her.

'That's it, you're nearly there,' said Natalie. 'You're nearly . . .'

'AAAARGH!'

The trellis gave way under my feet. Then the top corner went. Then the middle. If I didn't get off straight away, it would all come down with me on it. I let go with one hand, gathered some momentum, then swung towards the window.

« Older posts

I grabbed the windowsill, but the rain made my hands slip. Natalie grabbed them as I heard the trellis clattering to the ground. My legs kicked out with nothing to grip. My wet hands slipped out of Natalie's.

She grabbed my sleeves and kept pulling and soon my arms were inside. I hoisted myself in further, and with another pull, I was crumpled in a heap on Natalie's bedroom floor.

Straight away, she threw herself on top of me and we kissed for ages. Even if I live to be two hundred, or even as old as Doris is, I don't think anything will ever beat that feeling.

Then, afterwards, Natalie said, 'God, you're disgusting,' and got me a pair of her jeans and an Oh, Inverted World T-shirt, which fitted me perfectly. That doesn't make me a girl, OK?

'How did you do this?' she said. 'This is just . . . amazing.'

I told her about the entire scheme and how everyone had worked together to make it happen.

'I can't believe it,' she said. 'No one's ever gone to this much trouble for me before.'

'That's because we care about you,' I said. 'Obviously me more than the others, I mean, it would be weird otherwise. We'd have to, like, fight, or something. Which would be totally unfair because Gav and Greeny have the size advantage. And Harry can always use his strategic expertise, or failing that, his pipe, as a weapon. So really, me and Ad wouldn't stand a chance. But then, Ad would probably get distracted by a squirrel or something like that, so he wouldn't even be part of it.'

Natalie was beaming when I finally finished talking. 'I never thought I'd say this, but I've really missed listening to you talk absolute crap.'

I blushed and her smile faded.

'And I'm going to miss it even more when I'm gone.'

The control room stopped and watched.

'W-what do you mean?'

'Desmond is withdrawing me from Woodlet,' she said.

'And where are you going? King George? Belcote? Surely not Lowes Park?'

'He's sending me to a boarding school,' she said. 'In Kent.'

It was like someone had ripped out my heart and flushed it down the toilet.

Natalie started crying.

'He can't do this,' I said. 'You can refuse.'

She shook her head. 'I can't. And anyway, I've got to think about you and Clifton,' she said.

'Does he know about this?' I said.

'No,' she replied. 'If he did he'd be heartbroken.'

We held each other tight. 'If we could find him another job,' said Natalie, 'then that would be one less thing Desmond has over us.'

'He said no one would take him on because he's too old,' I said.

'He's not old,' said Natalie. 'He's just experienced.'

That last word echoed in my brain. Something happened. Some kind of connection. Experienced.

Control room, what does this mean?

Oh God, I don't know, said Hank, sobbing hysterically. *This is just so freakin' sad.*

Someone did use that word recently, you're right, said the much calmer Norman. *I'll see what I can find.*

I broke away from the hug and sat forward, rubbing my temples as if it would help speed up my brain.

'What's the matter?' said Natalie.

'How's, you know, the world of plastering?'
'Very good thanks, Joe,' said Jim. 'Too good, in fact. I mean I'm glad there's plenty of work coming in, what with the babies on the way, but there's so much, I'm having to turn away perfectly good business. What I really need,' he said, 'is another plasterer. A grafter, with plenty of experience.'

'Riker's beard,' I said, scrabbling for my phone.

'What?' said Natalie.

My display had gone all glitchy because of the mud and rain, but I managed to dial Jim.

'Hey up, Joe, where are you?'

'I'm at Natalie's,' I said.

'Oooh, Natalie's,' Mum trilled in the background. 'I'm so glad his lordship finally let him inside.'

'What can I do for you?'

'You know you said the other day how you needed a new plasterer? Someone with experience?' I said. 'Well, what would you say if I told you I've found the perfect person?'

'I'd say bloody hell, that's cheaper than putting an advert in the paper,' he said. 'Who is it then?'

I explained all of Clifton's skills to Jim and he seemed impressed, especially with the fact that he has done Natalie's massive house all by himself. He agreed to take him on on a trial basis, but I know he'll ace it.

Then we phoned Clifton, who sounded like he was doing a jig on the other end of the phone.

'Thank you so much, Joseph,' he said.

'Well, we did sort of owe you,' I said.

He laughed. 'And tell young Natalie not to be a stranger. She can visit whenever she wants. If Tuft ever lets her out.'

Natalie took the phone and said her goodbyes to Clifton. Despite everything, I know she's going to be really sad to see him go.

'Now all we have to do is figure a way out of this getting

« Older posts

me arrested problem,' I said.

'I don't get it,' said Natalie. 'What have you done, anyway? Other than become a nutter who runs around in his pants?'

'You must never reveal my secret identity,' I said. 'Besides, the Prince of Pants is not just a man, he is a symbol—incorruptible, everlasting.'

'Yeah, steady on, Bale,' she said. 'But seriously, what could it be? Desmond won't tell me.'

'The only thing I can think of is the website hacking,' I said.

Natalie frowned, then smiled. 'Then he's got nothing.'

'What?'

'Think about it.' She stood up and grabbed a shrunken head ornament off the shelf. 'I was just as involved in that as you were. And there's no way he's going to shop me to the police. Imagine the shame it would bring on him. Desmond Tuft's daughter going off the rails. He'd never live it down at the Masonic Lodge.'

'So you mean . . . '

'He's got nothing!' she said again.

After that, everything changed. We played music and danced around like a pair of idiots, laughing and planning what we're going to call our record label. We kept ignoring the phone ringing in the hall, and Natalie warned Charlie not to answer it, saying, 'It will only be Desmond.' Charlie was too engrossed in his books, anyway.

'And when we beat Seb, we're going to Buzzfest!' said Natalie.

I stopped dancing, which was a good thing because when I dance I look like a meerkat having a fit, but that wasn't why I stopped.

'What's the matter?' said Natalie.

'It's Seb,' I said. Hearing his name made it all come crashing back.

She sighed and pushed her fringe out of her eyes. 'What about him?'

'Did you two used to go out?'

'No. The creep makes my skin crawl. Who told you that?'

'Well, your mum and dad kind of implied it,' I said. 'So did Lisa. And Seb.'

She held my face with both hands. 'They're just trying to get in your head, Joe. Don't listen to them. And anyway, all that matters is you're the one I want to be with now.'

My face went all tingly.

'I mean, what other boy would lure my parents to a club outside town, get his mates to let their tyres down, and climb in through my window?' she said.

We kissed again. For ages. I don't know how long for, but it didn't matter. Nothing could ruin it.

Except the front door opening.

Sirens screamed in the control room.

Emergency, emergency. This was not part of the plan!

« Older posts

Why the hell didn't Harry text to tell me they were on the way back? I grabbed my phone. The screen was completely blank. All that water must have finally frazzled it.

Natalie's face was a picture of panic. 'You need to hide,' she said. 'I'll run and switch the cameras back on so they don't suspect anything.'

I glanced around the room in the desperate hope that Natalie's so rich that she has her own cloak of invisibility. No such luck. I got in the wardrobe. No, too obvious. I thought about hiding under the bed, but I couldn't even do that because there were these big drawers under there.

'WHERE IS HE?' Desmond yelled from downstairs.

'What are you talking about?'

'Do not lie to me, Natalie, you're in enough trouble as it is.'

Footsteps on the stairs.

I threw the drawer open and carefully climbed inside. Then I realized the flaw in my plan. It's very difficult to shut yourself in a drawer.

The footsteps got closer.

I nudged the side of the drawer under the bed with my body weight. Bit by bit, it shifted underneath.

'Come on, come on!'

The control room couldn't even look.

The door opened just as the drawer clicked into place. Everything went dark.

'I'm going to find you, you little creep,' Desmond shouted.

'Desmond, please, he's not here,' said Natalie.

I heard him pass right by me and go to the window. 'Then whose are these muddy footprints?'

Damn.

'They're mine,' said Natalie.

'But you haven't been out,' he said. 'And even if you had, why would your footprints be entirely located by the window?'

I heard the window open. 'The trellis has come off the wall. So that's how he got in.'

'Desmond, please.'

'I'm just glad we won't have this to deal with when you're away at school,' he said.

I heard what sounded like the wardrobe door being opened. I tried to control my breathing and stay completely still. Desmond is like some kind of bloodhound. The drawer on the other side of the bed opened.

Be prepared, Joe, said Norman. *This could turn nasty.*

Yeah, said Hank, *so when he finds you, kick him in the nuts and run like hell.*

'Whose are these sausages?' said Desmond.

'They're mine,' said Natalie. 'I got hungry.'

'I'm not leaving this room until I find you, so you might as well come out now,' he yelled. 'You're only making it harder for yourself.'

'You sound like a mad man, Desmond,' said Natalie. 'Give it up.'

'Charles?' Desmond called across the house.

There was silence for a second, before little footsteps came into the room.

'Yes?'

'Have you seen that boy here tonight?'

'I have no idea what you're talking about, Desmond.'

I think I was wrong about Charlie.

'Where did he get that book?' said Desmond.

Footsteps moved over to my side of the bed. Oh no. I felt the drawer moving. Light flooding into the darkness.

'Thought you could hide forever, Joe?'

'I'm not Joe,' I said. 'I'm some bed sheets. Now could you close the drawer, please?'

He grabbed me by the collar of Natalie's Oh, Inverted World T-shirt and pulled me out of the drawer.

'Let go of him,' Natalie cried.

Desmond set me down and stepped back.

'Just what did you think you were doing, trespassing on my property?' he said.

Just what do you think you're doing being a freakin' JERK? yelled Hank.

'I had to see Natalie,' I said. 'And you left me with no other choice.'

'I think you'll find you had one choice and one choice only,' he said. 'And that was to stay away.'

'But I don't want him to,' said Natalie. 'I love him.'

My whole face felt like a ball of flame.

'Oh please,' said Desmond. 'You don't know the meaning of the word.'

'And I suppose you do,' said Natalie. 'Locking me away like some kind of prisoner.'

Desmond ran his hand through his hair. 'Look, you're my daughter and I know what's best for you.'

He pulled out his phone.

'What are you doing?' said Natalie.

'I'm calling the police to have them arrest this criminal you supposedly "love",' he said. 'But first, I'm calling a certain gardener to let him know his services are no longer required.'

My eye twitched. 'Call the police if you want,' I said. 'I don't care. Nothing you can do can keep me from seeing Natalie. If you send her to that boarding school, I will follow her there.'

« Older posts

'Would you?' said Natalie, smiling.

'Yes,' I said. 'I'd hitchhike there and sleep in the drawer under your bed. You know, it's surprisingly comfortable.'

Desmond stared at me, shaking his head. 'I'd like to see you try,' he said. 'Anyway, I'm calling the gardener.'

Me and Natalie exchanged a glance. 'OK,' said Natalie. 'You know what, we don't even care about . . . what was his name again? I'd like to say Clayton.'

Desmond looked more unnerved than Ad did after we dared him to eat a whole jar of mustard.

'Fine,' he said. 'Here we go.'

He dialled Clifton on loudspeaker.

'Good evening, Mr Tuft.'

'Mr Golding,' said Desmond, still eyeballing us with what I thought was a hint of nerves. 'I am calling to inform you that I have decided to dismiss you from your employment. I feel that your actions constitute gross misconduct and leave me with no other option.'

Clifton took a deep breath. 'Thank you, Mr Tuft,' he said. 'I must admit I'll be sad to leave your employment. However, your decision to dismiss me does not stand, as I have already resigned.'

'R-resigned?'

'Yes, sir,' he said. 'Earlier this evening, I was offered alternative employment with a reputable local merchant. A position sourced for me by a wonderful young man called Joseph.'

Desmond looked at me like he wanted to rip out my rib-cage and play it like a xylophone.

'I have since spoken to the man with the job and it has been arranged that I start on Monday,' said Clifton. 'And let me tell you, Mr Tuft, I can already tell I'm going to like working for him. For one thing, and I don't mean to sound disrespectful, but he pays much better than your good self. And another thing, he doesn't seem like a man who would treat his employees like an inconvenience. Not that I'm saying you do, you understand.'

Natalie reached across and squeezed my hand.

'Is there a point to any of this, Mr Golding?' said Desmond.

'I don't suppose there is,' said Clifton. 'Other than the fact that I can't imagine why you wouldn't want your girl to be associated with young Joe. I have known her since she was a baby and I've never seen her this happy. Never.'

I looked across and saw those red patches on her cheeks.

'Point taken,' said Desmond. 'Is that all?'

'Yes,' he said. 'I am a good Christian man and there is no way I can say what I'm thinking right now. In fact, I imagine the good Lord would be very vexed with me if I said the words: you can take your job and stick it right up your—'

Desmond hung up. He stared at the ground for a second, before looking straight at me.

'Please . . . Dad,' said Natalie, as if the word was alien somehow. 'Don't make me go there. When have I ever had a group of friends who'd go to all this trouble for me? Never. Just . . . don't take it away from me. Please.'

Desmond glared at us both. 'You need to learn.'

'Oh, for God's sake, Desmond.'

I didn't know how long Catherine had been standing in the doorway. Desmond looked like he was about to cack himself.

'You just don't know when to let it go, do you?' she said.

'What are you talking about?'

'All those tests you were setting him?' said Catherine. 'Can't you see he's passed the biggest one?'

'But this wasn't a test,' said Desmond, then stopped. 'Hold on, did you know about this?'

'Of course I didn't,' she said, 'but come on. Somewhere giving away free toilets? I thought you were cleverer than that.'

Desmond huffed. 'But he's a . . . '

'I know,' said Catherine.

Wait, what does she know? What am I?

'But do you want to send your only daughter away? Is that what you really want?'

He grumbled. 'I suppose not.'

Desmond turned back to us and sighed. Then he held his hand out to me.

What the cocking hell is happening?

Proceed with caution, said Norman.

HI - YAH!

Extreme caution, said Hank. *I swear to God, I've seen Chuck Norris do this. He holds his hand out to shake, the other guy takes it, and HWAAA CHAAA! Broken neck.*

I slowly reached out and took his hand. He gripped it tight and shook it.

'It seems my wife is right for once,' he said. 'You have beaten me. And if you can beat the best, you can't be that useless.'

I looked at Natalie for guidance. She looked just as weirded out as I did.

'You orchestrated this insane scheme just for a chance to see my daughter,' he said. 'And it worked.'

'Well,' I said. 'Thanks.' Somewhere in the universe, Harry was giving me a telepathic bollocking for hogging all the credit.

'But that doesn't excuse your previous conduct,' he said.

'Sorry, w-what do you mean?' I said. I didn't want to admit to knowing about the website sabotage.

'Come on,' he said. 'Don't make me spell it out for you. Assaulting your teacher.'

« Older posts

'What? Are you serious?'

'Of course I'm serious,' he said.

'But I wouldn't do that, I mean the other way around, maybe—'

'You mean you didn't kick your teacher between the legs?'

'Not exactly,' I said. 'My boot did, but it wasn't on my foot at the time.'

'Oh,' said Desmond.

'Honestly, Mr Tuft,' I said. 'You can have me CRB checked if you want. I'm clean. I mean, in the interest of full disclosure, I was once falsely accused of stealing a fizzy worm from the tuck shop but that was thrown out due to lack of evidence.'

'OK,' he huffed. 'Fine.'

So he wasn't talking about the sabotage after all. Seb really is just making stuff up.

'So does this mean I can stay at Woodlet?' said Natalie.

'I suppose so,' said Desmond.

'And I can see Joe?'

Desmond stared me right in the eye, then back at Natalie. Then he nodded.

I finally allowed myself to breathe. Then he stepped close to me. 'But if you ever do anything like this again,' he said. 'Anything even approaching this, I will kick your bony arse from here to Norwich, do you understand me?'

'Yes, sir,' I said.

'Good,' he said. 'Now I will allow you exactly five minutes to have your little kiss goodnight or whatever it is you do, and then I want you out. And please, if your mother is picking you up, try and keep her from attacking me.'

'Yes, sir,' I said again as he stepped out of my face and left.

Wow.

'Um, thanks, Mum,' said Natalie to Catherine. 'I thought—'

'That I only cared about Charlie?' she said. 'Natalie, I'm just trying to help him reach his full potential. Like your father was with you, although I'd like to think I'm better at it than him.'

She brushed Natalie's fringe out of her face and kissed her forehead. 'You know, for such a bright girl, you can be really thick,' she said.

Huh. My mum says that about me, too. Except the girl bit.

Monday 19th November

Natalie's back at school! God, I'm so happy, that when we saw Mad Morris on the way to the Silver Club, I could have kissed him on his rich superhero lips.

The Colonel was really pleased to see us when we got there, especially Natalie.

'I'd just like to thank you,' said Natalie. 'For helping Joe.'

'It was nothing,' he said, then turned to me and winked.

« Older posts

'Hope it was worth it.'

As weird as it sounds, hanging around with a load of people old enough to be my great-great-great-grandparents, we had a great time. When they put the old music on, we got up and had a slow dance. The Colonel requesting that we swap partners so he had Natalie and I had Doris did slightly spoil it, though, but after what he did for us, we didn't mind.

Tuesday 20th November

Natalie's birthday today. I was beginning to think I wouldn't get to spend it with her.

At lunch, we had a little party and everything, partly for her birthday and partly to welcome her back to the *SOUND EXPERIENCE* fold. After a while, Harry tapped the side of his Coke can with his pipe.

'Comrades, I'd like to propose a toast,' he said. 'I can't begin to tell you how pleased I am to finally have our co-manager back in the ranks, as old Simon Cowley here was beginning to struggle. To Natalie.'

'TO NATALIE!'

'What you having a toast for?' yelled Pete Cotterill from the next table. 'Being a bunch of freaks?'

Gav leaned back so he was visible behind Greeny and Pete looked like he was about to die.

'Oh sorry, Gav, I didn't see you there. How you doing?'

Gav went back to his normal position and cracked his knuckles.

Natalie blushed. 'Aw, you guys are the best.'

'You're not wrong there,' said Harry. 'It's like I told Joe. We never leave a man or woman behind.'

'Yeah,' said Ad. 'But what about when you dared me to put my sister's dress on and do a pitch invasion at the school rugby final? You didn't wait for me, then.'

'That was different,' said Harry.

'Why?'

'Because it was *funny*.'

Ad shrugged and went back to his apple crumble.

'Anyway, as it's a special occasion,' said Harry, 'we thought we'd get you a surprise.'

'Ad's not going to dress as a girl is he?' I said.

'I will if you want me to,' he said.

Harry shook his head. 'You know, you could at least pretend not to be so enthusiastic about the idea.'

'Don't listen to him, Ad,' said Natalie. 'You are who you are. Own it.'

Ad grinned and dropped some crumble down his tie.

'So anyway,' said Harry. 'Here is surprise number one.' He passed Natalie an envelope. 'And here is surprise two.'

He took a candle out of his pocket and stuck it in her doughnut. He nodded at Gav. 'Do the honours, would you, old son?'

Gav lit it with his lighter.

'I know it's not much,' said Harry. 'We all just wanted to do something to mark the occasion, but to be honest, we're all skinter than Germany after the Treaty of Versailles.'

'Open the envelope,' I said.

I was dead excited about this. We'd made her a card, with doodles by me and messages and little bits by the other guys.

She opened it. 'Oh my God,' she said. 'You lot are the best mates ever. Admittedly the best friend I had before was a rabbit named Barry, but still.'

'Was he your pet, then?' said Ad.

'No, Ad, he was a wild rabbit who just happened to answer to the name Barry,' I said.

Natalie leaned over and kissed Ad on the cheek, and I'm sure he blushed.

'And here's the other thing as well,' said Greeny. 'You're coming to London!'

Her eyes went huge. 'No. Bloody. Way.'

I looked around the table. We were all grinning like idiots. Except Gav. If he grinned, the Earth would implode.

'Yeah,' said Greeny. 'And 'cause you're a girl and that, you get your own room. Harry goes with Ad, Joe goes with his old man, and I'm stuck with Farty McGoo over here.'

Gav nodded. 'I'm going to have a massive curry on the night, just to make sure I've got enough firepower.'

'For you it's one night,' I said to Greeny. 'But for me it's life.'

Harry pointed at me and Natalie. 'And I want no room-visiting after dark,' he said. 'Sometimes I think it's only me that cares about the moral fabric of our society DAMMIT!'

We laughed as Natalie blew her doughnut candle out.

'Did you make a wish?'

Seb and Lisa stood at the end of the table looking like a pair of hipster bookends.

'Yeah I did but you're still here so it clearly hasn't come true,' said Natalie, before exchanging a quick high five with Greeny.

'Ouch,' Seb laughed. 'That was a good one. Still, I'm surprised to see you here. I thought Desmond was keeping you apart.'

'Nope,' said Natalie. 'Despite your best efforts.'

'What do you mean, my best efforts?'

'Desmond knows you're full of crap, Sebastian,' I said. 'Your little scheme to try and break us up was as poorly planned as your last haircut.'

'What scheme?' said Lisa. 'What's he talking about, Seb?'

Seb stared at me. 'Nothing, babe,' he said. 'Stupid freak doesn't know what he's talking about.'

Gav shot out of his chair. 'Oi, no one calls him a freak. Except me.'

« Older posts

'Please, Gav,' I said. 'Don't rise to it.'

'Just say the word, man,' said Gav. 'Just say the word and I'll do him.'

'That won't be necessary, old boy,' said Harry. 'We're going to spank him so hard in the final, any beat-down from you would feel like being licked by a butterfly.'

Gav sat back down, never taking his eyes from Seb.

'We'll see,' said Seb.

'Oh, we'll see, all right,' I said. 'See you in Loserville!'

Everyone stared at me. Hank put his face between his knees.

'You know,' I babbled on. 'From . . . from Winnertown. Where we'll be. So . . . Ad, you say something now.'

Ad's eyes bulged. 'Dinner was all right today, weren't it?'

Seb slapped his hand down at the table, knocking Greeny's tube of Smarties over. 'You people aren't going to get away with what you've done.'

'Argh, some of them have gone on the floor!' yelled Greeny.

'Five second rule, mate,' said Ad.

'Oh yeah!' Greeny scrabbled on the floor for the lost Smarties before he ran out of time.

'Are you listening to me?' said Seb.

'I don't know, are you, Natalie?' I said.

'Stopped ages ago,' she replied. 'How about you, Harry?'

'I'm drifting in and out,' he said. 'I seem to remember

him mentioning something about us not getting away with doing something?'

'But what could we have done?' said Natalie.

'No idea,' I said. 'Maybe it was when we replaced his barber with Blind Trevor from Morningside?'

'You know what you did—to my car, and my dad's website,' said Seb. 'And you'll pay.'

We all looked at each other and then cracked up laughing.

'You'll pay?' Harry said through his laughter. 'You sound like a Bond villain, old son.'

Seb huffed and stormed off, dragging Lisa along with him.

We kept laughing long after he'd gone but I wonder if I was the only one who felt slightly uneasy.

9.45 p.m.

My phone is still knackered, so I've had to borrow one of Mum's old ones. It's crap. It doesn't have internet or games or anything. It just has texts and phone calls. It's just a phone! What's the point of having a phone if it's just a phone?

Wednesday 21st November

Got back from Natalie's tonight to a tense atmosphere—nothing unusual about that—but this was different somehow. Mum and Jim were sitting in the lounge with Doris. I got the sense that they'd all stopped talking when I walked in.

« Older posts

'Um, everything OK?' I said.

'Well, not really, Joe,' said Jim. 'My mum has decided she wants to leave us.'

Mum blew her nose into a tissue.

'What?'

'It's for the best, Joseph,' said Doris. 'I want my independence back. And with the new babies on the way, this house will be too full. I'm going to go and live at Morningside.'

'Don't be silly, Doris. We'd never want you to leave,' said Mum. 'Would we, Joe?'

I thought about it for a second. I think I knew what was happening.

'No,' I said. 'But if Doris wants to go, I think she should.'

Mum and Jim glared at me as if to say, 'Whose side are you on?'

'I go with her every week and she's really happy there,' I said. 'Plus, she'll get to be with the Colonel.'

'Who's the Colonel?' said Jim.

'Nobody,' said Doris, turning bright pink. 'He's nobody.'

So it's settled. Doris is going to Morningside. She's going to spend this weekend there on a trial basis, then she's moving in. Plus, Mum and Jim are going to Nan and Granddad's for the weekend, so the house is going to be empty.

Still, it's going to be weird without Doris around. Without anyone to make constant cups of tea and to sing songs from a billion years ago, and to pretend dolls are real babies.

'Look on the bright side,' said Natalie when I told her. 'If you can lose Gav for a while, we'll finally have some alone time.'

Must find Gav something to do. Maybe I could introduce him to a hobby, like rock climbing or kayaking or running really far away for a very long time?

Thursday 22nd November

'I hate to ride your back, old son,' said Harry on the way to school. 'But it's just over a week to go until the final and we still haven't got a warm-up gig.'

« Older posts

I screwed my eyes shut. Balls. With all the drama, I'd kind of forgotten about it. 'Do you definitely need one?' I asked hopefully.

Harry nodded. 'It simply won't do to arrive underprepared. Especially when I heard that DJ Bumface has had two gigs this week.'

'How did you know about that?' I said.

'Off his Facebook fan page,' he said.

'He's got a Facebook fan page?' I said. 'What a poser.'

'Actually, I think it's about time we took the step into the world of social media,' said Harry. 'Or would you rather us spread the word via carrier pigeon?'

'Yeah, I might get Gav on that,' I said. 'I don't do Facebook.'

'Bloody hell, old bean, are you ever going to get over that naked pensioners prank?'

'Sometimes, when I close my eyes at night, I can still see them,' I said. 'So much loose skin.'

'Seriously though, old son,' said Harry. 'We need fast action on this or we could be at a disadvantage. We have to be at the top of our game if we want to trounce Seb.'

'All right,' I said. 'I'll find you something tonight.'

'Marvellous,' said Harry. 'But be warned, if you fail, I'm emailing you more nudey pensioner material.'

As soon as I got in from school, I started the search for a gig. I tried clubs, pubs, open mics, everything. Nowhere had gaps.

'How are you getting on with the Facebook page, Gav?' I called over to him.

'Aight,' he said. 'Except I don't know how you spell "experience".'

'That's OK, I'll spellcheck it for you when it's finished,' I said.

Gav nodded. 'At least I got "sound" right, though,' he said. 'Everyone knows that's S O W N D, innit?'

I stared at him for a second. 'So, as I say, I'll spellcheck it for you when it's finished.'

Friday 23rd November

What a cocking day.

The gang met up at break time. I was nervous because I still hadn't secured them a gig.

'But this is getting desperate,' said Harry. 'Look, I'd even play a house party, if we were the type of people who got invited to house parties.'

'Hey, I invited you to mine once,' said Greeny.

'Yes, you told us it was fancy dress party, and yet we were the only ones who turned up in it.'

'Oh yeah, that was jokes, man,' said Gav. 'Didn't you come as the Monopoly geezer?'

Harry gawped at him. 'I was Winston bloody Churchill, old son.'

'Ain't that a dog off the telly?' said Gav.

'See, that's what I said,' said Ad.

« Older posts

'Look, I'm sorry,' I said. 'It's just, everywhere's booked up.'

Then Gav said the words that drove fear into me like a stake into the heart of a vampire. 'We got a free house this weekend.'

I eyeballed him.

'Think about it, man,' he said. 'Our peoples are away, Nan is going into the home. It'll be just you and me. Perfect for a party.'

'But, but . . . '

'That sounds like a capital idea, old bean,' said Harry. 'It's so good, I'll even forgive you your ignorance of our nation's greatest ever leader.'

I glanced at Natalie but she just shrugged. This was supposed to be our alone time.

'How about you, Greeny?' I said. 'Surely you won't be able to recreate all your effects in our living room?'

He bit into a cake. 'Shouldn't be a prob,' he said, spraying crumbs everywhere. 'Just need to resize the projection, make it smaller. The main thing is to practise timings, anyway.'

I sighed. 'Fine. But it can't go on too late and you can't play too loud . . . And we can't invite too many people.'

Harry chuckled. 'Joe Cowley, there. The spirit of rock and roll.'

'Promise me,' I said.

'All right, old boy,' said Harry. 'We'll play soft enough so we won't wake you. We'll even make you a Horlicks.'

'Kiss my—'

'Hello, Miss Tyler!' Harry cut in. 'What brings you out of the safety of the staffroom?'

I turned around and there was Miss Tyler, looking slightly nervous.

'Hey, guys,' she said.

I sat up and paid attention. Guys? A teacher called us guys? What the hell was happening?

'Listen, we're having a special assembly for you in the hall after lunch,' she said.

'Wicked, I get to miss Maths!' said Ad.

'For us?' I said.

'I've been told not to give too much away, it's supposed to be a surprise,' she said. 'But it is very exciting. For you and the school.'

Before we could ask any more questions, Miss Tyler was gone.

'What's all this about, old boy?' said Harry.

'I have no idea.'

'Well, I thought you were supposed to be our manager,' he said. 'Our commander. If you don't know what's happening then all is lost, surely?'

I sat back and rubbed my temples. 'It's probably just about the competition. They've heard you're doing well, and they just want to congratulate you. You know, to change things from announcing who's been sentenced to

Young Offenders.'

Harry took deep puffs on his pipe. 'I hope you're right, soldier.'

We got down to the hall after lunch to find all the seats full. The entire school must have been in there, from Year Seven to the sixth form. Mr Pratt was sitting on stage with the deputy head. Miss Tyler led Harry and Ad up on stage. I went to sit in the audience, but she called me back.

'No, no, Joe,' she said. 'Our guest has insisted you come up with the boys.'

'Guest?' I said. 'What guest?'

Miss Tyler winked and tapped the side of her nose.

We took seats next to Pratt. There was another empty seat next to him.

Remain calm, Joe, said Norman. *Whatever happens, remain calm.*

I'm not going to lie to you, man, this looks bad, said Hank. *This looks very bad.*

I stared out into the crowd. I caught a glimpse of Natalie. She looked worried as hell. I sent her a sneaky text.

What is going on?

I don't know. But this can't be good.

'Phone away, please, Mr Cowley,' said Pratt. Then his own phone beeped.

'Oh, he's here!' he said.

He got up off the chair and went outside. After a minute, he came back in with this smarmy, oily looking bloke. I stared out into the crowd. Natalie, Gav, and Greeny looked as worried as I felt.

Pratt stepped up to the lectern:

'Boys and girls, members of staff,' he honked. 'It is my honour to welcome our very special guest to Woodlet High, a school that until last year was under special measures. Now, it would be presumptuous of me to claim that the turnaround was all down to me, but it didn't begin until I took the helm, so . . .'

Everyone just stared at him. I could barely hear anyway, what with my heart pounding louder than a bomb.

'Anyway,' Pratt continued. 'Without further ado, I shall hand you over to our very special guest: the Right Honourable Member of Parliament, Henry Mangrove.'

Holy balls, said Hank. *This is it. This is what that douche meant when he said you'll pay. Man, you probably shouldn't have laughed.*

Mangrove stepped up to the lectern and shook Pratt's hand. I scanned the back rows and found Seb, leaning forward and grinning.

« Older posts

'Thank you, Mr Pratt,' said Mangrove. 'It is wonderful to be here at the rejuvenated Woodlet High. Now, while I am thrilled at the upturn in the school's academic fortunes, that is not the reason for my visit. No, I am here to recognize the excellent extra-curricular work undertaken by these three boys sitting here.'

There was a murmur in the audience.

'The Sound Experience, a DJ duo featuring Harry Hodgeley and Ad Lawrence, with their manager, Joe Cowley, have reached the final of a national music competition.'

I glanced at Pratt, who seemed to flinch. It must have been killing him after what they did at the prom.

'But that's not all,' said Mangrove. 'The thing that makes these boys an inspiration to so many is that they have achieved this as the world's only DJ duo . . . who are also a couple.'

There was a moment of silence. It was only broken by Pete Cotterill, who said, 'WHAT?' Followed by huge laughs from EVERYONE.

My eye twitched so hard it took my cheek with it.

Pratt tried to stop the laughter, but it was no good. It was like a force of nature.

I glared at Seb at the back, who was crying with laughter. So this is what they were planning. How the hell can you compete with a politician?

Eventually, the laughter stopped and Mangrove called us up to receive our Mangrove Citizenship Medals.

Harry motioned towards the mic, and Pratt waved him on.

'Thanks, everyone,' he said. 'This is all very unexpected. But we don't deserve these medals.'

Oh cock, he's going to tell everyone they're not a couple and ruin the whole thing. You'll be kicked out of the competition. Hank was going berserk in the control room.

I approached the lectern. 'Come on, Harry, let's leave it, hey?'

Harry put his hand up to silence me.

'This whole ceremony is a charade,' he said. 'Orchestrated by Mr Mangrove's son, Sebastian, to try and embarrass us.'

Oh Jesus Christ, here we go, said Hank.

'That is an outrageous accusation!' Mangrove said.

'Please, sir,' said Harry. 'We're not in Parliament now—you have to let me speak.'

Mangrove gave this really false smile, then sat back down, scowling.

'But we are not embarrassed,' said Harry. 'Why would we be? We're proud of who we are. Sebastian has been tireless in his efforts to get us out of the competition, and this latest one just shows him up as the small-minded bigot he truly is.'

This was the first time in my life I have ever wanted to hug Harry.

« Older posts

'Now, the reason Sebastian wants us out of this competition is because he is also in it, and is intimidated by our superior technical ability and style.'

You know when you say someone has a face like thunder? Seb's was like that times a million. It was like a tropical typhoon or something.

'I'm not sure why Mr Mangrove has had to get involved though,' said Harry. 'Perhaps he's trying to rehabilitate his image after his unfortunate comments about same-sex marriage.'

'How did you know about that?' Mangrove mumbled.

Harry took a deep breath. 'It was Sun Tzu in *The Art of War* who first used the phrase "know your enemy". This is a lesson Sebastian should have heeded, because if he did, he'd realize this method of attack would be completely useless on us, because we don't care what you think. Any of you. Now, if that is all, we'll be off.'

He dropped his medal on the ground and walked offstage. I exchanged a glance with Ad, and we followed. Natalie, Greeny, and Gav left their seats and joined us. The only sound was our footsteps. When Gav got to the bottom, he turned on the audience.

'When someone does a speech, you're supposed to clap, yeah?'

Immediately, everyone clapped. Everyone except Seb.

The six of us walked out of the hall and stood in the corridor.

'Great speech, Harry,' I said.

'Yeah, I'm so proud of you,' said Natalie.

'Ah, it was nothing,' said Harry. 'Listen to "We Shall Fight on the Beaches" and you'll hear a true classic.'

'So let me get this right,' said Ad. 'That geezer wanted to give us a medal for being gay?'

'That's the long and short of it, yes,' said Harry.

Ad shrugged. 'Still, it's the only award I've ever won.'

Saturday 24th November

God, I am freaking out. I have never thrown a party before. It's so stressful. How the hell can Gav be so relaxed?

'You know this weekend was supposed to be a chance for me and Natalie to have some time alone,' I said to him.

'Oh yeah,' he said, and then did a really obscene gesture with his hands.

'No, not that,' I said. 'But I was just wondering if you could, you know, make yourself scarce for a bit.'

'So you want me out on the streets?' he said. 'Thanks, man. Tell you what, I'll just go and sleep in Dad's van, shall I?'

'If you do, you'll have to take that sign off.'

'What sign?'

'No tools left in this van overnight.'

He smacked me around the back of the head and carried on stacking glasses on the kitchen worktop.

'Will we need to buy nibbles?' I said.

'Nah, man, I'm happy with the two I've got,' said Gav.

'That's HILARIOUS,' I said. 'But seriously, what do we need? Sandwiches? Chicken legs? Cheese and pineapple on sticks?'

'Bruv.' He got my shoulder in a Vulcan death grip. 'There's only three things you need for a quality party: booze, babes, and banging choons. And we got all three.'

'Booze?' I said. 'We don't have booze!'

'Chill,' said Gav. 'This party is strictly BYOB, you get me?'

'Byeob?' I said. 'What the hell's byeob? Some kind of drug? I won't have illegal substances in this house, Gavin! And anyway, how many people have you invited? Not too many, I hope. Oh God, I'm hyperventilating.'

'Bruv,' he said. 'You need to relax. I got this completely under control. Nothing bad's going to happen. Trust me.'

Sunday 25th November

Trust him? **TRUST HIM?** I must have been MENTAL!

Oh sweet Jesus, we are doomed.

People didn't start arriving until after eight, which was far from ideal as I wanted it wrapped up by half nine.

'Hey, guys,' I said, as a big gang walked in. 'If you could take your shoes off and leave them in the hall, that would be great.'

I don't think they heard me.

Harry and Ad were playing some soft warm-up music

while Greeny set up his projector. People started opening drinks and chatting. There were about twenty there. Enough. I listened out for anyone complaining about the lack of nibbles, and had some onion rings, bacon rashers, and Bombay mix on standby just in case. I also kept a look-out for anyone dealing byeob.

Natalie came up and squeezed me on the arm. She looked stunning, with her hair in this up-do thing I'd never seen her do before. I went all wobbly and everything, but that could have been due to my hunger, on account of there being no nibbles.

'Do you know any of these people?' she said.

I scanned the room. 'No,' I said. 'I thought Squirgy Kallow was here but it's just some girl with short hair.'

'How many have been invited, exactly?'

'I don't know,' I said. 'Gav was in charge of all that.'

She grimaced. 'Are you sure that was a good idea?'

I turned around and saw Gav pouring pepper into his eyes while a group of lads cheered him on.

'Gav,' I yelled. 'What the hell are you doing?'

'Things are looking a bit dry on the booze front, innit?' he said as tears streamed from his flaming eyes. 'I've heard this gets you well messed up.'

'If by "messed up" you mean "blind", then yes, you're probably right.'

Gav started laughing. 'You're all right, mate.'

« Older posts

My breathing went all short and high and I sounded like a hamster having an asthma attack.

'Gav,' I said. 'How many people have you actually invited to this party?'

'Like I said, bruv, just a few mates.'

'So you know everyone here?' I said.

He shrugged as he rubbed his streaming eyes. 'Yeah, why not?'

'You.' I grabbed some kid wearing a #YOLO T-shirt. 'How did you hear about this party?'

'Facebook, innit?'

My breathing shifted up another gear. 'You're going to have to elaborate,' I said. 'Do you mean you're friends with Gav and he invited you on there?'

'Gav? Who's Gav?' he said. 'Nah, I saw it posted on the Tammerstone Social page.'

'I see,' I said, my teeth gritted so firmly I nearly bit my own head in half. 'And how many members does this page have?'

'Dunno,' he said. 'About three thousand, something like that.'

THREE THOUSAND? said Norman. *Joe, you have to put a stop to this.*

Don't be such a freakin' sad sack, said Hank. *You can get three thousand in your house, no problem. You might want to throw the couch out, though. Create some space.*

I flew around to the front door to try and lock it, but was nearly trampled by another mass of people flooding in.

'What have you done, Gav?' I yelled as I was carried back into the living room.

'Everyone!' I stood on the settee and called out. 'There has been a misunderstanding, I need you all to—'

'SPITFIRE DISASTER!'

The *SOUND EXPERIENCE* cranked up the volume and drowned me out completely. Greeny's shapes started appearing above our heads, and soon the whole room was a writhing mass of dancing and other stuff I didn't really understand.

I grabbed Gav and dragged him into the kitchen. 'Delete this party,' I said. 'Now.'

'Delete the party?' he said, laughing. 'You can't just, like, delete a party.'

« Older posts

'I mean off Facebook,' I said. 'I don't want any more people finding out about this.'

He nodded and winked at me. 'I get ya, bruv,' he said, pulling his phone out. 'I'll do it. 'Cause you're a top man.'

'God, maybe pepper really does get you drunk,' I said.

He squinted at his phone. 'Mate, I can't see it, you're going to have to do it.'

I snatched the phone off him. Oh dear God.

SOWND EXPRIANCE PARTY
52 Monk Drive

Sat, 25th Nov.

Start 8.30 p.m.

See da 1 n only sownd expriance play at a house prtee! Its gna b wkd! BYOB!!!!

152 people like this.

'A hundred and fifty-two people, Gavin?' I screamed. 'Have you been snorting byeob?'

'It's chill, mate,' he said. 'Just 'cause they like it don't mean they're gonna turn up.'

I was about to combust with pure rage, but then I got distracted by some moron rearranging my fridge magnet alphabet so it said 'JOE SMELLZ OV W33' rather than 'JOE IS THE MAN.'

'Hey, put those back,' I said.

The moron laughed. 'Are you Joe?'

I gulped. I didn't want to give my name away where there might be criminal elements.

'No!' I said. 'My name is ... J-Jean Luc.'

I grabbed the magnet letters, along with an awful Year Seven mugshot of me that Mum put up there and took them up to Mum and Jim's room, where they would definitely be safe.

No one would ever use someone's parents' bedroom at a house party. That's just sick.

I felt the vibrations from the music through the floor-boards. *God, I can't wait until this is over.*

I walked out and found Natalie on the landing.

'Hello, you,' she said.

'I'm really sorry about this,' I said. 'This was supposed to be our chance for some time to ourselves.'

'There'll be plenty more chances,' she said. 'In fact, now might be good.' She smiled and nodded at my bedroom door.

The control room dimmed their lights. Hank watched through his fingers. *I'm totally not looking, you guys.*

I opened the door and she pulled me close for a kiss. With my spare hand, I found the light switch on the wall.

I broke off the kiss and turned around, and what I saw on my bed will haunt me for the rest of my days.

'OH GOD!'

« Older posts

'Jee-sus,' said Natalie.

'Haven't you heard of knocking?' said one of them.

'Please,' I said, covering my eyes with my hand. 'Just pull up your pants and get out of my room.'

When I allowed myself to look again, they were gone. I sat down on my office chair and Natalie perched on my desk.

'Well, that's ruined that,' I said.

'Mmm hmm.'

'Come on,' I said. 'We might as well go down. Someone has to stop this place going up in flames.'

The living room was so full, it was almost bursting. Sweat ran down the walls.

'I hate parties,' said Natalie.

'Me too,' I said. 'Shall we go outside?'

We pushed past a load of people I'd never seen before in my life and went out the front.

'Tell you something else,' said Natalie. 'I'll be glad when all this is over.'

'Me too,' I said. 'It's been nothing but stress.'

Natalie linked my arm. 'Still, I really hope we beat Seb,' she said. 'Spoiled little brat can't even play fair.'

'I know,' I said. 'God knows what else he's got up his sleeve to try and get rid of us.'

'Nah,' said Natalie. 'He's done now. I reckon Harry proper embarrassed him in that assembly.'

I glanced back through the window into the house. Dear

God, someone just puked into our houseplant. I looked away quick.

'He's such an idiot,' I said. 'Driving around in that stupid gold Jag.'

'Yeah,' said Natalie. 'Just like that one parked up the road.'

Oh.

We looked at each other. Without a word, we set off up the road to investigate the knobmobile.

We got closer, and sure enough, there was Seb sitting in the front seat. Natalie tapped on the window. He glared at us and wound it down.

'Yeah?'

'What are you doing here?' said Natalie. 'I'm pretty sure we had a no-tossers-allowed policy for this party.'

'What's he doing here then?' he said, pointing at me.

'Oh, my sides are splitting with the merriment,' I said. 'But seriously, why are you sitting outside my house? Are you in love with me?'

He picked up a cigarette and rolled it between his fingers. 'I'm not here because I'm in love with you,' he said. 'And I'm definitely not coming to your pathetic kiddies' party.'

'Then why are you here?' said Natalie.

He lit the cigarette and took a drag. 'I'm here as a concerned citizen,' he said. 'I have reason to believe that there are illegal activities happening at this property.'

Natalie sighed. 'So what are you going to do, call the police?'

Seb blew a stream of smoke in our faces. 'Already done it,' he said. 'Good night.'

He turned on the ignition and sped off up the road.

We ran back to the house and tried to squeeze our way through the crowd. No good. It was like trying to stick a sausage through the eye of a needle. I climbed up on the settee, clambering over that same couple from my bedroom, and tried to shout for attention. No one could hear me.

I tried to wave at Harry and Ad to get their attention. Harry was too absorbed in what he was doing, and Ad just grinned and waved back.

I looked down at my route to them. Completely blocked. I realized that there was only one way. I had to crowd-surf.

I let myself fall back into the crowd. At first I thought they were going to drop me, but they lifted me up with a cheer.

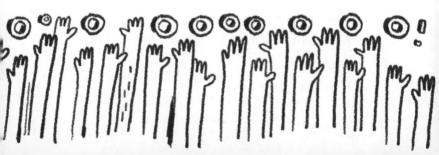

I must admit it felt good. Not the people touching my arse bit, but the being carried along by a giant wave bit.

I was enjoying it so much, I didn't even realize they were sending me the wrong way. When they dropped me, I was back where I started.

'Nice to see you getting in the party vibe, blud,' said Gav.

'No,' I said. 'I need to get to Harry and Ad.'

'Why?'

I thought about telling him the truth, but then I realized there was no way he'd assist in ending the party.

'I just wanted to tell them what a . . . bitching job they're doing,' I said.

Gav smiled. 'Aight, let's move.'

He strode out in front and started moving people out of the way. I grabbed onto the back of his shirt and followed in his wake. He was amazing, like a shark swimming into a shoal of fish.

We reached the front and Gav nodded. 'Glad to be of service, innit?'

'HARRY!' I screamed.

He didn't hear me, so I slapped him.

'What the bloody hell was that for?' was what I think I lip-read him as saying.

'We need to turn this off,' I yelled.

'WHAT?'

'TURN. IT. OFF!'

'No way, we're only just getting started.'

I scooched around the desk to the socket and pulled the plug. Everyone booed. I climbed up on a chair.

'EVERYONE!' I yelled.

'Hey, it's Jean-Luc!' I heard someone say.

'You all need to get out of here immediately,' I said. 'But please leave calmly.'

About thirty different variants of 'Why?' and 'Try and make me, you freak,' could be heard.

'Someone has called the police,' I said.

Straight away, everyone turned and stampeded for the door. They obviously didn't want to be caught in possession of byeob.

'Hey!' said Gav. 'Where are you all going? Are you going to let the filth spoil our good time?'

No one listened to him and within a couple of seconds the house was empty, except for the ƧOUNƉ EXPERIENƇE gang. And three people walking into the living room. Seb. And his two bodyguards.

'God, where were you hiding them, Seb?' said Natalie. 'In the boot?'

'Shut up,' he snapped back at her.

'Hey, don't speak to her like that,' I said.

One of the giant bodyguards rounded on me. 'Or what?'

I babbled something about writing a strongly worded letter and shut up.

'You best know yourself, man,' said Gav. ''Cause I'm gonna get you one day. Believe.'

Seb smiled and picked up a framed picture of me and Natalie that Mum had put on the mantelpiece. 'Can someone translate that for me?' he said. 'I don't speak Chav.'

'You're such a knob, Seb,' said Natalie. 'I bet you didn't even call the police, did you?'

He put the frame back face-down and laughed. 'You're even more gullible than your old man,' he said. 'And that's saying something.'

'So what is this, old son?' said Harry. 'You couldn't stand to take us on in a fair contest, so you have to keep cheating? That's poor form if you ask me.'

Seb turned on him and snatched the pipe out of his mouth. 'You know what I think is poor form, *old son*? Making me look like an idiot in front of that entire scummy school. And do you know why it's poor form? Because it made me angry. And you won't like me when I'm angry.'

Ad laughed. 'Hey up, mate, he's about to hulk up.'

Seb swung around and smacked Ad across the face with the pipe, knocking his glasses to the floor. He fell backwards and spilled his drink all over the equipment.

'YOU DID NOT JUST DO THAT.' Gav launched himself at Seb and it took me, Greeny, and Natalie to hold him back.

'What happened to my glasses?' said Ad. 'Has he done something to them? Is he flipping Vs at me?'

« Older posts

A bright red mark spread across his cheek. Only a true scumbag could hit Ad. It's like kicking a puppy.

'Oh, you're such a hard man, Sebastian,' said Natalie. 'Hitting someone when you've got your two pet gorillas with you. I'd like to see you try that when you're on your own. Hell, even I could kick your arse.'

Seb walked over to Natalie slowly. He stood close to her and traced a finger down her cheek.

Remain calm, Joe, said Norman. *J-just remain calm and everything will be fine. I'm sure it will be fine.*

No way, said Hank. *No freakin' way. Karate chop his ass. No one touches your woman.*

'Such a pretty girl,' said Seb. 'But such a big mouth.'

Natalie's expression thawed. She smiled flirtatiously.

Um, what the hell is this?

'I've been told my mouth is my deadliest asset,' she said.

Seb stepped closer. 'Oh yeah?'

She nodded and leaned in close to him. 'Well, second deadliest. My first deadliest is my knee.'

'Your knee?' he said. 'Why?'

'Well . . . ' she said, then quicker than Chuck Norris, brought her knee up and smashed Seb right in the balls. The impact made Boocock's mishap look like he was being tickled by a feather. Which is not an image I ever want to picture again. Seb screamed and bent double before hitting the ground.

'That's why,' she said.

The two bouncers stepped forward.

'What are you going to do?' she said to them. 'Hit a girl?'

Seb moaned into the carpet.

'No one hits Ad and gets away with it,' she said.

I looked at Natalie. Bathed in blue lights from the rig, she looked like an ass-kicking goddess.

The blast of a siren cut through the moaning and lights flickered through the window.

'Oh cock, the police are here!' I said. If Seb didn't call them it must have been one of the neighbours.

'Retreat!' Harry yelled, and ran out the back, with Greeny and Ad in tow.

One of the bouncers picked Seb up and they ran out, too. Me and Natalie went to follow.

'Come on, Gav,' I said to him. 'Get out of here before it's too late.'

'Nah,' he said. 'I've never run from the law and I ain't about to start now.'

I grabbed Natalie's hand and we got through the kitchen and out of the back door just as two police officers entered the house.

« Older posts

We stopped and peered in through the window, and watched as Gav ripped his shirt off and held his arms out wide.

'Come on then, copper,' he screamed. 'Let's 'ave it!'

GRRRRR

We turned and ran away, the sound of Gav being tasered ringing in our ears.

'All in all, I think tonight's been a big success,' I said to Natalie, as we dodged through the alleyways and into the park.

We saw two figures in the distance. It looked like Harry and Greeny, standing by the edge of the pit. Seb and his goons were nowhere to be seen.

'Where's Ad?' I said, when we got to them.

'This is not good, old boy, not good at all,' said Harry.

'He was running off ahead,' said Greeny. 'But he must not have seen this great big hole, and . . .'

'Lads.' We heard Ad scrambling to his feet below us. 'I think I might have hurt my wrists but I can't see.'

He walked into the light from the lamp post. 'What do you reckon?'

'Oh my God,' said Natalie.

'I think I'm gonna spew,' said Greeny.

'Yes, old boy,' said Harry in a shaky, faraway voice. 'I think you have hurt your wrists somewhat.'

I felt a sudden upsurge in my belly and turned around and puked. Hands are not supposed to stick out from arms at that angle. Ever.

Monday 26th November

After we took Ad down to A & E, where he was on first name terms with everyone, I went home to tidy the house.

The worst part wasn't the mess—I was expecting that. The worst part was when I plugged the equipment back in to test it and it blew up with a loud pop. Ad's drink had completely frazzled it.

When I'd finally finished cleaning at 4 a.m., Harry called.

'Hello?' I said, dreading the conversation that was about to take place.

'Two broken wrists, old son,' he said. 'They're keeping him in while they fix him up.'

« Older posts

I wasn't surprised. I thought he was going to need bionic limbs or something.

'Well, I may as well add to your bad mood now,' I said. 'Your gear has had it.'

There was a pause. I could feel my overtired brain whirring slowly.

'What do you mean, had it?'

'Totally kaput,' I said. 'Ad's drink blew it up.'

There was another silence. 'Well, it doesn't bloody matter at the moment, old son,' he said. 'Because we're out, anyway. Without Ad, there's no Sound Experience.'

I picked up a pair of boxers between my little finger and thumb and dropped them into a bin bag. 'I can't believe he's winning like this.'

'He might not win though,' said Harry.

'Yes, but he has, hasn't he?' I said. 'He's knocked us out.'

'This is a sad day, comrade,' he said. 'A sad day indeed.'

I got a couple of hours' sleep and was woken up by Gav coming in.

'What happened?' I said.

'Bruv, I am knackered,' he said. 'Tell you what though, that taser gives you a wicked buzz—you should try it sometime.'

'No thanks,' I said. 'What did the police do?'

'Well, believe it or not, this ain't the first time I've been busted,' he said. 'So they've given me this.'

He lifted the leg of his jeans to reveal a plastic band.

'What, jewellery?' I said. 'This country is too soft.'

'It's a tag,' he said. 'They've got me under surveillance, man. On lockdown. Means I can't come to London, innit.'

'We won't be going, anyway,' I said. 'It's over.'

Harry asked me to call Bangaz and tell them we're withdrawing, but I can't bring myself to do it.

9 p.m.

Mum, Jim, and Doris arrived home today. Gav hasn't told them about the tag. He reckons he can keep it a secret for the entire month he has to wear it. Yes, I can't see anything going wrong there.

« Older posts

Tuesday 27th November

Me, Harry, Natalie, and Greeny went to visit Ad in hospital. He had to have his arms put in plaster, so even if he could get out, there's no way he could operate the equipment. Which we don't even have.

'How are you, old son?' said Harry.

'Rather frustrated, to tell you the truth,' said Ad.

'I'm not surprised,' said Harry. 'I mean, with your hands out of action, you can't even scratch your general, can you?'

Greeny laughed. 'You should defo get one of them fit nurses to sort that for you.'

'Hardly,' said Ad. 'My frustration stems from the fact that I will be unable to compete in the competition.'

We all looked at each other. 'Are you, um, all right, Ad?' I said.

'Perfectly fine,' he replied, scrunching his nose to keep his glasses on. 'The morphine has been helping with the pain.'

'It's just, you seem different,' I said. 'Like, you're using sentences with, you know, words in them.'

'Well, it is rather curious,' said Ad. 'I feel much more clear-headed since my admission. Perhaps it's having the time to think.'

'I think I know what's happened,' said Natalie. 'For most people, morphine causes hallucinations and skewed perceptions. Maybe, because you might say Ad's perceptions are already a bit, um, skewed, the morphine has evened him out and made him . . . normal.'

We all stared at him. It was like entering a wormhole to another dimension.

'What the devil are you looking at?' said Ad. 'I'm as normal as I've ever been.'

'This is some serious *Twiglet Zone* crap,' said Greeny.

None of us said anything.

'Anyway,' said Ad. 'You still need to do this.'

'Do what?' said Harry.

'You need to go to the final.'

Harry chewed on his pipe. 'How can we? We have no equipment, no muscle, and now, only half the act. Plus, Joe has already withdrawn us, haven't you, Joe?'

I stayed quiet and avoided eye contact.

'Joe?'

Ad kicked his heel into the mattress. 'You can make this happen, I know you can. What about when Natalie was being held prisoner by her dad? Kept under lock and key? Did we give up then?'

'No, but this is different,' said Harry.

Ad narrowed his eyes at Harry. 'When the Luftwaffe flattened London in the Blitz, did Churchill give up?'

Harry sighed. 'No.'

'And, Joe,' he said, 'would Captain Picard surrender this easily?'

« Older posts

He knows us too well.

'Well then get out there and do it,' he said, then winced.

'Are you OK, Ad?' said Natalie.

'Yes, it's just the morphine must be wearing off.'

'Do you want me to get you a nurse?' said Natalie.

'Yeah,' said Ad with a dopey grin. 'And make sure it's one of them fit ones.'

And he was back.

'I don't know how we're going to do it,' said Harry as we left the hospital.

'Yeah, I mean he was tripping his tits off in there,' said Greeny. 'He probably thinks we can ride down to London on magical unicorns and play the tunes by slapping our bum cheeks.'

'Let's think about this logically,' said Natalie. 'What we need first is equipment.'

'And unless you've got seven hundred quid, there's no way we're going to get it,' said Harry.

We stood around trying to think of something. I even started stroking my chin as if that would somehow help. It didn't.

'I've had an idea,' said Greeny.

'The world really has gone mad,' said Harry. 'What is it, old bean?'

'Well, ain't you and Nat's dad bessie mates now, Joe?' he said.

'I wouldn't go that far.'

'Yeah, but you're all right,' he said. 'And now you're on good terms, and you're both businessmen, this could be one of them opportunities for him, couldn't it?'

I thought about it. I mean, it wasn't ideal but if it was our only hope . . .

'No way,' said Natalie. 'We won't do it, will we, Joe?'

I hesitated. 'But it might be the difference between us competing and not.'

'It's worth a go, surely?' said Harry.

Natalie opened her mouth as if to argue. It seemed like she couldn't think of a good reason though. 'OK,' she said. 'Let's do it.'

'Let me get this straight.' Desmond paced in front of his grand fireplace and swished brandy around in a glass.

'You want me, the managing director of the region's leading supplier of quality WCs, to give you—the person who wrecked my wall trellis—a loan to buy new equipment, so you can go and beat my business protégé in a DJing competition?'

None of us would make eye contact with him. 'Yeah, kind of,' I said.

Natalie squeezed my hand as Desmond stared us all out. Then, in a split-second, his expression turned from stony to smiley.

'Fine,' he said. 'How much do you need?'

'Is that it?' said Natalie. 'What's the catch, Desmond?'

Desmond pinched Natalie on the cheek. 'So cynical, this daughter of mine,' he said. 'And she's quite right to be, because there is a catch.'

Here we go, said Hank. *He wants your soul.*

'The way I see it, this is an investment,' said Desmond. 'Because you're better than Seb. You must be. Otherwise, why would he want you out so much? So I think in the future, if this all goes well, and you grow a few more hairs on your chests, this . . . SOUND EXPERIENCE and I may make a lot of money together. I could mould you into a real commercial entity. And maybe I could find a new protégé.'

He held out his hand to me. My pulse thudded in my temples. I reached out my hand but before I could take his, Natalie slapped it away.

'No,' she said. 'I'm sorry but I can't do this. The deal's off.'

I thought Harry's head was going to explode.

'Fine,' said Desmond. 'Good luck finding a new way of raising capital.'

Natalie ran up to her room. I went after her, leaving Harry and Greeny to make awkward small talk with Desmond.

She was sitting on the end of her bed with her head in her hands.

'I'm really sorry, Joe,' she said. 'I just couldn't let that happen.'

I sat down next to her. 'But I thought you wanted us to win.'

'I did,' she said. 'But some things are more important.'

Wednesday 28th November

I was poking my lunch around the plate, too depressed to even contemplate eating it. The mood was pretty low in our camp since Natalie threw away our only lifeline and wouldn't say why. Things didn't improve when Seb swaggered over.

'Do one right now before I rip your neck off,' said Gav.

'Noticed you walking a bit funny today, Seb,' said Natalie. 'Hope you're not still sore.'

He sneered. 'I heard about what happened to your gear, and your boy.'

'Seriously, if this chump doesn't leave here in five seconds, he's going out the window,' said Gav.

« Older posts

'So I suppose that means you won't be coming to the final,' said Seb. 'That's a shame.'

'If you're so good, old son, why were you so worried about us, anyway?'

'Pfft. I was never worried.'

'Then why were you so bothered about getting us out of it, then?' said Greeny.

'I became bothered, my fat friend, when you people made it personal,' said Seb. 'Because I always win. And I'm not about to be beaten by a gang of outcast freaks.'

Gav threw his knife and fork down, launched himself out of his chair, and grabbed Seb around the neck. Before we could stop him, he had him up against the wall.

'Gavin James, put Sebastian down, immediately,' Mr Pratt yelled.

Gav looked over his shoulder at Pratt, shrugged and dropped Seb, who then landed in a wheezing heap on the floor.

So now Gav has an electronic tag and, because he's broken his good behaviour bond, is suspended for two weeks. What next? The chair?

7 p.m.

OK, OK, OK.

Gah.

Right. Something weird has happened. We were gathered at Harry's for what he called a 'crisis summit' to try and come up with a way to get our equipment back. Rejected ideas included (1) breaking into Seb's house in balaclavas and stealing his gear as revenge and (2) applying for a grant. What's weird is that the balaclava thing was what we came up with first. Anyway, we asked around and found out it's too short notice for a grant, so we were back to square one. Natalie still refused to take Desmond's offer, and I could tell Harry was getting racked off about it.

'This is ridiculous,' he said. 'There is an offer on the table that would allow us to continue, and you won't take it. Whose side are you on, anyway?'

'How dare you say that to me?' said Natalie. 'After everything that's happened.'

'Exactly.' Harry jabbed the air with his pipe. 'Everything which included saving YOU from captivity, or did you forget about that?'

I didn't know what to do. My girlfriend and my best friend were having a row. No matter who I stuck up for, I'd be screwed. I tried to think of something diplomatic to say and came up with nothing. Then my phone started ringing.

'Quiet please,' I said. They carried on yelling at each other.

'SHUT UP!' I screamed. They both stared at me. How's about that for diplomacy?

« Older posts

The number wasn't one I recognized. I answered it anyway. Any distraction was welcome.

'All right, Joe?' said Ad. 'Put the news on right now.'

'Um, OK.'

I switched the news on. It was showing a report about morris dancers.

'That's great, Ad,' I said. 'Have they increased your morphine dosage by any chance?'

'Just wait,' he said.

'Let's hope they can find a new place to jig, eh?' said the newsreader. 'In other news, a fifteen-year-old Tammerstone boy has won a payout after breaking his wrists at an archaeological dig site. Winnie Bailey has more.'

'What do you reckon, Joe?' said Ad down the phone. 'Do I look fit or what?'

Everyone started going crazy. The argument was forgotten. Ad appeared on TV in his hospital bed.

'Well one minute I was walking through the park, the next I was in the pit with my hands all crooked,' he said.

'Tammerstone Council has apologized to the Lawrence family and offered them a one-thousand-pound out-of-court settlement,' said the news lady.

'Cocking hell!'

'We would have held out for more, like,' said Ad's dad. 'But Ad mentioned that he wasn't wearing his glasses at the time so we had to take what we could get. I love the boy but he doesn't know when to shut his face.'

'So what do you reckon, mate?' said phone Ad. 'Pretty sweet, yeah?'

'I could bloody kiss you, you clumsy BASTARD!' Harry yelled.

As soon as the news finished, my dad called and congratulated us on our new windfall. 'You should hire yourselves some hot dancers, guys. That would be P H A T.'

I told him about what happened with the gear and he offered to give us a bridging loan to buy new stuff until Ad's money came through. Even though me and my dad have our differences, I wasn't about to refuse.

Anyway, Ad was discharged from hospital later on just in time to see our new set-up. WE'RE BACK!

9 p.m.

Well, not really.

As soon as we had the gear, we went back to Harry's garage to rehearse. Harry tried to run through the tracks by himself but he couldn't do it. It was too much for him to keep up with.

'This is useless, comrades,' he said. 'I can't do it single-handedly. I need a replacement Ad.'

'I can't do it,' said Greeny. 'I have to operate the visual effects console.'

'Gav would have been the obvious choice, but he's under cocking house arrest,' I said. 'How about you,

Natalie? You love their music—I mean you actually listen to it for pleasure.'

Harry gave me a look.

'As do I,' I said.

'I'd be too intimidated,' said Natalie. 'The music is so powerful, I wouldn't want to risk messing it up.'

'Plus, your whole gimmick is that you're a gay couple,' said Greeny. 'If they see a girl up there, they're going to start asking questions.'

I felt my ribcage tighten.

'So that just leaves you, Joe,' said Natalie.

Control room, we have a situation here, said Norman.

A situation? said Hank. *Yeah, just like a train crash is a situation.*

'No,' I said. 'No way.'

Natalie stepped close and put her arms around me.

'What happened to Ad,' she said. 'That was Seb's doing, you know.'

'I know,' I said. 'But, I, I just . . .'

'One of the reasons I love you is your loyalty to your friends,' she said. 'Now are you going to grow a pair and do this, or are we going to have a falling out?'

Oh cock.

Thursday 29th November

After school we went straight over to Harry's for rehearsal.

I've had this weird sick feeling in my stomach since yesterday. There's no way I can go on stage in front of all those people and play music I don't even understand. It's impossible.

Harry showed me the equipment, what all the buttons do, and when to press them.

'We have two days before we leave for the final,' he said. 'So I hope you're a quick learner.'

'Me too,' I said.

He clapped his hand on my shoulder. 'Look, if you can memorize all that *Star Trek* trivia, there must be room in that brain of yours to remember when to press a few buttons. I've taken on as much of it as I can and left you with the easy bits, OK?'

My guts felt like they were made of rice pudding.

By the time we were finished for the night, my ears were ringing, partly from the music and partly from Harry constantly shouting at me.

'No, the explosion doesn't come in until "Spitfire Disaster"!'

'You were early with the 808!'

'You were late with the 808!'

'What do you mean, "What's an 808?"'

In the end, he took my sampler and 808 (apparently, some kind of drum machine) and said he'd try and make them less daunting for 'people of limited musical ability'. Arse.

When it was just me and Natalie left, she asked me what it was that was keeping me from picking it up.

« Older posts

'I don't know,' I said. 'I just imagine that I'm stood on stage in front of hundreds of people and I freeze.'

'Come with me.'

She grabbed my hand and led me up to her bedroom. Scary make-up wearing men scowled at me from the walls and the smell of incense tickled my nose.

'Lie down on the bed.'

I did as I was told while Natalie went scrolled through her iPod.

She docked it and this soft music drifted out, accompanied by what sounded like whales calling.

'This, um, isn't your usual kind of thing,' I said.

'This isn't what I listen to for pleasure,' she said.

'So what's it for then?'

'Just lie flat on your back.' She walked over to the bed. 'I've been reading up about hypnosis.'

Alarms bells rang in the control room. No. Not hypnosis. I remembered seeing a stage hypnotist once, when I was on holiday. He convinced this poor bloke he was a chicken. It was all fun and games until he ragged his trousers down and laid an egg on stage. Well, I say an egg . . .

Natalie sat down beside me and started rubbing my temples. It was nice. I felt myself drifting. *No. That's what she wants to happen. Fight it.* I opened my eyes.

'What's wrong?' she said.

'You're going to make me think I'm a chicken,' I said.

'I'm not going to make you think you're a chicken,' she said. 'You act like a cock enough as it is.'

I gave her the stinkeye.

'Sorry,' she said, laughing. 'You walked right into that one.'

'I suppose I did.'

'Just relax,' she said. 'Let yourself go. You trust me, don't you?'

'Course I do.'

'Then let yourself sleep,' she said. 'Let the music pull you under.'

I closed my eyes and tried to make the most of my last few seconds before I became a chicken forever. The music drifted and swirled like a river. I felt myself falling asleep and, as much as I tried to fight it, I was gone.

While I was under, I remember still hearing little phrases coming through:

'These people aren't there to judge you. They are your friends.'

'You have prepared for this, you are competent. You will be fine.'

'When you see the sampler and the 808, imagine they are the controls on the bridge of the *Enterprise*.'

'Above all. Be like Picard. Be like Picard . . .'

Be like Picard . . .

Be like Picard . . .

'Welcome back, Mr Sleepyhead.'

When my eyes finally readjusted, I saw Natalie looking down at me.

'How are you feeling?'

I started clucking like a chicken.

She laughed and slapped me on the shoulder.

'Yeah, I feel fine,' I said. 'How long was I out for?'

'About half an hour,' she said. 'You make some interesting noises when you're asleep.'

I sat up and rubbed my eyes. 'Oh God, I didn't fart, did I?'

'I don't think so,' said Natalie. 'It was all coming out of the other end.'

I scratched the back of my head. 'Really?'

'Yep. First of all you were snoring for a bit, then you started talking. Saying some nonsense about some blokes called Norman, and I think the other one was Frank.'

'Hank,' I said, then immediately grimaced.

Nice going, numbnuts, said Hank. *Tell the girl you're insane, she's not likely to run a freakin' mile.*

Calm down, Hank, said Norman. *It's not that bad.*

Calm down? said Hank. *He's about to tell her all about us, and we're not even REAL!*

'Who are they?' she said.

'My, um, my . . . my uncles,' I said.

She gave me a weird look. 'You dream about your uncles?'

'Yep.'

'If I fetch you a doll,' she said, 'can you point to where they touched you?'

I laughed and grunted a little bit, which was proper embarrassing.

'Come on, Joe,' she said. 'I know they're not your uncles.'

You are the WORST LIAR IN THE WORLD, Hank yelled.

'All right,' I said. Then I told her everything about Norman and Hank and the control room. I'd never told anyone about it before, not even Harry and Ad.

'It's really weird and I'm sorry, and if you want to chuck me, I'd totally understand,' I ended up saying.

Natalie smiled, then kissed me. 'I'm never chucking you,' she said. 'You'd have to do something monumentally stupid for that to happen.'

'And you don't think I'm weird?'

'Joe, I had an imaginary friend until I was fifteen,' said Natalie. 'So, no, I don't think you're weird.'

'An imaginary friend?' I said.

'Yep,' she said. 'Her name was Minnie.'

'And why did you get rid of her?'

'I didn't,' said Natalie. 'She just disappeared because I didn't need her any more. Because I've got you guys, now.'

I smiled. 'Just don't tell Ad about her though,' I said. 'Because he'll probably try and ask her out.'

Friday 30th November

'YES! "SPITFIRE DISASTER"!' I yelled as we got through it for the third time.

Harry stared at me with what I thought might have been awe. He's made these laminated colour-coded sheets to stick over my gear. He had numbered all the buttons as well, telling me what order to press them in. When I had my cue, Harry would nod at me and I would press the appropriate button. The thing is, after a while, I didn't even have to look at him. I knew it. I knew what I was doing! I just imagined that I was Picard on the bridge of the **ENTERPRISE**—Data was on an away team, and it was down to me to pilot the ship.

'I must say, I'm impressed,' said Harry. 'You're actually starting to pick this up, old bean.'

'It's all down to Natalie,' I said. 'She's sorted my head out.'

'Cripes, what did you do to him?' said Harry. 'On second thoughts, don't tell me, it's probably too rude.'

'You can tell me though,' said Ad, finally allowed out with his arms encased in plaster. 'Just whisper it—I won't tell no one.'

We'd all signed his plaster, and we may or may not have drawn some doodles of willies on it as well—I couldn't possibly comment.

'What do you think, Ad?' said Natalie. 'Isn't he doing well?'

'He's doing wicked,' said Ad. 'To be honest, after everything that's happened, I'm well impressed that we're still going. After I broke my wrists and our gear got took, I'd wrote it off.'

We all stared at him. 'But you were the one who told us to go for it,' said Greeny.

'When?'

'When you were in hospital, old son,' said Harry.

'Did I?'

We all nodded.

'I can't believe you listened to me,' said Ad. 'I was proper off my nut on that Morphy Richards stuff. I could have been saying any old guff.'

'Well we're glad you did, because now we're going to

London and we're going to kick Seb's arse,' said Natalie. 'Isn't that right, guys?'

We all shouted our approval when my phone rang. Mum. *Good God, what's happened? Is she calling to shout at me for walking on the carpet or something?*

'Joe, it's time to say goodbye to Doris,' she said.

'What, already?'

'Yes, a place has become available at Morningside,' she said. 'We're going to take her this evening.'

When I got home, they were ready to go, all bags packed and in the car.

'We're gonna be back before seven, yeah?' said Gav.

'Yes,' Jim snapped back. 'What's so important that you have to rush back, anyway? I know you find old people "freaky" but I would have thought you'd be able to grin and bear it, just for today.'

I could see Gav searching for a lie. 'It's just . . . ' he said. 'I got . . . homework, innit?' He hasn't told them about his suspension, either.

Jim and Mum couldn't have looked more stunned if Gav's head had sprouted wings and flew out of the window.

'Fine, we'll get you back for seven,' said Jim, before turning to me. 'I didn't realize you'd be this good an influence on him.'

If only he knew.

It was proper sad taking Doris to Morningside, but she seemed happy. As did the Colonel. He wasn't even bothered that she had a baby she hadn't told him about.

Saturday 1st December

So here we are. It's the night before the final and I'm lying in my hotel bed staring at the ceiling. I've given up on the idea of sleep so I'm going to write this.

We had to tell them one of our party wouldn't be coming, so now they've put Harry, Ad, and Greeny together. Greeny was not impressed because he thought he was getting his own room, but even he had to admit it's a good thing, really. He is not to be trusted alone with a minibar.

Dad and Svetlana picked me, Harry, and Ad up from my house after school, just in time. Jim was interrogating Gav as to why he wasn't going.

'I told you, it's homework, innit?'

'Don't give me that,' he said. 'Something else is going on here.'

When I saw Svetlana's car pull up outside, I could have whooped with joy. 'WE'RE OFF THEN,' I yelled as we ran out of the house. 'Wish us luck!'

I was nearly in the car when Mum shuffled after us. 'Good luck, my darling,' she said, kissing me all over my face. 'And be careful. If anyone offers you drugs, what do you tell them?'

« Older posts

'No,' I murmured.

'You'll look after him, won't you?' she said to Harry and Ad. They nodded.

'Thank you,' she said. 'And good luck.' She gave them both kisses on the cheek. Ad didn't speak for another three hours.

We loaded our stuff into the back and got in. Through the open window, we quite clearly heard Jim screaming, 'YOU'VE GOT AN ELECTRONIC TAG?!'

'Drive,' I said to Dad. 'Quick.'

We picked up Natalie and Greeny and soon we were on our way. Being able to sit on the back row with Natalie made up for the fact that my dad was being a tool as usual, playing rap songs at deafening volumes and shouting things like, 'This is my jam,' and, 'Superfly shizzle todizzle.'

The unlikely combination of Harry and Svetlana was quite amusing, though.

'So, Svetlana,' said Harry. 'That's an unusual name. Joe tells me you're from Russia.'

She sighed and flipped through her magazine. 'Yes.'

'Fascinating place,' said Harry. 'Instrumental in the fight against the Nazis, but arguably committed equal atrocities themselves. Tell me, have you ever visited Lenin's tomb?'

'What?'

'Never mind,' said Harry. 'So, were you mail order, or what happened there?'

We stopped at the services to use the toilet and to empty Ad's sick bag. How the hell did I forget travel sickness pills again? Me, Natalie, and Greeny were the first back in the car.

'Hey, Joe,' said Greeny. 'While we're alone, like, I just wanted to say thanks.'

'What for?' I said. 'You've just had to hold a plastic bag under Ad's face while he chundered.'

'Yeah, but I wouldn't swap it for nothing,' he said.

'That's weird,' I said.

Greeny chuckled and rubbed his mouth. 'What I'm trying to say is, I've never really had mates before, and now I have, and it's all down to you.'

'Oh,' I said. 'Don't worry about it.'

'That goes for me, too,' said Natalie. 'You're all right, Joe Cowley.'

It was quite a nice moment until Ad got back in the car with a bag of Haribo and a bucket of candyfloss.

'Oh god, what is this going to look like when it re-emerges?' I said.

By the time we'd all polished off the four tubes of Pringles Greeny brought along, we were almost there. London. Just looking out at it through the window made me feel excited, and scared, and very small somehow. Even the tramps are crazier here. We saw this one bloke fighting a lamp post.

« Older posts

He made Mad Morris look like a fluffy hamster.

We approached some traffic lights and Dad whistled. 'Yo, shorties, check the pimped-out Jag to the left. Gold. Very bling.'

Me and Natalie looked at each other. Surely not.

I looked out of the window and saw the personalized number plate:

`DJ S38`

'Everybody, over to my side!' I yelled.

Dad stopped at the lights so that we were slightly ahead of Seb. To begin with, he didn't notice us all waving at him from the windows, but when he did, it was the best moment I have ever witnessed. He looked like the bloke from that Scream painting. Even worse when the waving changed to obscene gestures. Lisa looked horrified, too.

'Who'd have thought, out of all the douches in London, we would run into him?' said Natalie.

'It's like chaos theory,' said Harry. 'Except instead of a butterfly flapping its wings, it's a Jag-driving rich boy slapping Ad. What say you, old son?'

'Who cares? Joe's mum kissed my face today,' said Ad.

The hotel we're staying in is proper posh. Even the biscuits with the tea-making facilities look expensive. Dad keeps saying stuff about it being 'Totally boho-chic with a hint of Bauhaus,' as if he has any idea what he's cacking on about.

We went down for dinner after we checked in. Dad said it was his treat. I ended up sitting next to Ad and somehow got given the duty of hand-feeding him. His garlic bread starter wasn't too bad, but then he looked at what he wanted for his main.

'I reckon I'm going to have spag bol,' he said.

'Really?' I said. 'Why don't you have something less messy, like steak?'

'Nah,' he said. 'I proper fancy some spag bol.'

'Oh sweet Jesus.'

'You think you've got it bad, old boy,' said Harry. 'Someone's got to wipe when that comes out the other end.'

'Well, that's put me off my starter,' said Natalie.

'Wicked,' said Greeny, as he yoinked it off her.

After dinner, and post-dinner cleaning of both Ad and myself, we went out for a walk. Me and Natalie went off on our own to look at the club where the final is tomorrow night. It's this huge place right near Trafalgar Square called Silk Kitty. When we got there, people were starting to queue up outside.

Natalie squeezed my hand. 'You nervous?'

I nodded.

'You'll be fine,' she said. 'Remember: be like Picard.'

'S'up, young'uns?' I looked over the road and saw Dad waving at me from the queue. Svetlana didn't look up from her phone.

« Older posts

'We're going to check what the dilly yo is in this clizzub and bring you the four-one-one *mañana*,' said Dad.

I wondered at what exact point he stopped speaking English. Was it when he met Svetlana or before?

We took Dad's arrival as our cue to get the cocking hell out of there and go over to Trafalgar Square itself. We stood by one of the big fountains. It was nice, with all the Christmas lights up, too, but kind of made me want to wee.

'Whatever happens, Joe,' said Natalie. 'I'm proud of you.'

'What about if I puke and faint?' I said.

'I know you won't.'

'But what if I do?'

'You won't.'

'But what if?'

She grabbed me by my collar and kissed me.

'That was just like our first kiss,' I said.

'And I've still yet to find a better way of shutting you up,' said Natalie.

After that, we went back to the hotel, Natalie went to her room and I went to mine. I climbed into bed and eventually managed to drift off to sleep. A few hours later, I was awoken by Dad and Svetlana coming in. I decided to pretend to be asleep. The idea of talking to Dad after he'd been clubbing was about as appealing as licking a tramp.

I surreptitiously pulled the covers over my head to block out the sound of them giggling as they got into bed. The noise stopped for a minute, then started up again, with more giggling and moving around.

Then sounds of kissing.

It's OK, Joe, said Norman. *Just keep your head under the covers and it'll all be over before you know it.*

Screw that, said Hank. *This is the stuff therapy is made of. You have to do something, man.*

I cleared my throat. They carried on. I cleared my throat again, louder. That didn't do anything.

'Oh, Svet, baby . . . '

'REALLY?' I sat up in bed.

'Oh, hey, son,' said Dad. 'We thought you were asleep.'

'Well, you thought wrong.'

I lay back down. Silence. I was starting to drift off when the giggling started again.

'That's it,' I said. 'I'm going out.'

'Where are you rolling to at this time?' said Dad.

'I don't know,' I said. 'Reception?'

'OK,' he said. 'But don't come back for about fifteen minutes.'

Svetlana said something in Russian.

'Make that twenty.'

I shuddered as I threw my clothes back on and left the room. I went and sat in reception but the bloke there kept looking at me weird so I went back to walking the corridors.

I texted Natalie:

« Older posts

Are you up?

Yep. Why?

I'm outside.

She came to the door in her Iron Maiden pyjamas.

'Hello, you. Do I need to call security and report a prowler?'

'God no. Dad and Svetlana have come back and let's just say if I stay in there I'm going to hear some things,' I said. 'Some really grisly things.'

The door across from us opened and Harry stood there in his boxers. 'What did I tell you two about room visiting after lights out?'

'Sorry, Harry,' I said. 'What are you doing up, anyway?'

'Not that it's any of your business, but the maids have left all these extra pillows in our room so I'm building a fort,' he said. 'But I won't go back to my construction until I see you walk away.'

'Hey, Harry,' Ad called from the bathroom. 'I need a bit of help with the wiping.'

Harry shuddered, then pointed at us. 'You got lucky, old son,' he said, then disappeared back into his room.

'So, do you want to, um, do something?' I said.

Natalie smiled. 'Like what? It's the middle of the night.'

'Maybe we could build our own fort?' I said.

She laughed. 'I think you need to get some sleep. It's a big day tomorrow. Maybe we'll make one tomorrow night, yeah?'

I puffed out my cheeks and nodded. I knew she was right but I didn't fancy the idea of going back to my room to hear sounds that could make me vomit all my internal organs.

She blew me a kiss. 'Goodnight, Joe Cowley.'

'Goodnight, Natalie Tuft.'

Sunday 2nd December

When I got back in last night, Dad and Svetlana were asleep. God. I never thought I'd say this but compared to these two, sharing a room with Gav isn't that bad.

After breakfast (feeding Cheerios to Ad after you've only had a couple of hours' sleep should be the dictionary definition of 'pain in the arse'), me and Natalie headed out to the **STAR TREK** museum. We had a great time, and had our photos taken with the complete bridge from **THE NEXT GENERATION ENTERPRISE** AND the console from **VOYAGER**.

'When my Auntie Sandra blathered on about how visiting the Vatican was a truly spiritual experience, I thought she was full of crap,' said Natalie. 'Until now.'

'Yeah,' I said, pointing at Picard's seat. 'This is like the Sistine Chapel for geeks.'

Natalie looked around. We were the only ones in there. People are philistines. 'Hey,' she whispered, 'go and sit in Picard's chair.'

I gawped. 'But there's a velvet rope. You're not supposed to cross the velvet rope!'

'And you're not supposed to climb up people's houses and jump in through the window, but sometimes needs must,' she said. 'Go on, it'll help you become him tonight.'

I gulped. She was right. 'OK. I'm crossing the velvet rope.'

I ducked underneath and no alarms went off, which was a relief.

I walked over to the chair as the control room sent a message to my buttocks that they were in for a treat.

I sat down. At first I thought it was just like any other chair, but then it hit me. I was sitting on history. This was the very chair that Picard sat in when he commanded the **ENTERPRISE**. There was a little LCD display with the names of all the crew in the arm. A shiver ran up my body. I felt invincible.

'Hey!' An employee dressed as a Klingon came tripping in. 'Get out of Picard's chair, you'll compromise the bum grooves!'

5.30 p.m.

I'm back in the hotel room now, having a break from rehearsing. I've been listening to the tracks on my iPod, and pressing the buttons on the unplugged gear. I'm doing OK, but I keep forgetting that breakbeat in 'Kamikaze Attack'.

God, listen to me—a couple of weeks ago I didn't even know what a breakbeat was.

Yeah, and you still don't.

SHUT UP, HANK.

The others have gone down for dinner, but I couldn't. My stomach feels like I've swallowed an angry squirrel. Plus, if I do an Ad, at least there'll be nothing to bring up.

Two hours until soundcheck.

Maybe I could run away? Grow a beard and join the circus?

Goddamn it, said Hank. *When did you become such a wuss? If you screw up, there's only gonna be what, five hundred people there? It's not like you're ever going to see 'em again!*

I think what Hank is trying to say is, just try your best, said Norman.

I'm thinking about Seb. About him trying to kiss Natalie, telling Desmond all those lies about me, and slapping Ad.

I'm ready. Let's kick some rich boy arse.

« Older posts

Wednesday 5th December

I think I'm ready to write what happened now.

We lugged all our gear around the corner into Silk Kitty. Dad and Svetlana went for drinks in another bar. Great. The only thing worse than my dad in a nightclub is my dad drunk in a nightclub.

The place was even bigger than I imagined.

'Just imagine what it'll look like when it's full, old bean,' said Harry.

'I feel sick,' was my reply.

This lad called Rory showed us to our dressing room.

'The one and only Sound Experience,' he said. 'We've been digging your vibe at Bangaz HQ.'

Harry shrugged as if to say, 'Well, obviously,' and stuck his pipe in his mouth.

I paced up and down the dressing room, trying to slow my palpitations before I had a cardiac arrest.

'Bloody hell, old son, you're making me seasick,' said Harry. 'Can't you just sit down and worry quietly?'

I sat on the bench against the wall and my leg started shaking uncontrollably. Harry's pipe chattered in his mouth.

'Seriously, old bean,' he said. 'Just relax. If you're this bad now, what are you going to be like when we're live on the radio?'

Norman spat his coffee out.

'Live on the radio?' I said. 'Live on the cocking radio? When were you thinking of telling me about that?'

Natalie stroked my arm. 'It'll be OK, Joe.'

'OK?' I said. 'OK? This is the opposite of OK. This is . . . KO. Knock out! I am literally knocked out by this news.'

'To be fair, it is run by Bangaz Radio,' said Greeny. 'You should have probably guessed some radio would be involved.'

My eye started twitching.

'I shouldn't even be up there,' I said. 'This would never have happened if Ad hadn't fallen down that pit. Stupid archaeology! Leave the past in the past!'

I sat back down and felt the full horror of what was about to happen hit me. I couldn't remember when that breakbeat was supposed to come in. Every time I went through it in my head, it would all turn to mush. I was going to mess our set up in front of five hundred people, and God knows how many listening at home. It was going to be like when I was an innkeeper in the nativity play and instead of saying 'There's no room at the inn,' I just weed myself and burst into tears. But a billion times worse.

'I'm just going out for some fresh air,' I said.

Harry looked up from his book. 'Go with him, Natalie,' he said. 'I think Private Cowley presents a flight risk.'

'I'm not going anywhere,' I said. 'I'll be fine on my own. Trust me.'

« Older posts

'So,' said Natalie as we got outside. 'Are you feeling any better?'

Before I could answer, my phone started ringing. Gav.

'What the hell, man?' said Gav. 'Why ain't you been answering your phone?'

'The club's underground,' I said. 'There's no signal. What's up?'

'Oh man, oh man, oh man.' I'd never heard him sounding this scared. Even when he thought our bedroom was haunted.

'Look, calm down,' I said. 'What's happened?'

'It's your mum,' he said.

A hot flood of panic spread over my skull. 'What about Mum? Is she OK?'

'I don't know, man, these pricks ain't telling me NOTHING!'

Natalie stared at me open-mouthed and leaned closer to listen.

'Who?' I said.

'These paramedicals,' he said. 'Man, what have I done?'

'Please, Gav,' I said. 'Just tell me what's happened.'

He took a shaky breath. 'Me and Dad have been arguing about my tag,' he said. 'And then he found out about me being suspended and that made him worse. Anyways, your mum shouts at us to shut up, but we just carry on and ignore her. But then she kind of starts moaning and holding her belly. And there was all this pissy stuff all over the floor.'

'That means her waters have broken,' said Natalie. 'She's gone into labour.'

'She ain't due for weeks though, right? What if the twins, you know . . . '

Gav trailed off and what sounded like sobs hiccupped down the phone.

'What if something happens to them?' he said. 'It'll be all my fault. Dad was right, I ain't nothing but trouble.'

Natalie grabbed the phone off me.

'Listen, Gav,' she said. 'This is not your fault, OK?'

'It is, it is.'

'No it's not,' she said. 'Besides, just because a baby is premature doesn't mean there'll be any complications.'

The sobs started to get slower. 'Yeah?'

'Yes,' said Natalie. 'Now stop being a big girl. They're going to need you to be strong, OK?'

'Yeah,' said Gav. 'Thanks.'

I sat down on the kerb with my head in my hands. Natalie sat next to me and rubbed my back.

'Everything's going to be fine,' she said.

'How do you know?' My words echoed down the drain below me.

'I just do,' she said. 'And if anything, this should put this whole thing into perspective.'

'What do you mean?' I looked up.

'Well, no matter what happens, there's going to be two

« Older posts

little people back home who are going to change all your lives forever. What's a poxy DJ competition when you compare it with that?'

'I guess so,' I said. 'I just wish I could be there.'

'I know you do,' said Natalie. 'But it's probably for the best. I mean, if you got sick at the sight of Ad's floppy wrists, imagine what seeing two babies squeezing out of your mum's flue would do to you.'

'Flue?'

'Yes, it's very quaint, isn't it?' she said.

We stared out across the street as the rain started to come down. Panic gripped me by the throat and wouldn't let go.

'I need to leave,' I said. 'I've got to find my dad and get him to drive me home.'

'And let down your friends?' said Natalie. 'Come on, we both know you're not going to do that.'

'But my mum—'

'Is going to be fine,' she said. 'I promise. Plus, I think we both know your dad will be in no state to drive.'

I sighed. I knew she was right.

'All right, superstar DJ,' said Natalie. 'Shall we go in?'

An hour before the start of the show Rory came by with the running order:

1. KRYPTIDZ
2. DJ Krazy
3. *THE MAELSTROMS*
4. *DJ Flossie*
5. THE SOUND EXPERIENCE
6. DJ Filthybeatz

'It's the same as the heat, old beans,' said Harry.

'Yeah,' I said. 'And remind me who won that?'

'This is different, now,' said Harry. 'Our tunes are better, our effects are better, and now we have a reason to win.' He tapped Ad's plaster.

'Ow,' said Ad.

Half an hour before show time this bloke walked into the room, carrying a big mic. I'd been trying to get some signal on my phone in case Gav had any more updates about Mum, but had no luck.

'Hey, hey, party people, welcome back to the Bangaz Buzzfest final, I'm here, right here, right now, with another of the finalists, the wicked Sound Experience.'

I eyed up the door, but some sound technicians were in the way. Harry stood next to me, as if he could tell what I was thinking.

'Guys, what does it mean to you to be in the final?' He shoved the mic under my chin and I froze.

« Older posts

'I'll field that one, old boy,' said Harry, grabbing the mic. 'It's an honour and a privilege,' he said. 'But one that we have fought hard for. Like when the RAF shot Jerry out of the skies over the channel.'

The bloke laughed nervously. 'Wicked. Anyway, you guys have created mad buzz as the first gay couple DJ duo in the country. The gay community has been bombarding us with messages of support for the Sound Experience. That must be wicked, right?'

'Oh yes,' said Harry. 'To be gay icons is a wonderful thing. Lady Gaga, Madonna, Cher, they're our heroes.'

'How about you, man?' he said, pointing the mic at me.

'Well, yeah,' I said, feeling weirdly guilty. 'But I'm not actually an original member, I'm just a replacement.'

Harry and the interview bloke glared at me.

Goddamn it, just say something, said Hank. *This is dead air!*

'Still gay though!' I blurted out. 'I'm as gay as the day is long.'

I give up, said Hank.

'Riiiiight,' said the bloke. 'Anyways, good luck for tonight, hope you smash it!'

After he left, Harry put his hand on my shoulder. 'Gay as the day is long?'

The others went out to watch when the show started. I

couldn't. I just stayed in the dressing room and paced, going through the buttons again and again in my mind—where the breakbeat comes, when the explosion sample has to be triggered. No wonder Ad puked as much as he did.

After a while, Natalie came in.

'How's it going?' I said.

'The first two have been good,' she said. 'But they just don't have the substance that the Sound Experience have. But then, I would say that. How are you feeling?'

'Like I'm about to go to the gallows,' I said.

Natalie smiled. 'Don't forget—you're Picard,' she said. 'You compromised his bum grooves and everything.'

'But this is all . . . so unlike anything I would ever do,' I said.

'I know,' she said. 'But so are a lot of the things you've done lately. But you've done them because you had to. You've done them for me, or for your friends.'

I gulped.

'And whatever happens,' she said. 'We're going to make a fort tonight, remember?'

She held my hand. 'Come on, let's go up.'

We joined the others on a balcony overlooking the club. I had my *SOUND EXPERIENCE* coat on. The dance floor below was swarming. It was like that party at my house to the power of a hundred. The Maelstroms were on stage playing some kind of music that I could not determine the quality of because I DON'T GET IT.

« Older posts

A table of judges sat stage left, making notes. Natalie pointed out DJ Swizz in the middle. To be honest, I wouldn't have recognized him if he'd smashed me in the face with an 'I am DJ Swizz' knuckleduster.

A bright pink flash caught my eye near the front of the stage. It was Dad, dressed in neon, dancing and waving glow sticks around.

I swear, if he tells anyone I'm his son, I will kill myself.

I glanced over at Harry, who was leaning over the railings and watching The Maelstroms closely, as if he was studying them.

I tried to go through the sequences in my mind, but my thoughts kept returning to Mum and the babies. What if something went wrong?

The Maelstroms finished and the radio guy, some bloke called Mad Tony, told the crowd to 'make some noise'. Which my dad did by blowing a vuvuzela.

After a couple of minutes, he introduced the next competitor. The last one before us. Sweat started pouring down my forehead and into my eyes. I suddenly became very aware of my braces. They felt like boulders in my mouth.

'All right, party people,' said Mad Tony. 'This next girl

is the baddest DJ to come out of East-bourne since, well, anyone. She's foxy, she's crazy, she's eighty-four years old, let's give a massive Bangaz welcome to DJ Flossie!'

We and the rest of the crowd watched in amazement as a little old lady hobbled up to the decks in a bright pink jumpsuit and started playing massive party anthems. The crowd went wild.

Harry came over and nodded appreciatively. 'She may not have the best chops in the world,' he said. 'But she's got an angle, all right.'

Rory gave us the thumbs up. 'It's time.'

Natalie hugged me tight. 'You're going to be brilliant, I know it,' she said. 'I love you.'

'I love you too,' I said. 'And if I make a complete arse of myself, do you promise you won't chuck me?'

'Cross my heart,' she said. 'If that kind of thing were a problem, I'd have dumped you at Water World.'

I had to hold onto the handrails on the way down the stairs. My knees actually knocked together like Shaggy out of *Scooby Doo*.

We waited by the side of the stage. I stared at the green sign above the door:

EXIT

« Older posts

I wished I could.

DJ Flossie finished her set to deafening applause and the crowd chanting her name.

'Follow that, eh, old boy?' said Harry.

My teeth were chattering. I turned and looked at Greeny. He was chomping on a Crunchie. How could he eat at a time like that?

'You're going to be fine,' said Harry. 'Just hit that break-beat and you'll smash the rest.'

My shaking got worse.

'Us even being here should be considered a victory, you know, soldier?'

'OK, guys, are you ready?' said Rory.

'Yes, sir,' said Harry.

I nodded and said something that sounded like, 'Meer-rherrgen.'

The control room beeped and buzzed.

Don't get too worried, Joe, said Norman. *Try and enjoy it.*

Yeah, said Hank. *And if you mess up, just smash the gear and crowd-surf. Rock and roll!*

'All right, people, we're down to the penultimate act of the night. They've got a huge buzz right now, and you lot love them—go wild and crazy for the Sound Experience!'

The roar from the crowd made my brain vibrate. I climbed the steps and looked out. I had to shield my eyes from the spotlight, but I could make out some blokes holding up a banner saying 'We Luv the Sound Experience'.

My dad shouted up, 'Go on, Joey, show them how us Cowleys roll. Whoooooooo!'

Harry started 'Dive! Dive! Dive!' and we were away.

NOD.

Green 1.

NOD.

Red 1.

NOD.

Blue 1.

And so on. I had no idea if the noises I was triggering were any good, but the crowd sounded like they were going for it. Greeny wrestled with his effects box next to me and made amazing plane holograms fly through the air.

I glanced up at the balcony. I knew Natalie would be up there somewhere. Oh crap, a nod. Orange 1.

Harry brought the song to a close, but kept a beat going. A small 'Sound Experience' chant went up.

'Seb must be hating this, old son,' Harry shouted over the noise.

My body shook with the adrenaline surge. I didn't know whether to smile or scream.

'All right, "Spitfire Disaster",' said Harry as he launched straight into it. We carried on with the same system of nodding and colour-coding. Even though I was barely moving, I was panting.

« Older posts

Coloured lights danced in front of my eyes. What the hell was happening? I glanced up at the big screen on the wall and saw myself on there. My braces were catching Greeny's lights and reflecting them out into the crowd. People were going crazy. They must have thought it was a part of the act. I knew no matter what Seb had planned, he could never beat my technicolour robo mouth.

By the end of 'Spitfire Disaster', I was covered in sweat. As was Harry. Greeny looked like he'd stepped into a shower fully clothed.

The next track was 'Kamikaze Attack'. The one I kept messing up. My heart rate accelerated and I felt myself drifting on the verge of hyperventilation.

Harry nodded at me. I screwed my eyes shut.

'KAMIKAZE ATTACK'! The sample boomed out over the PA. It was so loud, my eyes involuntarily opened and I could see everyone in the club dancing to the beat.

NOD.

Green 3.

NOD.

Red 3.

The breakbeat approached. I glanced over at Harry hunched over his console, furiously working the dials, doing half of Ad's job as well as his own.

It's coming.

Oh crap. What was the button?

Control room, help me out!

Um, um, I think it's Blue 3, said Norman, frantically shuffling his papers.

No way, it's Orange 3, said Hank. *Trust me*.

Blue 3, said Norman.

Orange 3.

Blue 3!

The breakbeat is coming. Harry nodded. I closed my eyes. Blue 3.

The music stopped and the breakbeat boomed, before the rest came crashing back in. Even though the music and the crowd were deafening, I still thought I could hear Natalie and Ad cheering.

Greeny leaned over and slapped me on the back and Harry gave me a quick thumbs up. We powered through the rest of the track and segued straight into 'Victory'.

Green 4.

Red 4.

Blue 4.

My teeth flashed like a demented Christmas tree.

Orange 4.

« Older posts

Green 5.

Red 5.

Blue 5.

DONE!

It's over! The crowd went mental. Me, Harry, and Greeny shared a sweaty, three-way man-hug.

'We did it, old son!'

'SOUND EXPERIENCE, SOUND EXPERIENCE, SOUND EXPERIENCE!'

'Bangaz people, go mental for the Sound Experience!'

As we walked off the stage, my legs were shaking even more than before, but this time it was pure relief. I'd never had a feeling like it before in my life. I knew that no matter what, I would never have to get up on stage and do that EVER AGAIN.

I nearly collapsed into Natalie's arms when we got back upstairs. She kissed me, and didn't even complain about how disgustingly sweaty I was.

'I told you you'd do it!' she said.

'Yeah, well done, lads,' said Ad, who was attempting to eat a tray of nachos with runny cheese and salsa.

Loads of random people came over and gave us back-slaps and congratulations. Then I felt one slap that was a little harder than was comfortable. I turned around.

'Hello, Seb.'

'Shut up, freak.' He pushed me aside and stood between me and Harry. 'How did you . . . '

'Do that?' I said. 'I have absolutely no cocking idea. But I did it. Sorry.'

'OK, OK, party people, are you ready for your final contestant?'

Seb gulped and ran his hands through his stupid hair.

'Now the Sound Experience aren't the only special act on tonight—DJ Filthybeatz is the son of a politician!'

The crowd started booing while Seb looked like he'd started pooing.

'And not just any politician—Henry Mangrove!'

The booing got louder. They must have heard about his dad's 'views'. Our crowd were furious.

Seb's mouth dropped open. I think his shades were the only thing keeping his eyes in. Ad started chuckling.

'What are you laughing at, you stupid monkey?' said Seb. He grabbed Ad by his collar.

'Let go of him, now,' said Natalie.

'Why should I?'

Before Natalie could threaten any more violence, the nachos that Ad had balanced on his casts toppled over and splatted against Seb's silk shirt, leaving a massive cheese and salsa stain all the way down it.

He leapt back and screamed.

'Guys, go crazy and please try not to throw things at DJ Filthybeatz!'

Seb tried to brush his front down, but it just made it worse. He marched past Harry and Ad, stopping by me to say, 'You just wait.'

When he took to the stage to a chorus of boos, I wondered what the hell he meant by that. I didn't worry about it too much because I was just so ecstatic to have got it out of the way. I started to wonder if we could win this thing. Watching Harry, Ad, and Greeny rock the dance stage at *BUZZFEST* would be ridiculous.

Seb started playing, and the only person cheering in the whole room was Lisa. It was brilliant. Even his bouncers looked embarrassed.

The gang that made the *SOUND EXPERIENCE* banner were chanting, 'We're here! We're queer! Get used to it!'

The look on Seb's face was brilliant, and I don't know, because it all sounds the same to me, but I think he kept messing up.

I gave Ad a thumbs up. 'You got him good, mate,' I said.

'What you on about?' he said. 'I was enjoying them nachos.'

Me and Natalie watched with our arms around each other. To be bearing witness to Seb's epic failure together was weirdly romantic.

'I'm so proud of you,' she said.

'Aw, it was nothing,' I said. 'It was easy really.'

'Really?'

'God no,' I said. 'I think it's going to give me night terrors.'

Natalie laughed. 'The important thing is we got here, and we blew that idiot off the stage. No matter what happens, he can't hurt us any more.'

The beat slowed down and a chipmunk helium voice started singing something about 'Oh, I miss you, come back to me.'

All the screens around the venue changed from the generic Bangaz logo to a DJ Filthybeatz one. The boos got louder.

Then the logo disappeared and changed to a picture. It was Seb with his arm around a girl.

'Nice,' I said. 'Showing the world that no matter how much of a douche you are, there'll always be someone desperate enough to go out with you.'

I looked at the girl again; she had brown hair over half her face, but she seemed . . .

Holy crap, what's your girl doing on that screen with him? said Hank.

No, that's not her, said Norman. *She doesn't have purple hair.*

Don't you think that might be out of a bottle, numbnuts?

Natalie's face was frozen with horror.

« Older posts

'N-Natalie?'

'I can't believe it,' she said.

'Why are you?'

Look, their families have been friends for years, said Norman. *There's nothing about this photo to suggest anything untoward.*

The photo changed to one of Seb and Natalie kissing.

You were saying? said Hank.

I felt sick. My eye twitched. My stomach heaved.

The photo changed. This time it was Natalie kissing him on the cheek and making a peace sign.

My face went hot. I felt tears brimming in my eyes. I turned around. Lisa made brief eye contact with me and looked as horrified as I felt. I looked down at the stage. Seb's mouth was twisted into a smirk.

Oh dear, said Norman.

I let go of Natalie and ran for the exit. I had to get out. I felt like a fool.

'Joe, wait!' Natalie came after me, along the corridor and into the foyer. I tried to get away, but she caught me.

'Please don't go,' she said. 'I can explain!'

'How can you explain?' I said. 'Was that Photoshopped?'

Even though I knew it wasn't true, if she'd have said yes, I'd have believed her.

She shook her head and looked at the ground.

I pushed tears away from my eyes with the ball of my palm. 'I need to go,' I said.

'No!' She grabbed me tight and pulled me back.

'Look,' she said. 'Me and Seb . . . We used to have a thing . . . It was ages ago. Like, last year. But I ended it because he changed, OK? He got too close to my dad and started turning into him. Why do you think I was so scared about the same thing happening to you?'

My hands were trembling. I felt like a cretin in my blood-stained *SOUND EXPERIENCE* coat.

'But why did you lie?' I said. 'I asked you and you said it wasn't true.'

A tear rolled down her cheek. 'I don't know. I just . . . I don't know, OK?'

'You just didn't want me to know that I was second best,' I said. 'He goes off with someone else, so you just settle for a geek with no money.'

'Joe, that's horrible,' she cried. 'I love y—'

'Don't,' I said. 'I need some time to think. I'm going for a walk.'

The streets were busy outside and the air was cold enough to almost freeze the moisture to my eyeballs.

Harry was leaning against the wall with his back to me.

'No, Mother, I promise you if I was going to come out, you'd be the first to know . . . Yes, I know what the radio

said, but it's not true. It's like a gimmick sort of thing . . .
No, Ad's just a friend. So is Joe . . . What do you mean
I've never had a girlfriend? How do you know? Look, just
because I'm picky doesn't mean I'm . . . '

I walked away, not knowing where I was heading. I just
had to get away from that club. How could Natalie have lied
to me like that? After all we'd been through, as well.

My phone buzzed in my pocket. I didn't want to speak to
Natalie. It wasn't her, anyway. Text from Gav.

My heartbeat ramped up a gear. With all this crap, I'd
almost forgotten about Mum. I opened it.

**2 GIRLS BRUV! BORN ON DA LIVIN ROOM FLOOR!
THERE CALLIN EM HOLLY N IVY. UR MUMS FINE N
ALREDY SEEMS A BIT LESS MENTAL. PEACE, G.**

So we've got baby sisters. It was a weird thought. But
I promised myself at that moment that I'd look after them.
That I'd teach them right from the start that it's wrong to
lie. Then, fifteen years from now, some poor idiots like me
would be spared a lot of trauma.

The thought of Natalie and Seb together was like a kick
in the stomach. Did she love him like she loved me?

I remembered that day on the bench in school when she
told me she'd only ever snogged one boy, and he was some
French guy, and yet there was photographic proof that she
kissed Seb. How many others could she have been lying
to me about?

I kept walking and walking until I ended up by the big fountain in Trafalgar Square. I stood next to these weird merman statues and looked up at it, lit up in different colours.

Natalie kept trying to call me, but I switched my phone off. I needed to be alone.

I wished I never bothered with this whole thing. I should have just let Seb win, because regardless of the result, he has.

The square was busy with people staggering around, laughing and singing. One bloke stumbled over and said, 'Nice jacket. What have you got down it?'

'Blood,' I said. 'And if you don't leave now, my urge to kill will only reawaken.'

He left pretty quickly after that.

I stood there staring at the water for what felt like hours. Then a voice beside me made me jump.

'All right?'

I turned, a part of me hoping to see Natalie, but it wasn't. It was Lisa.

'Any room around this fountain for me?' she said.

'Yeah, it's pretty big,' I said. 'There is another one over there though, if this is too crowded for you.'

Lisa didn't say anything, but then her face crumpled and she burst into tears. I didn't know what to do.

'What's . . . what's the matter?'

« Older posts

'Seb's dumped me,' she sobbed.

'Really?' I said, trying to make it clear that I wasn't interested in the slightest.

'It was horrible,' she said. 'He came off stage and everyone was booing him, and I asked him what all those pictures were about, and he just flipped at me. Saying, "None of your business," and, "I'm done with you anyway, you've served your purpose."'

'So he was using you?' I said.

She nodded.

'Hurts, doesn't it?' I said.

'What do you mean?'

I sighed. 'Nothing.'

I didn't have the patience to explain it to her.

We both stared at the fountain, changing from green to red. Lisa hugged herself. She was only wearing a dress.

I puffed my cheeks out. 'Do you want my coat?'

I took off the *SOUND EXPERIENCE* coat and gave it to her. She smiled as she put it on.

'You've always been a nice guy, haven't you, Joe?' she said.

'I don't know,' I said. 'Maybe I'm too nice, that's the trouble.'

'What do you mean?'

'Well, look at Seb: he's a complete bastard and he's got everything,' I said. 'Being nice does you no favours.'

Lisa shrugged. I dug a penny out of my pocket and dropped it into the fountain. The wind made my fingers numb.

'What do I need to do, anyway?' said Lisa. 'No boy I've ever been out with has cared about me. Not really. They just think I'm easy, or they just want to look cool, to prove a point. None of them has ever cared about who I was, or what I wanted.'

'I did.'

'What?'

I rubbed my eyes. 'I did,' I said. 'I would have done anything for you. I was even ready to dump my best friends, just because you asked me to.'

She stared at me, open-mouthed. 'Really?'

'Yes,' I said. 'Stupid old Joe. Never learns. I was obsessed with you . . . for years, and then you finally say you like me? Can you imagine, even for a second, what that must have been like?'

'Are you serious?'

'Of course I am,' I said. 'Not everyone has other motives, all right? Maybe if you'd have known that, things could have worked out different.'

Lisa dropped her purse on the floor, leaned forward, and kissed me.

No, Joe, this is wrong, said Norman. *Stop this immediately.*

Are you kidding me? said Hank. *So, he already has a*

girlfriend. She's a liar! He's just getting his own back. Plus, you know as well as I do how many years he dreamed about this. Just let him have his fun.

I wanted to stop. But like Hank said, it was fun. Lisa ran her fingers through my hair and grabbed my hand and put it on the small of her back.

Over the rushing of the fountain, I thought I heard a voice. To begin with, I thought I was hearing things, but the voice got louder. It was saying the same thing over and over again. I couldn't make out the words to begin with, but they gradually became clearer.

'Oh my God.'

'Oh my God.'

'OH MY GOD.'

'OH MY GOD!'

I broke off the kiss and spun around. I saw where the voice was coming from. Natalie was standing there, staring at us. Her face was frozen into an expression I've never seen before. Hurt, angry, I don't know. Even now, I can't un-see it.

'How could you, Joe?'

My chest tightened.

'Natalie, please.'

I took my arm from around Lisa and ran after Natalie. She weaved through the crowds and I kept bumping into drunk people. When she reached a clearer part of the square, I managed to grab her arm. She turned around. Black trails ran down her face.

'You b-bastard,' she sobbed. 'How could you?'

'I'm sorry,' I said. 'I was upset . . . she made the first move.'

Natalie clenched her fists. 'You shout at me, you make me feel like crap, for something that was in the past, and then you run away and do this?'

'But you lied to me about Seb!' I said. 'Doesn't that make us even?'

She snarled at me, actually snarled, which more than answered my question.

'I didn't tell you about Seb because I wanted to forget about him. I wanted to pretend it never happened.'

Natalie wrenched her hand from mine and started running away again. Hot, stabbing pains ripped through my brain. I ran after her again and caught her. She stopped but didn't turn around.

'Please, Natalie,' I said. 'After all that's happened it can't end like this. It just . . . it just can't.'

She slowly turned around and looked at me. She'd stopped crying and a strange kind of hardness had crept into her face. Only her trembling chin gave her away.

« Older posts

'I loved you, Joe Cowley,' she said.

'No,' I said. 'Don't say it like that, I—'

I felt all the breath leave my body. She'd punched me in the stomach. I crumpled into a heap, my knees tucked underneath me, and my forehead on the cold floor. I heard her run away, but I couldn't stop her.

This is it, I thought. *My life is over.*

As I sucked air back into my lungs, I felt a hand on my back.

'Yeah, sorry about that,' said Lisa. 'I don't want you getting the wrong idea about what happened there. I was just sad, you know?'

I didn't say anything.

'It might be all right,' she said. 'Maybe . . .'

'Please,' I wheezed. 'Just leave me alone.'

I felt warmth spreading over my back. 'I've given you your coat back,' she said. 'Don't want you freezing to death.'

'I don't care,' I said.

There was a pause. 'Right,' she said. 'So, I'll see you around, maybe.'

Her footsteps faded away into the distance.

My tears formed a puddle on the ground underneath me. I needed to move, but I couldn't.

This is what happens when you listen to him, Joe, said Norman. Everything is ruined. Your record label? Gone. That trip to the Star Trek museum in LA you planned? Gone.

Your future happiness together? Gone. And for what?

I screwed my eyes shut, hoping that if I wished hard enough I could go back in time and never bother getting involved in this stupid competition. Back to the holidays, when we were happy. That day when the sun made her hair shine and she bought two ice creams just to cool her lip piercing down. That's where I wanted to be. No matter what happens, I will never be that happy again.

I don't know how long I was curled up in a ball like that. People walking by avoided me. I heard one woman ask her partner if he thought I was OK, and he said, 'Leave him. It's probably just a student doing some performing arts bollocks.'

My legs went completely numb, but I didn't care. I had nothing to go back to the hotel for. The only thing I had to go home for was Holly and Ivy. But what kind of brother am I going to be to them, anyway? I'm an idiot.

« Older posts

I sensed two people standing next to me.

'What do you think he's doing?' a voice whispered.

'I don't know, old son,' the other replied. 'Probably praying to Mecca or something.'

'My nan goes there every week—I wonder if praying to it helps them win or something?'

'You're a very special boy, Ad.'

I felt a tap on my back. 'Are you, uh, OK, old bean?'

'No,' I said. 'Natalie has finished with me. It's over. Everything is over.'

There was an awkward pause, then I heard Ad whisper, 'What do we do?'

'I'm, uh, I'm very sorry to hear that, Joe,' said Harry.

'Um, yeah. I am and all,' said Ad.

Another pause where I could only hear the fountains and the background noise of the city.

'How about we stand you up, eh?' said Harry. 'No matter what's happened, it won't make it better lying on the floor.'

'I don't care,' I said. 'Just leave me.'

'What's happening, Harry? Has he gone mental?'

'I can hear you whispering, Ad. I'm not deaf,' I said.

'Right.'

'In case you were still bothered, old boy, we didn't win the competition.'

I didn't reply. I hated the competition.

'That granny won,' said Ad. 'We came second. Seb came

nowhere. After his set, he grabbed the mic and called the crowd a bunch of freaks.'

'He had to have a police escort off the premises,' said Harry. 'You should have been there.'

'I don't care,' I said. 'I don't care about anything any more.'

'That's it.'

Harry grabbed me under my armpits and dragged me to my feet. I nearly fell back down because my legs were so numb. He picked my coat up and put me in it.

'Come on, that's quite enough of that,' he said. 'Let's get you back to the hotel. I'll conduct a recce and do away with all the sharp objects and potential nooses before I leave you.'

'Not funny, Harry,' I said.

I started stumbling towards the hotel, but my feet didn't want to work, so Harry put my arm over his shoulder, and Ad put the other one over his, and they helped me along.

'Look, old boy,' he said. 'Maybe in the end, this will be a good thing.'

'How can this possibly be a good thing?' I said. 'I've just lost the love of my life.'

'But your life has only just started, soldier,' said Harry. 'Surely you're not going to settle for the first girl who comes along?'

I blinked hard. 'Where else am I going to find someone like her?' I said. 'Who's beautiful and funny and who likes the same things that I do, and who likes *me*? Nowhere. She was the only one, and I blew it.'

Harry squeezed my shoulder. 'Come on now. The world is a big place, old son.'

'Yeah,' said Ad. 'I mean, don't get me wrong, I love Nat, but you could be getting plenty of action out there. Especially when we're at Buzzfest.'

'Buzzfest?' I said. 'But we lost.'

'Second place get VIP tickets, remember?' said Ad. 'We're finally going!'

'I'm not going,' I said. 'It won't be the same.'

'Come on, where's your spirit?' said Harry. 'We'll be going to Buzzfest this summer, when we'll have finished our GCSEs. It will be the party to end all parties, old boy.'

'But I . . . '

'No buts,' Harry cut in. 'With the Experience finally getting a fan base . . . '

'A gay fan base,' said Ad.

'. . . Which is the best fan base in the world,' Harry continued, 'and us finally getting to Buzzfest after years of trying, I've got a feeling that tonight is just the start of another big adventure.'

'Oh cocking hell,' I said.

BEN DAVIS

Since he was a little boy, people told Ben Davis he would
grow up to be an author. He didn't listen at the time,
because he thought he was going to be an astronaut
or play up front for Man United. When he reached his
mid-twenties without a call from NASA/Fergie, he realized
that maybe they had a point and started writing again.
First, Ben wrote jokes for everything from radio shows to
greeting cards. Then, he moved on to stories. He chose
to write for young adults, largely because his sense of
humour stopped maturing at the age of fifteen. Ben now
lives in Tamworth with his wife and his big, wimpy dog.

Find out more about Ben at the
Not So Private Blog of Ben Davis:
bendavisauthor.blogspot.co.uk

You can also visit his website:
bendavisauthor.com

Sunday 1st January

So here's the thing. I've decided to start writing a blog. A private one. The idea is that it'll help me sort my life out, because quite frankly, it can't get much worse . . .

1. I gained the nickname Puke Skywalker after vomiting over Louise Bentley on the waltzers.
2. I am subjected to daily wedgies by my arch-enemy Gav James.
3. My so-called best mates are trying to get me killed in a bid to win £250 on You've Been Framed.

This cannot go on! I have to do something, or I'll end up like Mad Morris down the park who thinks he's Jesus. By the end of next term, I'm going to be a completely different person.

At least, that's the theory . . .